In 1947, the Village Theate[...] [...]y invitation only" Grand Opening. T[...] [...] were excited to have the opportunity to see a movie without navigating their way across the bay to downtown San Diego. Gregory Larson's parents sat in the red plush seats of the Village Theater to see the Best Picture of the Year, *Gentleman's Agreement.* The film so moved them that their son, born months later, would be named for the film's lead actor—Gregory Peck.

World War II was over, and the Baby Boom Generation was born. In the decades to follow, Gregory Larson became enamored with UCLA co-ed Raquel Mendez. Meanwhile, on the Jersey shore, Abby DiFranco held hands with her boyfriend, Navy hero Jack Adams. All four lovers were destined to face the sexual and cultural revolution in America, headlined by the mayhem of the Vietnam War, the debilitating posttraumatic stress disorder that ensued, the corruption of America's political leaders, and the insidious breed of terrorism that originated in the Middle East, eventually spreading across the Atlantic Ocean.

To escape these tumultuous times, the two couples turned to the movies, often a source of inspiration, humor, and hope. But soon even their quaint Village Theater fell victim to the ravages of time and profit margins. Consequently, their favorite cinema was boarded up. Its Art Deco design became dilapidated, and its once spectacular murals of the San Diego skyline vanished into faded, grimy walls and torn curtains. The Village Theater's long-time projectionist mused, "Some awfully sad things that happen just change you, I guess."

When does someone find the courage to face his or her tragic past and haunting loneliness? *The Restoration* begins with a gentleman's agreement that binds Jack Adams and Greg Larson. But it is the women in their lives, Abby DiFranco and Raquel Mendez, who understand that by restoring the Village Theater to its original grandeur, they are actually restoring themselves—heart and soul. In *The Restoration,* it becomes clear that "you have to break down walls to reconfigure, remodel, and renovate…you have to leave the best memories and create new ones."

# Praise for

## *Meetings at the Metaphor Café*

"*Meetings at the Metaphor Cafe* reads like an invitation...an invitation to sit down amongst its characters and relive your youth. With the turn of every page, you are transported back to a time when the world was new to you, sitting among friends, sipping a latte, discussing love and the meaning of things, and discovering life all over again like it was the first time. Along with the characters, the readers are sent on a journey toward rediscovering themselves and reconnecting with what really matters at the heart of who they are. All the while, the book reads like a who's who and what's what of the 20th century. As a teacher, I can say that this book is a MUST read for any high school English or history class. *Meetings at the Metaphor Cafe* should be in the hands of every teenager in America, and those of anyone who once was one!"
**-Danielle Galluccio, Trinity Montessori School, Adolescent Academy Director**

"This debut novel rings with authenticity. *Meetings at the Metaphor Café* is a must for anyone looking for a little meaning and a lot of inspiration, whether you are a new teacher or a lifelong student."
**-BaBette Davidson, Vice President, Programming for Public Television–PBS**

"*Meetings at the Metaphor Café will* challenge the minds and hearts of teenagers everywhere"
**-Bruce Gevirtzman, author of *An Intimate Understanding of America's Teenagers***

"Robert Pacilio's novel works on many levels. It's enlightening—an open window into the teenage soul. *Meetings at the Metaphor Cafe* should be required reading for teenagers and their parents."
**-Linda Vanderveen, Board of Education Member–Poway Unified School District**

"I thoroughly enjoyed this book. Mr. Pacilio inspires the reader to be a better person and gives us faith in our new generation of youth. The take-home messages, however, engage a much wider audience and offer life lessons that build resilience and encourage a positive outlook on life, encouraging both youth and adults to make a difference in our society. This book is a must read for students, educators, and all the people who believe in positive change."

**-Michele Einspar, Director, Transformative Inquiry Design for Effective Schools**

"This is a wonderful book and should be required reading for all history and English teachers. I hope that many read it, and in some way recognize parts of themselves and once again relive those magical moments."

**-Bill Orton, San Diego District Director of High School Counseling**

"Maddie, Mickey, Rhia, and Pari are so real I actually can *see* them sitting in any classroom. Students will relate to their diverse life experiences and their common bond of needing to make sense of it all. They will see parts of themselves in the characters and feel that the diaries are a true window into the sometimes confusing journey through high school life. Teachers will be challenged and inspired by Mr. Buscotti's brilliant example of one way to be a responsible and caring guide on that journey."

**-Linda Englund, Ed.D., A.P. English Teacher**

"Not only did I enjoy your book very much, but I learned so much about what is possible when it comes to turning a classroom into an experience. My students are captivated by the book and have transformed into more caring people, thoughtful and responsive."

**-Kristen Gall, 8th Grade Teacher Terra Del Sol Middle School, Lakeside, California**

# Robert

# <u>Pacilio</u>

To
Michele
I'm so glad you
were restored !

# The

# <u>Restoration</u>

*Robert Rankin*

## WHEN I FALL IN LOVE

Words by EDWARD HEYMAN Music by VICTOR YOUNG

This is a work of fiction. All the characters and events portrayed in the novel are either the products of the author's imagination or are used fictitiously with the exception of the actual restoration of the Village Theater, the mention of the Helen Woodward Animal Shelter, and the description of the Hotel Del Coronado's Crown Room. The death of Anthony Buscemi in the Vietnam conflict, the "Brown Water Navy" and its swift boats, the use of Agent Orange, and the Battle of Hamburger Hill are based in fact. The film *Gentleman's Agreement* did open the Village Theater in 1947, and the film *Some Like It Hot* was indeed filmed at the Hotel Del Coronado and did star Marilyn Monroe.

Pre-publishing technical assistance provided by LOTONtech (http://publishing.lotontech.com).

# Also by Robert Pacilio

*Meetings at the Metaphor Café*

*Midnight Comes to the Metaphor Café*

How old would you be if you didn't know how old you are? – Satchel Paige

To my wife Pam—who restores me

# Part One:

# "The Movie Palace"

# Chapter 1

## *The Projection Booth—2000*

"When did I first come here?" The old man's eyes seesawed to the discolored walls. "You mean, this projection booth?"

"No, Joe. *Here*—the Village Theater?"

"Oh, well, when I got invited."

"Invited?"

"Well, yeah. See, Abby, the Village Theater sent out invitations for its grand opening. Back then, you had to get invited, you see. I still got my invitation. Kept it all these fifty-three years."

Joe Pappas shuffled toward a table beside the monstrously large projection machine. On the table was a hodgepodge of old movie reels, tools, a few magazines, and some knickknacks for which Abby Adams could not possibly guess their use. From the table's drawer, he withdrew a slightly yellowed envelope—inside was the invitation dated March 18, 1947 for the movie, *Gentleman's Agreement*.

"That's when they used to call this the Movie Palace," Joe said proudly as he placed the invitation in Abby's hands.

Joe's knuckles brushed against his soft, well-manicured, silver goatee in an effort to recall some memory of bygone days. The faded blue Navy cap came off, revealing the feathery, soft white hairs on top of his head. He leaned on his cane and bowed at the waist so he could glance out the window of the projection booth. He gazed down at Gregory Larson and a few other men who huddled near the torn screen that— like most everything in the movie theater—had seen far better days.

He looked back at Abby and brightened at a long forgotten memory: "Now, coincidentally, 1947 was the same year that Greg Larson was born."

"How do you know that, Joe?" Abby peeked out of the projection window as well.

"Oh, I hear voices, you know. People tell me their stories. I was friends with his folks—but that's a long story."

"Oh, I've got time, Joe. That's part of why I asked you to meet me." Abby smiled. She had been taking notes, hoping that Joe's recollections would stir up interest in the article she was submitting to the local paper about the restoration of the theater. Joseph Pappas was a lovable island treasure—a man everyone simply called Joe. He was leaning on a stool, his cane supporting his light frame in his abandoned Village movie theater on Coronado Island.

Joe replaced his cap. "Well, if you got the time. Let's see. You probably didn't know that his parents named him after that famous actor in *Gentleman's Agreement*—Gregory Peck."

"Really? He never mentioned his parents to me." Actually, many of the details of Gregory Larson's life were cloaked in mystery.

"See, his mother—she was Jewish. Her husband—he wasn't. They were so taken by that particular movie 'cause they just felt that Hollywood had finally had the guts to tell what it was like for Jews in this country, what with all the prejudice towards them. Gregory Peck played a writer who pretended to be a Jew…"

"Ah, like the book *Black Like Me*," Abby quickly interjected.

"…oh, I never saw that one…where was I?"

"Um, he pretended to be a Jew…" Abby, angry that she upset the rhythm of Joe's story, made a note to herself—*just let the man talk.*

"Okay, so anyways, that film won the Oscar for Best Picture that year. Did you know that?" The question was rhetorical in nature. "And, Janis—Greg's mom—pregnant as she was, told me she was naming the baby, if it was a boy, after Mr. Peck 'cause she admired what he had done." The old man readjusted his cap, stroked his chin, and looked straight into Abby's brown eyes. "And he was a boy alright. He sure lived up to that name, didn't he? He practically grew up in this theater when he was a kid—then later on, he sat up in the balcony a lot with his dog." Joe glanced back out the window at the men down front.

"Greg sure has made something of himself. Now he and a bunch of people are trying to get this old place opened again. I wish 'em luck. Heck of a guy, Greg."

Abby just looked down at her notes; her pen was frozen in place. This story had taken a direction Abby had not expected. Joe continued his ruminations on Gregory Larson's personal life: "Always with his dog, he was. Never settled down with a gal. Some awfully sad things that happen just change you, I guess." Joe started to fiddle with some of the knickknacks on his old worktable.

Abby sat quietly. Then she finally glanced up. "Yeah. I know what that's like."

Joe realized his mistake. They both pushed the conversation back where it belonged.

Abby looked up at the posters on the walls of the booth. "You said you 'hear voices' and 'people tell you stories'—what else comes to mind?"

"Oh, I seen the young ones in the balcony holding hands the entire movie; the boy'd be coppin' a feel. I'd hear arguments; sometimes they'd turn into a fight and the gal would storm outta the show." He shook his head in mock disbelief.

"But then, sometimes people would applaud when a movie ended. Kinda funny since there was no one there to really applaud for. It was their way of sayin' that they liked it—and they wanted others to know. Like that movie *Gentleman's Agreement*—boy, they sure clapped when it was over."

Abby understood. Being a history teacher for nearly thirty years, she knew that a picture was worth more than a thousand words of any textbook. And the Village Theater revealed more about history and the people who lived it than one could imagine. Joe was living proof.

The memories were still rolling from reel to reel for him—fond memories. "And I saw movie stars—real ones, too—like Marilyn Monroe. She would sneak in when they were filming *Some Like It Hot* there at the Hotel Del. Boy, she was shy. Hardly said a word. Not what you'd think. Loved her buttered popcorn and a Coke, though. She was a giggler—must've seen that movie *Gigi* five times. 'Course, it won Best Picture in '58, I think. Oh, and she was smart, too. Really. Forget all that crap you hear, Abby. She told me once, 'Joey, you got a beautiful theater here and the best popcorn. And you don't show all those crappy movies they keep advertising, you know?' And I said, 'Yes, Miss Monroe, but I plan on showing yours.' She laughed and said, 'This new one, it's awfully funny, Joey. The two fellas I'm in the movie with are a riot.' Then she headed in to see *Gigi* again. She was fantastic. And she is the only person who ever called me *Joey*."

The old man stood up, stretched his legs, reached for his old wooden cane, and gazed around the booth. "It all came to an end in about '98—for me, anyway. They said, 'Who wants to see just one movie playing at a theater?' I guess they forgot that we used to have double features. So they closed me down. I guess ownership didn't care that Orange Avenue is a street with lots of shops where people meet and talk."

Abby stood up with him, looking at some of the posters that were pushpinned into the dingy walls: *Rear Window*, *Cinema Paradiso*, *Forrest Gump*.

Joe looked at the remnants on the table. "I don't remember who did it, but somebody left some reels of a movie up here. Maybe on purpose, I guess, 'cause on the reel it has the title dated 1971—*The Last Picture Show*. Now as I recall, they made that in black and white, and had that new actress Cybill Shepherd—now, she was a looker. What I'd give to see her again." He sighed. "To see anything in this place again." His goatee got his attention, and he dropped the film reel back on the table.

"So you were the projectionist for how long, Joe?"

"Well, I worked here when it opened. Stayed until I got drafted. Korea. '52. Now, that was just a God-awful mess. Guess it worked out, though—but what a price, huh?"

Abby knew the exact price. She had recited it too many times to count in her class.

Suddenly, Joe smiled, "Hey, I don't wanna be all doom and gloom, Miss Abby." He yanked off his hat and ruffled what was left of his hair. "I do remember a time—it lasted maybe ten years or so. Started here about '75 and lasted until they closed down the place. At midnight on Saturday nights, we showed *The Rocky Horror Picture Show*—now, that was a really weird scene. But I gotta tell you, the audience—lots of kids, mind you—they had a great time, singing, dancing, in costumes—and they knew every single word of that crazy movie. You know what? After awhile, so did I." He laughed for the first time. It made Abby smile. She had a sense that he was much more than what met the eye— a soul who managed to transcend time.

Joe started heading down the steps, taking them slowly, with his cane hooked around his forearm. But he knew every cracked tile, the warp in the banister. The distance from top to bottom was ingrained into his descent. When they got to the lobby, Abby knew that this effort had taken up enough of Joe's energy for one day. Joe pointed his walking stick: "Well, now the windows have been boarded up. The old ticket booth out front, too. Poor gal. Out there all alone."

Abby looked around. The seats were faded red, and the snack bar was cluttered with garbage and dust. The murals on the walls had a ghostly appearance. They were still there, but you could only make them out if you remembered what they used to look like.

Joe moved close to her. "I guess that's just the way of things. The past just disappears, huh? When you get to be my age, you feel like you're all used up. It seems like people just want to junk it all. So I guess all those voices I hear are all up in heaven. Maybe all them son- of-a-bitch villains went straight to hell, huh?" As he shuffled into the lobby, he dug his hands deep into the pockets of his baggy khaki pants. His soft flannel shirt seemed like a blanket around his thin frame. His expression had changed, bending to the will of time.

Abby hugged him tightly, but before she could thank him, he repeated something that she knew haunted him. "Abby, I've been just waiting for the wrecking ball."

What Joe didn't know was that Abby Adams and Greg Larson packed a bigger blow than any wrecking ball.

# Chapter 2

## *Closing Night—1998*

The Village Theater's last picture was a tearjerker, and Abby Adams could not stop crying as *Saving Private Ryan's* credits cycled through. As the damp ball of tissues overflowed the grasp of her slender hand, Abby noticed the old man walking slowly down the center aisle. He stopped at the front of the screen, dead center stage, and gave a drawn, weary smile as the music from the soundtrack faded down to a whisper.

"I just gotta thank all you folks for coming out all these years. This'll be the last show. I don't want to say too much 'cause...well, you know. Anyways, this old Movie Palace is closing tonight. Lotsa memories. So thanks." He bowed his head, tipped his old Navy cap, found a break in the curtains that no one had ever noticed before, and disappeared. And the Village Theater vanished as well.

Abby looked down into the depths of her oversized purse. "Jack, I'm a mess. And then he tells us this. It's terrible." She fished for one more tissue in her seemingly bottomless purse.

Jackson Adams simply pursed his lips. He had the look of a man who had been beaten by an unrelenting force. "It's the way of things, Abby."

"Well, it sucks. And this is an island..."

"A peninsula."

"I know that, Jack, but who wants to cross the bridge to see a movie? And I love this old place." She looked around from wall to wall. "It could use a little sprucing up..."

"More than a little." Jack knew the seats were worn; the carpet had come up in places; the floor was sticky; the curtains were more faded than any business should allow; the sound system wasn't crisp; and more often than not, the audiences were too small. Tonight was the exception, as word had spread of the closure. People wanted to see one last picture. But even so, the audience occupied maybe two-thirds of the seats. Jack had the keen eye of a carpenter whose business card read, "Jack of All Trades," and he saw how much time and money it would take to keep the old theater running. Ownership had tossed in the towel. He understood when things were worn beyond repair only too well.

Meanwhile, his adoring wife of twenty-four years was delivering a soliloquy about all the movies she had seen there since she had agreed to move to San Diego's Coronado Island in the autumn of 1971. "I think the first movie we saw here was *Butterflies Are Free*. Oh my God, do you remember that movie? Goldie Hawn and the blind guy? It was so cute. Remember the ending, when she comes back to him when he thinks she is going to leave him for some sleazeball Hollywood type and he is lost and about to have a panic attack? Then Goldie walks into his apartment and tells him he can't have a panic attack without her. Oh, it was so touching. Jack, they don't make comedies like that anymore." For Abby, history and the cinema were on parallel tracks that took her all over the country…and beyond.

Jack was getting antsy, ready to stretch his long legs.

Abby kept her monologue running as they shuffled out of the theater. "Remember *A Room with a View?* God, I loved that movie. We saw it here, too."

Jack merely nodded, as was his habit. His mind was on something that troubled him.

By now the couple had reached the street and were heading south to the famous Hotel Del Coronado for their usual cup of coffee and a pastry that they were in the habit of splitting.

Jack finally interrupted her *A Room with a View* summary: "Abby, you remember everything. I must've forgotten that one." Jack glanced back at the *Village* sign that hovered above the theater like a sword pointing down to the stony street. "Anyway, I'm gonna miss this old place, too." Jack then turned and looked straight down the street.

Abby began to open her mouth to ask what he had thought of *Saving Private Ryan,* but she caught herself. It was enough to get Jack to see a war movie. She knew how restless he was—how anxious these films made him. She knew what bubbled up to Jack's surface, often making him grow quiet, sometimes for days. She wanted to talk, though—especially about the first twenty minutes of the film, when they hit the beaches of Normandy. *Horrifying,* she thought. Almost so realistic that it made you forget you were watching a movie.

But Jack never forgot. Two tours. Vietnam. 1966. 1969. One he enlisted in proudly. The other—he was dragged back out of guilt, determined to finish what was started. It all ended badly. The patrol boats on which he served were in constant danger from sniper fire; however, the sniper fire didn't stop when he returned home.

It had taken years for Jack Adams to finally go to the VA Hospital and see a psychiatrist. His epiphany had been rattling around in his brain for so long that it just came howling out of his lungs as tears welled up in his reddened eyes.

*It was all bullshit, Doc. We took a hill, got orders to backtrack. In country, we made friends with the farmers, only to find them booby trapped. They sprayed orange defoliant on us, and the chemical companies told the higher-ups it was all safe. We knew that was bullshit when the trees were bare and our throats burned. We came home, and people spat at us when we returned. Then we couldn't find jobs. All bullshit, Doc. Pure and simple.*

He had to push it all away. Far away. The only film that really made him laugh at it all was *Good Morning, Vietnam*. It made the bullshit visible to everyone. He laughed so hard he cried. Back then he did a lot of crying.

It was part of the reason he finally went to Washington, DC to see The Wall. As he and Abby slowly walked its long, pitch-black contours, he was overcome with emotion—so much so that Abby stepped away and just let Jack be. She stood near a middle-aged man strumming his guitar to the song that she knew was an anthem to Jack's embittered generation of Vietnam vets—"Born in the USA." She made a mental note to teach that song one day.

She saw that Jack had found the name of one of his best friends. As so many did that day, he made an etching. He placed his fist on the name as if to signify that they would remain together somehow. He had touched The Wall many times, but the name Anthony Buscemi was one that mattered more than most. Abby wondered why, but knew well enough not to ask. She knew it would take a while before Jack could get words out of his tightened throat.

The man with the guitar packed up his instrument. Abby found herself drawn to him.

Abby said to him, "I'm glad you play music here. But you're not asking for donations. Why do you do it, if you don't mind me asking?"

He did not look up from the guitar case. He just kept adjusting the strap and such, hesitating to reply, measuring his words carefully. He didn't seem angry at her for asking nor did he act insulted, as if she was wondering if this was a chance for him to profit from the tragedy of others.

Abby sensed her error and his unease. "I'm sorry. I shouldn't have been so crass. It's just that your music just seemed to…I don't know…soften the blow. My husband is out there finding names. Too many, I'm afraid. So what I really want to say is just *thank you*."

He looked up. Pushing his long, wavy brown hair behind his ears, he made eye contact with Abby. "It's okay."

They paused. Abby nodded. She turned toward Jack. From over her shoulder, she heard the man's voice. "My big brother is up there, Miss." Abby pivoted toward him. "So, I get out here when I can. We were gonna be in a band. He was the drummer. So I just play for him, you know." He picked up his guitar case. Nodded to Abby and slowly walked away.

Jack finally came back to her. They finished their somber walk to the end of the monument. Their reflections on the black walls made it feel as though they were casualties too.

No shit.

Abby knew *Saving Private Ryan* must have had a powerful effect on her husband. It wasn't until he stirred his coffee and took a bite of the slightly larger half of a chocolate croissant that he finally spoke softly to her. "I knew guys like Tom Hanks' character, Abby. Cool on the outside, but when no one was looking, shaking—small stuff, but you noticed it no matter how much they tried to hide it."

Abby knew that was as much as she would get from her husband. She knew he had delivered his favorable "review" of the film. She would have to wait until she was at school and in the safety of the faculty lunchroom to talk about the movie with colleagues who, unlike Jack, had never pulled a trigger and killed a man.

---

Walking in the opposite direction that evening down Orange Avenue, Gregory Larson loosely held the leash of his dog, Aussie. Aussie was the second version of Aussie; like his predecessor, he was, of course, an Australian shepherd. Aussie regularly visited the balcony of the Village Theater. He was Greg's date more often than not, and his bowl was a part of the old place. Top row. Left corner. A few biscuits would hold him over.

He had just heard Joe Pappas' speech about the theater closing. Greg wasn't going to miss the last night—even if *Saving Private Ryan* premiered that night. He hadn't known just how much that last scene would affect him. He wished he had someone to talk to about it. Talking to Aussie would just have to do.

"Pretty scary movie, huh, Aussie? Man, your ears were up those first twenty minutes, buddy." Aussie looked up at him as if he was supposed to comment. This was a routine for the two of them. "Jesus, it gave me the shakes."

Greg Larson had every reason to feel the way he did. He was, like Jack Adams, in Vietnam in 1969. Though he was only deployed for three months in country, he found himself involved in the battle that began to turn the tide of public sentiment against the war—the Battle of Hamburger Hill, in which he helped launch 450 tons of bombs along with 69 tons of napalm.

But Greg Larson was one of the lucky ones—no physical damage to his body. The drinking and the drugs had started before his draft, but the war had intensified everything. His soul shattered a month after Hamburger Hill, when he unexpectedly received his orders to go home. Thirty years later, he still managed the symptoms of a wound that never healed.

Greg walked past the hardware store that he now owned. Coronado Hardware was a mainstay on the island. He had always found it remarkable that a hardware store could have everything to repair a home, and during his darkest days, the store's former owner, Norman Barnett, knew that down his aisles Greg Larson could also find just the balm to temporarily soothe a young man's broken heart.

Greg understood Private James Ryan, who was afraid he was starting to forget his brothers who were killed in the war; he couldn't picture their faces. "Fear will do that," Greg said out loud to nobody but Aussie, who seemed to nod his head as he marched toward Greg's small, quaint house two blocks away. Captain Miller tells Private Ryan to think of a favorite memory of each of his brothers, like he does when he pictures his wife pruning rosebushes.

Greg stops. A small tug on Aussie's leash.

*Giving Raquel the ring. Her smile. Their kiss.*

He shakes his head. "Sorry Aussie, let's keep going."

---

Abby was surprised when Jack looked up from his coffee, which he had just refreshed, and asked her, "Abby, did I *earn it?*"

Abby knew what he was asking, why he questioned himself, and how silly it was—but also how predictable it was. *Of course, he is thinking about the last scene of the film, when Private Ryan looks down at Captain Miller, who gives him his final command.*

Jack Adams did not emerge unscathed from Vietnam. Damage to his lungs from defoliants like Agent Orange, painful knee issues caused by time and shrapnel wounds, and the wounds inflicted that one can never see had weakened his strong, powerful body. But Jack Adams "soldiered" on as everyone's fix-it man.

Abby's eyes immediately became watery.

"Jack, you can't possibly be serious. Look at us. We've raised three children who adore you, and even more importantly, I love you and I always have—since the day you walked into my parents' house in Jersey with that uniform..." Abby needed another tissue, but she had exhausted her supply. Jack's offer of a napkin had to do.

"I didn't mean to make you cry. I guess sometimes movies like this just make me think about things I never want to think about. Sorry." Jack put a ten-dollar bill on the table.

Abby knew at that moment that when her teacher friends asked her what she thought of the film, she would tell them they needed to see it for themselves to understand the sacrifices made by men just like her Jack, a man for whom the phrase *earn it* was a badge of honor.

# Chapter 3

## *New Year's Eve—1970*

Greg Larson was drunk when he saw *Love Story*. He went by himself, too miserable to be around anyone else, and he knew he would be equally depressed when the movie ended. He needed to be alone and wallow in his misery. Ah, but what to see? His only choice as he walked down Orange Avenue was a ridiculously sappy movie called *Love Story*.

Greg thought. *Just what I need. Some guy who has his heart cut out of him—by what, cancer? Car accident? Some random act of unkindness?* He didn't give a damn. He had what he needed tucked under his jacket, and he bought a ticket to the last showing of a movie that guys only went to when dragged by their girlfriends.

Everyone knew how this movie ended. Women brought a wad of tissues stuffed into their purses. Greg brought an entire bottle of Jack Daniel's, a Christmas gift to himself. *Have yourself a merry little Christmas,* he snorted as he sipped away the two hours watching Jenny's and Oliver's lives play out in a melodrama that seemed farfetched in one sense—but really, *shit happens every day. I know.*

---

Four years ago, Greg embarked on his dream. He was offered a scholarship on the strength of his left arm to play baseball for the UCLA Bruins. When his high school coach told him that pro scouts were in the stands, Greg was pleased but stubbornly determined to go to college first. In 1966, the big signing bonuses were not so tempting, and college meant a way out of Vietnam and into the dorm rooms of UCLA coeds.

His parents glowed with pride. His dad was retired Navy, and they lived in a tiny house on Coronado Island. Greg thought about enlisting in the Navy, but his old man told him that the war in Vietnam could wait. He had a gift and he ought to see it through. Besides, Greg wasn't naïve, and neither were his folks. By then, the war was getting worse by the month. Greg figured baseball might just be his ticket to fame and fortune. If that didn't work out, he'd have a college deferment and degree, and by then, the war would be over. He figured that the worst case scenario was that he'd become a CPA.

But life threw Greg Larson a wicked curve.

During his freshman year, he pitched in relief. He had a great slider that broke wildly. Sometimes too wildly. But his best pitch was the one he made to the girl in the next dorm over from his.

Raquel Mendez was a force. Her parents lived in Mexico and had sent her to America for "the education they had never dreamed of." She was going to double major, she told him, in education and dance. Her goal was to teach elementary school. She loved children, and she hoped to teach near the border in San Ysidro, where she felt she could give back to the Hispanic community. She hoped she could convince her parents to come to America one day and they could all become citizens. But that seemed so far away, and it required patience and persistence, not to mention money.

When Greg got the chance to talk to her alone in her dorm room a few hours before their English class, he found himself terribly distracted. He struggled to pay attention to her explanation of Mark Twain's personal views on slavery, as Raquel sat cross-legged across from him in a tight, baby blue UCLA T-shirt. Her long, pitch-black hair was twisted up in a knot and somehow held in place with a pencil. Mark Twain was the farthest thing from Greg's mind. *Raquel Mendez was so gorgeous.*

"Are you listening to me?" Raquel feigned anger.

"Yeah. Of course I am, Raquel. So Twain *was* a racist?"

"No, he was a product of the South. The preachers back then...Wait. Did you read the article the professor assigned?"

"Well, I was getting to that." English had never been his best subject. And frankly, baseball took up more of his time than he had anticipated, as did his math classes. Of course, the freedom to flirt with girls had been too intoxicating to ignore. Especially this girl.

Raquel rolled her eyes, but smiled knowingly. "I hope you are not some dumb jock."

"Raquel, come on, you know me. I'm a math guy. See, in math there's always a correct answer."

A beat.

"Sorry, I didn't mean to call you dumb." She smiled at him in a way that made Greg understand she was toying with him.

Raquel wore less makeup than most of the girls Greg knew. Her skin was a creamy light brown. Her Spanish accent slipped out frequently, enticing him, drawing him closer to her.

Greg begged for mercy. "Really, I was gonna read it. It's in the library on hold…for me. Honest." He just stared at her lips. Red, puffy lips. He had no idea how obvious he was to her.

Instead of explaining the article, Raquel did what she really wanted to do. After all, he had those hazel eyes, and he wore his hair like her favorite musician, Jackson Browne—long and parted slightly to the side. She leaned forward, put her hand around his neck, and pulled him to her, kissing him softly.

Her lips slowly released her hold on him, and she whispered, "There. Are you happy now?"

Greg Larson didn't open his eyes; rather, he slid off the edge of his seat and gently pushed her back onto her bed. "Well, I could be a little happier if you would let *me* kiss you this time."

Raquel wrapped her arms around his neck and closed her eyes.

Their study session didn't end until long after their English class had been dismissed.

As *Love Story*'s theme song droned on, Greg's bottle drained steadily. His eyes blurred, and his mind wandered to a time when his life held so much promise. All the innocent joy of his freshman year vanished into painfully acute tendinitis in his left elbow. It happened when he threw the slider. The pain shot down his arm from his elbow every time. He knew it was bad. Real bad.

His coach told him to rest it. He did, but when he tried to pitch again that season, he had to be shut down. It was over. His coach was kind, but honest—he was done. His scholarship ended abruptly after his sophomore year. Despite Raquel's encouragement and their passionate relationship, Greg began to feel sorry for himself. His grades slipped as his math courses became more and more difficult. His parents offered to have him stay at UCLA; they would find a way to afford it, they told him. He gave it a half-hearted attempt for the first quarter of his junior year, but something was wrong.

Raquel had two years left to go on her degree and another for her teaching credential, but Greg's exit strategy from college made him feel like a mouse confused in a maze. He became angry, then depressed. When the fall quarter grades came out, his upper division math classes showed the results of his lack of motivation. He had never failed anything in his life. Now his once powerful arm and proclivity for numbers had left him. He felt impotent. He may have been lost, but he wasn't alone. Raquel hadn't abandoned him.

He never enrolled in the winter quarter. That decision changed everything.

His naiveté became apparent when he lost his II-S deferment status. He was drawn to the Navy. Halfway through what would have been his junior year, a recruiter made it all seem so simple. "You've done two years at UCLA, Greg. You could move up so fast in the Navy. You're smart, Greg. This could be a great career. Wasn't your dad a Navy man?" Greg was looking for a world in which things made sense again. A place where he could be a winner. What he had forgotten was that he was the prime age for *induction* into military service—more commonly referred to as *draft eligible*.

Raquel tried to understand. She kept hoping that she could delay him until the war was over. In 1968, when Bobby Kennedy was assassinated just a few miles from campus, the only hope for immediate American withdrawal dimmed. President Nixon had a far different agenda.

None of that mattered when the draft notice came in the mail. *Army.* That meant infantry. That changed everything. He had waited too long. The Navy ultimately did not need him. "America needs ground troops right now. You should have enlisted when you had the chance. Sorry, son," was all he could recall a Navy recruiter saying.

So, as was the custom in those turbulent years, Raquel and Greg were married, ironically, by a justice of the peace. He put a ring on her finger—a ring he promised was only temporary until he could save up more money and afford a better one. The size of the ring really did not matter to Raquel; only he mattered. Because her parents could not be there, neither were Greg's. Their vows were equal parts love and fear. They inhaled the passion of each other's breath during the days they had left together. They spent as much time as they could naked and embracing—holding on, as the expression goes, to dear life.

He would train for six weeks. Then, at the beginning of 1969, he didn't realize one break had come his way; he would be stationed for two months at Fort Irwin as an artillery specialist. The Army knew he was smart enough to shoot missiles and calculate distance. During those months at Fort Irwin, Greg and Raquel saw each other as often as they could. Raquel sensed he had suspended his emotional free-fall. His persona was changing. He was valued. He had structure. She prayed he would be somewhat safer behind the lines. Vietnam's invitation came, and their last goodbye twisted their hearts so badly that talking became nearly impossible. He swore to Raquel the Soldier's Promise—"I'll come home. I'll be careful. I'll write."

And he kept all three.

His exodus after just four months stemmed from the letter that Captain O'Rielly handed to him. Private Gregory Larson knew that a letter from the Army wasn't a good sign and neither was the look on his CO's face. Not now, when he had at least eight months left to serve.

**DATE: 21 June 1969**

**TO: Private Gregory Larson**

**RE: Raquel Mendez Larson**

**The United States Army regrets to inform you of the passing of your wife, Raquel Mendez Larson. She died on 14 June 1969 in a traffic fatality. She died at the scene. The Army has few details; however, your parents and the parents of the deceased have been notified. You are hereby ordered to fly stateside to make funeral arrangements. You will be contacted by the CO at Fort Irwin. Await further orders.**

**Our sincere condolences to you and your family,**

**Lt. Colonel Harold Jenkins**

**United States Army**

Captain O'Rielly waited as Private Gregory Larson read the letter. O'Rielly had delivered bad news before, but never something quite like this. Parents died. Brothers. Uncles and Aunts. Sisters. But never a wife of someone so young. He finally made eye contact with Private Gregory Larson, who looked at him in shock. O'Rielly wanted to say something, anything that could make this all go away. Instead he said, "Son, I am so sorry. Greg, you need to go home to your family. I have told Colonel Jenkins that you should be re-evaluated before redeployment to 'Nam. I really don't want you back here, son. You have already given enough." With that, Captain O'Rielly did something uncharacteristic. Instead of placing his hand on a shoulder for support, he moved to embrace his artillery gunner. As he did so, Private Gregory Larson broke down such that, if not for Captain O'Rielly, he would have collapsed into the dirt and weeds beneath his feet.

Raquel never saw him coming. Chances were the 16-year-old boy driving stoned with a learner's permit never saw her. According to the police report, he ran a red light and hit her broadside going 50 mph. Raquel never regained consciousness. Her limp, broken body had to be untangled from the wreckage. She had been driving to the post office to mail a letter to Greg. The police found it in her car. It didn't have a stamp on it yet; it was, however, stamped with blood. For want of a single United States postage stamp, their dreams had been crushed and mangled.

That letter peeked out from the breast pocket of Greg's uniform as he spoke to the doctors at the hospital a few days after the Army had sent him from one tragic landscape to another. He kept thinking about how *his* casket, with a flag draped across it, should have been the consequence of war. How Raquel's eyes were supposed to be filled with tears, not his. *Why is my every decision the wrong one?*

He could not remember the order of the doctor's words. All Private Gregory Larson could understand was:

"Raquel. Autopsy. Pregnant. Three months. Baby. Hopeless. So sorry."

He never knew. No one did. She had been waiting for the first trimester of her pregnancy to be complete. Raquel wanted to make sure her pregnancy would come to term. Her mother's miscarriages decades earlier had spooked her.

So now Greg knew the letter's purpose. He also knew he could never open it and read her final words. He just couldn't. It had been delivered at the cost of two lives.

---

As *Love Story* came to its pitiful climax, Jenny and Oliver discovered that she had some mysterious terminal disease, and they held hands and counted the days until she walked into the Boston hospital and died.

And in the dark recesses of the Village Theater's balcony, Private Gregory Larson thought: *So simple. So nice and tidy. So peaceful.*

*Bullshit.*

*I never got a chance to say one single word to Raquel. Not even "Goodbye."*

He finally decided to leave the theater. A kid in an usher's uniform came in to clean up. Private Gregory Larson tossed the Jack Daniel's bottle into the trash. His love story would haunt him for the next thirty years. All he had left of her was folded in an unopened envelope.

The last thing Raquel's lips touched.

# Chapter 4

## *In the Jersey Snow—1971*

Before she was Abbigail Adams, Abby DiFranco was a Jersey girl. She knew in middle school that she wanted to be a teacher. Some people just know. American history always fascinated her. She started teaching at twenty-one years old, and in 1971, she was munching on popcorn and watching Jeff Bridges make out with Cybill Shepherd in *The Last Picture Show*; the lovers are bored in their stifling Texas town. It is so dull there that even its movie theater is closing down due to lack of patronage.

Sitting next to her, holding the hand that was not going back and forth to the popcorn tub, a handsome young man of twenty-four tried to wait. He was wearing his uniform; the pin attached to his breast read "Adams." He had trouble sitting still, and his arm pulled her to him; his fingers grazed the side of her breast. But her eyes were glued to the screen. His were glued to her dark brown hair, which was pulled into a ponytail; her bangs brushed her eyebrows. The soft, red lips parted for another kernel of popcorn. Jack could barely contain himself. He wanted this movie to end. He wanted to kiss her now. Deeply.

Finally, she turned to him and smiled with the look that made it clear: *I know exactly what you are up to, soldier. You are just gonna have to wait.*

Waiting was all they did. She was too poor to move out of her parents' house. Her job paid her $6,000 a year. And he lived in Navy housing, bunking with two other guys—waiting for the call to be transferred to his dream assignment: Naval Base San Diego. His second tour of duty had finished, and he knew the war was going badly of late.

Thanksgiving was tomorrow. He had much to be thankful for. Mostly he was thankful he was alive.

They had been dating for nine months. He adored her. She studied history; he felt like history had stamped its indelible mark on his rear end. He so wanted his life back. He wanted to be in love, to return to a vision he had believed in before the war had swept it away—the American Dream.

He could not be sure how she felt about him. She knew his moodiness. He had issues. She loved the government, and he had grown to hate the part of it that had betrayed him and thousands of soldiers, sending them off to fight a war that politicians just did not have the willpower to want them to win. And the people back home? By now, they were just sick of it all. The caskets. The "friendly fire." The My Lai Massacre. Kent State. He pushed it all out of his head.

Abby's hoop earrings dangled and brushed against the crook of her neck. Jack stared at her petite features, mesmerized by her more than any "picture show." When she would talk to him about her students, Abby's passion was infectious and made him forget Vietnam. She gave Jack Adams hope that things would start turning his way.

Thanksgiving dinner at Abby's parents' house reminded him of *Meet the Press*. Between slabs of turkey smothered with gravy, politics were front and center. Abby's parents were level-headed. They were not fans of President Nixon, but they knew that Lyndon Johnson had gotten the country into this mess in Vietnam.

Abby's parents were sensitive to their daughter's new love—Jack. Jack in uniform. Jack in battle. They knew that despite all his bravado, he was scarred from the war and angry at the way he had been treated by the people who were supposed to have his back. They knew happiness eluded him—except, of course, when he dated their oldest daughter, Abby. They knew Abby had fallen in love with him. Nevertheless, they were unsure of how secure Abby's life would be with Jack. Respect was one thing, but giving their daughter away to a man who had just come home from a jungle and had lived to *not* tell about it was unnerving at best and frightening at worst.

Jack Adams waited again. Waited until dinner was finished. Waited until the dishes were done and people were too full and needed a break before pumpkin pie. Then he wrapped his dark blue Navy pea coat around him as Abby also bundled up. He opened the door to the chilly Jersey air. She made sure her cinnamon-colored scarf was tucked in under her chin just right, and then they strolled down the snowy front walkway for a talk that would forever change their destiny for better or worse.

"I've received my orders." Jack said this looking straight ahead, as was his habit.

"Oh. Orders to where?" Abby couldn't help shivering. She tried to hide it, but it was not the cold. It was her nerves.

"Well, I got what I wanted. What we talked about."

"San Diego?"

"Yep. I bet it is a hell of a lot warmer there today. Probably seventy-five degrees. We'd be walking down some beach today."

For the first time, he glanced at her. His dark, chestnut hair had gotten a bit too long by Navy standards. He had to do something about that. His hazel eyes took in Abby's reaction. It scared him when he saw her teeth chatter.

They stopped.

Abby knew what this meant. He was leaving town, with or without her. She held his hand but pivoted so she stood in front of him. They were face to face. Abby DiFranco needed him to say it. What did he intend? What did *he want her to do?* Only then would she know what she would be able to consider. She loved her hometown. Loved her job. Loved her family. Why couldn't things just be simpler? Now she was the one waiting.

"I gotta go, Abby. I want to go. I know how I feel about you. I just don't know if you love me enough to give up all this and be a…"

"A what?" Abby looked up at him unblinkingly.

"…a Navy wife." He had said it. Not eloquently. He hadn't exactly asked her to marry him. It simply did not go as he had planned. But he seemed bewildered. Less than a year ago, he had fought for his life. And now, after spending nine months with the woman he loved, he could not for the life of him *get it out.*

"What are you asking me, Jack? 'Cause I'm freaking freezing here, and I'm scared and worried, and I don't know what we are saying to each other. So I need you to just say it, *now.*"

He grabbed her around the waist and hugged her close. He closed his eyes and whispered into her ear, "Please come with me. I know what I am asking of you. We don't have to get married right away if you're not sure. We can wait and see if it works out. But I love you, Abby. I love you. I need you. I want you with me. And if you want to marry me—well, I want that more than anything."

He was so afraid of her reaction that he held on to her longer than he needed.

"Jack, I love you," Abby said as she pulled back and felt her whole body shake. "Are you asking me to marry you? 'Cause if you are…" She froze, almost literally. Why did the biggest decision she had to make in her life have to come with such sacrifice? She knew the problems they would face: her parents' deep concerns, three thousand miles away from family and friends, her job lost, a war still raging. What if the unimaginable happened and they called him back to Vietnam? Who knew how this crazy war would end or when?

Her hesitation melted like the snow on his shoulders.

"…if you are, then I am telling you right now, yes. Yes. Yes, I will marry you, but…"

Before she could say another word, her big strong soldier, who had faced the Viet Cong, mortar fire, leeches, defoliants, and more snakes than he could bear, let out a sigh of relief that doubled him over as if he had just taken a Smokin' Joe Frazier punch to the gut. He sprang back up, smiling as wide as Abby had ever seen him smile. He grabbed her again by the waist, hugged her close, and then spun her around. He kissed her, and then she felt something unexpected. The tears in his eyes had splashed onto her red, numb cheek. And at that minute, she had stopped shaking. They looked at each other and broke into an insane laugh. She wiped her tears, and then his, into her mittens.

They would work out the details. Those didn't matter. All that mattered was that the snow fell softly. Abby kept thinking how crazy all this was. Perfectly crazy.

"Jack, I just realized I'm going to be Abbigail Adams, a history teacher. I guess the name fits."

Jack just gazed forward, nodded his head, and squeezed her hand.

# Chapter 5

## *Monsters at the Village Theater—1974*

Abby Adams had never seen her husband Jack laugh so hard, so loud, and for so long at any movie. But her stoic, hardworking husband just howled at the genius of Gene Wilder and Marty Feldman and the utter nuttiness that is a Mel Brooks comedy like *Young Frankenstein.* Abby thought that Mel Brooks' genius was not just in making people laugh, but also in making people laugh at their fears—in this case, taking that most horrifying monster, Frankenstein, and transforming him into a song-and-dance man "Putting on the Ritz."

And finally, Abby too could laugh.

---

But there was no laughter in the DiFranco household when Abby first confronted her mother, Helen, with the news that she had "made an engagement" with Jack Adams.

"A what?" Helen asked.

"Well, he asked me to marry him, so I'm engaged."

"Wait. Start over. He proposed to you?" Helen's excitement was muted by her daughter's obvious trepidation.

"Mom. Yes. He proposed. And I said yes, but I told him that I had, have…worries." Abby's hands formed a ball that knotted just below her throat.

"Worries?" Helen, ever patient, tried to decipher the message that her daughter stammered over.

"Yes. Mom, Jack has orders to go to San Diego, and, well, he doesn't want to leave without me…and so he asked me to marry him, and I said 'Yes, *but*,'" Abby explained.

Helen remained calm. "Dear, '*Yes, but*' is a seriously mixed message. But what?"

"But I have to leave my job, you and dad, everyone I know! For God's sake, it's practically on the other side of the world!"

"Abby, calm down. It's San Diego. It's beautiful. Your father and I have vacationed there. But that's not the point; none of this matters. You realize that, right?" Helen reached across the dining room table and took Abby's hand. Helen gently pulled them toward her. "Listen to me, dear. First, calm down and breathe, okay?"

Abby, all of twenty-one years of age then, did not speak. She merely nodded.

"Good," Helen continued. She gazed at her oldest daughter, who in many ways mirrored her own petite features: olive skin, brown eyes, and brown hair that now required coloring to fight off the gray roots.

A beat.

"Do you love Jack? I mean really, *truly* love him?" Helen's voice resonated calmness blended with wisdom.

Abby had heard that voice many times in her life. Unlike many of her friends who abhorred their mother's advice, Abby had been gifted with a mother whose insight knew the time and the place. Abby nodded and uttered one word: "Terribly."

Helen smiled. "And he loves you 'terribly' as well. I can see that, honey."

"Yes, but I told him I didn't want to *get married* until things are settled there and I know that it is right for me." Abby's eyes pleaded for her mother's approval.

"Hum. Well, I understand. But, Abby, you are making one of the most important decisions of your life. You can't always have everything aligned just so. You have to have faith that the two of you can see things through. I know that's not what you want to hear, but if you want to marry Jack, then you need to accept that and all that comes with it." Helen looked directly into Abby's eyes.

Abby began to cry. "I will try...to not miss you and Daddy and everybody...and try to not be so alone...I can't believe I'm crying. Mom, I love him so much." She caught her breath. "We are shopping for a ring later today...and we will come over tonight to tell you and Daddy. But Jack will have to leave soon for San Diego, so I guess we will make the wedding plans here...but I will fly out and look for a teaching job, and we'll try to get by...and I will try to..."

Helen stood up and reached for the tissue box. "One thing at a time, Abby." Helen waited calmly. Her daughter was facing a woman's dilemma, but it was compounded by the fact that her daughter was going to be a Navy bride; military life was capricious.

"Honey, I promise you I will see you after you are settled. Daddy and I will come out there as often as we can. I mean, it's San Diego—and we need to get out of the freezing cold, you know."

Abby nodded. Her tears subsided to sniffles.

Helen smiled. "Your father and I do respect Jack, but we worry about all he has been through in Vietnam. He and I will talk about all this, but, Abby, it is not about us. It is about you and whether you feel this is what you want. Love can overcome many things, but are you both sure—really sure—you are ready? Do you understand Jack well enough?"

"Oh, Mom, we both try. He is so kind. He cares about how I feel, about all I have to sacrifice. He would do anything for me. I feel the same way. I can't let him go, Mom. I love him so much."

Helen's right eyebrow lifted. "I understand, Abby. I do. I felt that way once, too." She corrected her posture, sitting taller. "It will take your father a little time to get used to the idea of you being far away, but that is what life is, dear. Life is change. He will understand, trust me." Helen was resolute.

Abby's smile came an instant before she pushed out her chair and embraced her mother. "Oh, Mom. How come I'm so lucky to have you guys?"

They held onto each other tight. They both knew how lucky they were.

Later that evening, Abby and Jack came into the DiFranco home to announce their plans to the family. Abby's engagement ring created a good diversion for Jack, who approached Abby's father, Fred. "I will never stop loving her, Mr. DiFranco. I will take care of her, I promise."

"Jack, I'm trusting you with my daughter."

"I know, sir. She is the most important person in my life." Jack did not blink as he looked at Abby's devoted father.

A beat.

"That's all I can ask of you, Jack." They shook on it.

For Fred DiFranco, a handshake was sacred.

---

So on a summer's day in 1971, they wed. It took some time to get all the principal cast members in one of life's most dramatic moments to gather under the New Jersey sunshine. Hotel rooms needed to be reserved. Flights booked. Dresses ordered. Bridesmaids chosen. Groomsmen groomed. Settings set. The cake baked. But there was nothing too frivolous about the marriage of Abbigail DiFranco and Jackson Adams, except that they insisted on a real band that could play for a few hours or so. Their wedding song was an old-fashioned standard. After all, wedding nights were meant to be "Unforgettable."

---

Two years had passed since they had departed the Jersey Shore. Abby finally found a teaching position after six months of being a substitute. During those six months, she was known as an energetic, young teacher. Then she caught a break—one of the teachers she subbed for became pregnant, and Abby was hired on for the rest of the year. That was all she needed. Word spreads fast on an island, and when the school year ended, the principal of Coronado High School hired her to teach social science. She became the first female teacher in the school's History Department in the summer of '72. Abby's salary wasn't much, but it at least allowed them to get on a better financial footing and see a movie, Abby's guilty pleasure.

But distance remained an issue. She missed her family. She knew that Jack wanted to stay in California. He loved the outdoors. He took up surfing. They could drive three hours and go skiing. Jack knew that San Diego was a city that was beginning to grow, and construction work of all kinds was in demand. He knew exactly what he wanted to be when he left the Navy as a petty officer, second class in May of 1973.

Fortunately, Helen understood her daughter's loneliness, and her trips out West, with or without her husband Fred, came every four months. That kept Abby from being too homesick when the Navy dominated Jack's time.

In the summer of 1973, Abby and Jack both knew that the time had come for a decision. The United States Navy became Jack's past. Jack's future involved two partners, former Navy men, who were going to open shop as a "one-stop construction group that could be hired out for jobs big and small"—as they advertised. The business was called "Jack of All Trades." Jack invested the most and thus owned the majority share of the business, which had a storefront in a tiny office off Orange Avenue.

Jack sat down on the beach, gazing at the surf at sunset, and held Abby's hand. "I know this is hard for you, Abby. But when I proposed and you accepted, you said we would have to wait until things were right. And I know you risked everything to come here. And I know you miss everyone…"

Abby looked at Jack. She knew he would continue to stare out at the ocean. Eye contact had never been his forte. There was already a lump in her throat. She had known this time would come. She was so overjoyed to have a job, to enjoy her students, to see her mom occasionally, but most importantly, to know that this man loved her unconditionally. She was just afraid because she knew that something very important could change everything, and she was just barely adjusting.

"I know, Jack. I know I have to decide, and I know it can't wait much longer."

"Abby, tell me what you are afraid of."

"I want us to have children, Jack."

"I know that, Abby. So do I. We've talked. You know that is just as important to me. Why does it frighten you?" Jack felt that sometimes Abby could be a complete mystery.

"We talked about two or three children. Jack, we are just getting our feet under us. I just got my dream job. I mean, then we'll be back to maybe one paycheck…"

"Abby, Abby. Hold on, sweetheart. I love you. One thing at a time." Jack paused and said, "Look out there, Abby." The sun had set on the horizon. He saw it. So did Abby. The green flash. He turned to face her, knees in the sand.

Jack spoke tenderly. "I believe in us, Abby. I want to be the father of your children. I will do anything to make that work. I'll work nights if I have to. Maybe you can teach part time. I don't know. It's about faith. Abby, I will never let you down."

Abby knew she needed to simply jump *heart first*. She buried her face in Jack's soft cotton shirt. "I know that, Jack. That's why I came here— why I love you so much."

Abby faced him, and just as the high tide tickled their bare feet, she finally swept away the fears, the miles, and the loneliness.

That night, their breath blew hot, their bodies rose up to meet in a manner that consumed them, and their eyes glowed with fire. Clarity only came to them when the morning light peeked across their bed to awaken them.

Six months later, as Abby watched *Young Frankenstein's* happier-than-ever ending and the townsfolk's fears of a raging monster quelled, she felt—for the first time—a kick.

"I think our baby likes comedies, Jack." Abby squeezed her husband's hand and placed it on her belly.

"Let's just hope ours is not a little monster," Jack winked.

# Chapter 6

## *Norman Barnett's Hardware Store—1974*

Thank God for Norman Barnett.

In 1948, Norman Barnett opened Coronado Hardware three doors down from the Village Theater. It was the go-to place on the island for everything one could think of. Despite the fact that the Navy took his only son, Larry, and returned him in a flag-draped casket, Norman Barnett was not an angry man. To the contrary, he still proudly displayed the American flag in his window and made sure the Navy guys got whatever they needed, even if they couldn't pay for it just then…or ever.

But his proudest accomplishment was the restoration of Private Gregory Larson. Greg was his son Larry's best friend and teammate in high school. Greg threw strikes and Larry caught them. On the baseball diamond, they were on the same wavelength, but in the classroom, Larry Barnett's big heart could not make up for his small academic stature. While Greg drove up the freeway to UCLA, Larry thought that no college was worth the drive. So right after graduation, he shipped off with the United States Navy.

Norman Barnett was a proud father of three. His two older daughters had careers, husbands, and kids, making him and his wife, Doris, doting grandparents. However, Larry's shortcomings at school did not diminish his parents' pride in their son. Norman was a GI in France during World War II, so he knew the cost of war and that the price of freedom was steeped in blood. He was no fool. But stopping his son from enlisting in the Navy was like stopping the rain from falling.

Besides, Norman supported the war in 1967 and still did when he buried his son in 1968. Larry was hit by gunfire as a part of the "Brown Water Navy" that patrolled Vietnam's rivers and coastline. It was mere coincidence that this was the same type of swift boat action that Jack Adams had served on just two years earlier.

Norman and Doris Barnett's longtime friendship with the Larson family meant that they hastened to arrive at the hospital's emergency room with Greg's parents on the night that Raquel Larson was killed. All four hoped that the worst could be avoided.

At Raquel's funeral, Norman Barnett made a promise to Greg that he would do anything to help him move on with his life. Norman Barnett was determined to not lose another son to the war.

After five months of battling the demons of grief and depression, Greg, with the option to take an honorable discharge from the Army, made a pivotal decision. He could have stayed on at Fort Irwin. His CO knew that he was a damn good artillery specialist. He had a knack for explaining things to newcomers. But Greg had had enough of Army life. Despite all the discipline that the Army afforded, he still drank too much. Cried too much. The world pissed him off far too much. He just needed to go home. Fortunately for Greg, Norman Barnett's hardware store provided a safe haven—and Norman would not take no for an answer.

When Greg went to work at the hardware store, it was a natural fit. He got along fairly well with people and even better with gadgets. He was at his best when he was explaining how things worked—except, of course, why horrible things happen to the people who least deserve it. Only Norman's patience saved him from a nosedive into despair. Norman had only one rule: be sober at work. Greg honored that, but made up for it when the evening's demons appeared.

He lived that way for the longest time. Routines. Work, eat, drink. Repeat five times a week. Sometimes Greg worked an extra day to keep his mind off the loneliness and the bottle. Then in '71 he got Aussie. Aussie went everywhere with Greg. He was an older rescue dog and probably would have been put to death had Greg not grabbed him. Aussie rescued Greg, alright, but he only lived two more years. When he died, Greg knew that he had done right by Aussie and that Aussie had done right by him.

So he drove all around the county looking for another Australian shepherd, and when he found one at the Helen Woodward Animal

Center, he named him Aussie, too. They were quite a pair. Greg got along far better with him than with the women he dated.

---

*Young Frankenstein*'s humor seemed to escape Greg Larson's date, a girl named Diana—*or was it Diane or Dena? Damn it. I forgot her name.* It was easy for Greg to do because she spent various parts the movie in the bathroom or, as Greg suspected, smoking a reefer in some inconspicuous spot. She wasn't the brightest girl he'd ever met, but a discussion of humorous irony was not why he was on a date with her.

"So, like, that was a really freaky movie," she said as she stumbled out of the lobby and onto Orange Avenue.

"Well, which part?" Greg smiled. "You missed some of the funniest scenes."

She stopped, looking dead serious, and said, "At first, I thought it was some kinda horror flick. I mean, shit, it's Frankenstein. I mean, like, people were laughing. I guess I don't get it. I mean, like, you were laughing."

"Yeah. It's a comedy."

"It's freaking Frankenstein, Greg! What's so funny about a monster? And, like, why was it in black and white, for God's sake?"

*Ah. She doesn't get it.*

Despite the fact that Greg had himself imbibed more than a bit before the date, he kept his senses about him, mostly. He knew where this dialogue would lead, and it had nothing to do with why he was dating her. All he had to do was take in her look: black hot pants; a tight red top that revealed exactly what she was advertising; big, flowing, Farrah Fawcett hair; and a stoned look that screamed, "I want to get laid in the worst way!" But first, of course, he had to make a stop at a bar. And even though satire wasn't her strong suit, there was no mistaking what was. She sizzled like a firecracker in bed.

Soon afterward, she passed out.

There were times when he could temporarily put Raquel out of his mind and enjoy the company of a woman, albeit an unconscious one. Perhaps it was better this way. A string of Dina's and Diane's only reminded him that they were never even remotely like his Raquel. He didn't really try to look for her. It was safer to soak in the booze and the girls who sat next to him at the bars. He looked for disposable women, and he made sure he recycled them, one after another. He wasn't sure who claimed the lead as the more pathetic character in this quixotic farce.

On the way to work the next day, Greg felt miserable. One thought that he simply could not shake from his mind that morning—many mornings—was that he didn't have the courage to look for anyone like Raquel. He was afraid to try. Friends kept telling him that he would never replace Raquel, but undaunted, they kept trying to set him up. He usually passed on those women. All he kept thinking as he strode into Norman Barnett's sanctuary was this: *There's nothing down any of these aisles that can fix my broken heart. Ain't that a damn shame.*

Gregory Larson had no idea what shame was until he crossed the only bridge to the island.

# Chapter 7

## *The Coronado Bay Bridge—1983*

On June 14, 1983, Greg Larson got himself good and drunk at a bar in Old Town. It had been his favorite place to go with Raquel when they were traveling back to his hometown and spending the summers together.

It was the fourteenth anniversary of Raquel's death.

Aussie was welcome everywhere Greg went, but on this night, Greg just wanted to be utterly alone.

As he brooded over the remnants of an empty pitcher of margaritas and too many tequila chasers, Greg played the pathetic role of the "What if I...?" martyr. His well-rehearsed regurgitation of rhetorical questions played like a constant loop in a *Time-Life* offer on TV. *What if I had never blown out my pitching arm? What if I had taken better care of myself? What if I had not been such a pathetic jerk and not bailed from UCLA? What was I thinking? Didn't I realize that dropping out would screw everything up and get me drafted? What if I had just joined the Navy and not waited around? What if I had never been to Vietnam? What if Raquel had had a simple postage stamp? What if she wasn't at that corner on that night at that precise moment?*

*And what if I had just changed one thing—just one? Maybe I wouldn't be here without her.*

The now empty glass in his left hand made his anger revert to a lazy, sleepy drone.

The bartender told him he would get him a cab. Greg told him to forget it. He was fine. And he would have been if he were just going to stumble across the street to his house on the island. But Old Town required passage across the Coronado Bay Bridge. Still, Greg had no worries.

A cop dragging him from the front seat of his car: that was the first vivid memory Greg Larson had on the bridge. He had passed out; however, his car had remained fully engaged. When he sideswiped the Honda in the outside lane of the bridge, both cars screeched and spun, with the bridge railing doing the most damage to the Honda. Greg's own steering wheel made a nasty gash across his forehead. The blood flowed freely down his forehead and into his eye sockets. He was a mess.

Another cop had a rag on his head fairly quickly. Greg tried to stand, only to find that his knees seemed attached improperly. The cop didn't need to test him for alcohol—it was perfectly clear that this man was drunk. But once Greg could gain his bearings, the cop would test him anyway.

The EMTs appeared to Greg almost like they were pulled out from behind a magician's curtain. He heard not sirens. The red lights and blue flashes were just part of the act. They were poking and taping. They murmured numbers. They frowned at him. He got the distinct feeling that he was a villain—but in what? He passed out again.

He reappeared in a bed. The ER bustled with noise. He saw a label on a monitor next to him, and in big red letters it said, "Mercy Hospital." He began to cry. He could not stop, even when the nurse came by and he tried to muster up a sense of manhood. It was no use—*Lord, have mercy. What have I done?*

His eyes followed the nurse, a tall, angular black woman whose lanyard identified her as Carmen. She did not speak to him right away nor did she smile, although she did make fleeting eye contact with him. Instead, she inspected some bags above him. Checked the monitor. Jotted down some words on a clipboard. She began to step away from him, but then she stopped, turned, and said, "Mister, we all do stupid things. You were just very lucky tonight. Lord knows what could have happened."

Greg stopped sobbing, and he looked so pathetic that this hardened veteran of emergency room drama took pity on him. Carmen's difficulty stemmed from the fact that she knew he instigated the chaos.

But then she came back to him and delivered more healing than bandages could ever assuage. "Can you tell me your name?"

Greg nodded.

"Tell it to me, please."

"Private Gregory Larson."

"You're in the service?" She checked the information on her clipboard taken from his wallet's contents; there was nothing about being in the service.

"No, I used to be."

"What? When?" The nurse's confusion increased as one eyebrow arched upward.

"When it started."

"Um, Mr. Larson, when what started?" Carmen glanced at the monitor momentarily.

"What I did tonight, nurse."

"Do you know what you did tonight?" She tried to not sound too brittle.

"Car accident."

"Well, that is the first thing you've said that makes sense."

"Anybody…hurt? Besides me, nurse?"

His nurse looked down at him and touched his swollen wrist. "Mister Larson, that's why I said you're a lucky man. There's no telling how much you had to drink tonight, but you could have killed someone mighty easily. No, sir. The woman you hit was just shaken up a bit. Her toddler doesn't have a scratch. Thank the Lord for car seats. She was a pretty good driver, too. Because she managed to hold the cars together until I guess your foot slipped off the accelerator and you two came to a stop on the bridge. At least, that's what the cops told the EMTs."

Then she placed her hands on her hips and looked him straight in the eye. "So now I'm telling you. You are a very lucky man, Private Gregory Larson."

She stood erect—the voice of compassion morphed back to her normal business cadence as her job's hectic missions reclaimed her. "I will be back to check on you. The doctor will come by in a few minutes. Just rest, okay?" And she slid around the curtain.

A woman holding a toddler peeked through that same curtain, at first to see if he was the right person and then to see if he was conscious. Just that glance made her recoil. That was all she needed to see. He was alive. His face obscured with a bandage. She didn't want to look at him, really. She just needed some form of closure.

Just then, Nurse Carmen appeared next to her. "Well, dear, you seem to be just fine. The doctor has discharged you, so you are good to go. And how is this brave little man doing?" She touched the puffy chin of the woman's little boy.

"Oh, we're both fine," she said. The woman felt that her nerves required her to keep talking things out. "Luckily, years of driving in the snow and ice back East helped tonight 'cause we skidded a ways." She blew out a sigh. "Thank you so much for all you did tonight, Nurse—I mean, Carmen." Then she nodded her head in the direction of the man surrounded by the aqua-colored curtain. "He seems to be okay?" asked the woman, balancing her one-year-old on her hip.

"Oh, well. He's got a pretty good-sized gash and stitches, Miss." Then Carmen, after looking around for an eavesdropper, said in a hushed voice, "I must say, I have seen a lot of drunk drivers in my day, but I feel sorry for this guy. He has some issues that he has to deal with. When he was dozing off, he kept muttering something about some girl named Raquel and his baby...something painful. For a minute there, I thought he was talking about you. 'Course, you're not this Raquel person. There is just a pain in him, Miss. A deep pain. But I don't often see them—drunk drivers, I mean—so...so *remorseful*. Well, anyway, here I am going on like I'm a psychiatrist. The point is that the Good Lord has been watching over you—all three of you—tonight."

She took Carmen's words to heart. Like a reflex, she hugged her boy tightly and then hugged Nurse Carmen.

Inside the curtain, Greg felt dull, constant pain from his heart up to the top of his head. He realized that there was a large bandage across his forehead that barely allowed his eyes to peek out from under it. Some dried blood on the parts of his face that were not bruised had not been cleaned up yet, and his hair was covered with those light blue nets they make people wear.

But the physical damage to Greg's body paled in comparison to his emotional realization of what he had almost caused. *Fourteen years ago. A woman and a child.*

Just beyond that aqua curtain, the woman knew that the man had been drinking. She knew it was his fault completely. She knew that this man could have destroyed the lives of her and her family. She had every right to scream at him: *What the hell were you thinking driving drunk, you stupid fool?*

The woman looked up from her son, who was enjoying the nurse's attention, to Carmen. "My husband wouldn't be so kind to that guy. He wants to come in here and rip his throat out, but I made him swear he wouldn't come in here. There's been enough damage already." She diffused the danger of that remark with a quick addendum: "I'm only half kidding."

"I wouldn't blame him one bit," Carmen said, and she looked up at the ceiling. "I'm glad you appealed to your better angels, though. Besides, we have enough trauma in here tonight. I gotta check on someone. You know your way out, honey?" Carmen added over her shoulder, "You just need to rest up, and you'll be fine."

---

When Carmen reappeared by Greg's bed, Greg asked her again if the person he hit was okay. He had gained a sense of composure. "Yes, Mister Larson, we just discharged her and her little guy. He is a doll.

Not a scratch on him. You, on the other hand, are gonna take a while to mend."

There didn't seem to be much more to say, but the nurse felt something inside her telling her that the best medicine to heal this poor man could only be administered from inside his own soul. So she leaned over to fix his pillow and softly said to him, "Listen, I gotta go. My shift is almost over. But you need to promise me this—never, never do that again, Private Gregory Larson. You hear me? The Lord works miracles, but he's a busy man. He doesn't have the time or the patience to teach a lesson twice."

They looked into each other's eyes. He knew she showed him tender mercy.

---

The woman and her boy made the slow walk down the hallway. They turned the corner and went into the waiting room.

Only then did Abbigail Adams crumble into the arms of her husband Jack and her two other children.

Only then did the tears pour down her cheeks.

# Chapter 8

## *Coffee and a Movie—1983*

In the month that followed the crash on the Coronado Bay Bridge, Jack realized he was also heading for a collision—only his was to occur on Orange Avenue.

*Accidents happen.* Jack understood that. *But some idiot driving drunk almost killed my wife and child.* Jack couldn't help but be pissed off. Abby seemed to forgive the driver for some mysterious reason. All she told Jack was that his nurse said that he carried pain and that he was so remorseful. All Jack could think was, *Damn it, Abby, the guy was a drunk. If I ever meet the jerk, he'll feel real pain.*

Of course, accidents bring police reports, phone calls from insurance companies, and such. Eventually, Jack got the police report in the mail; it revealed the name of the driver. The guy's name was Greg Larson, and he lived on the island. Jack didn't know him. *That's probably a good thing, 'cause there is no telling what I would do.*

By now, Jack's business was thriving. He had taken sole proprietorship; his partners had moved away. So just when things were going well, Jack now had to worry about fixing Abby's car.

*I need this like I need a hole in the head. Thank God that Jake was okay.*

Jack had Tommy and Carly to worry about, too. Tommy was seven years old, and Carly was five. Abby taught at the high school, and Jack was concerned with all that was on her plate.

*It was only an accident for God's sake. Relax.*

But Jack knew it was not just a matter of relaxing. Abby knew about the episodes he experienced. The anger. The dreams. They came and went. Sometimes it presented itself as anxiety. His doctor told him lots of vets felt the same way. "You're lucky all you have is an anxiety disorder, Jack. I've seen much worse."

Somehow, that didn't dispel Jack's fears. Abby insisted that he see a psychiatrist. The VA had some good ones. Her girlfriends recommended a doctor who worked with Vietnam vets.

*Yeah. Yeah.*

But her accident made things worse. Jack had the doctor's business card burning a hole in his wallet: Dr. Harold Tillson, M.D. *Maybe, just maybe, I will.* But the fact that he needed to pick up some more drywall screws set other things in motion.

---

Coronado Hardware's owner, Norman Barnett, and Jack knew each other well. It seemed that the hardware store became Jack's second office. Jack also knew Norman's manager, a guy named Greg, but their conversations were limited to construction supplies.

*Haven't seen Greg these past few weeks. Probably on vacation.*

So when he walked in and grabbed what he needed, Jack froze at the counter. He stared at the bandage across Greg's forehead. Suddenly, it became obvious. *Greg. Greg Larson. Oh, my God. I've known this guy for years.*

No such connection registered on Greg's face. The name *Adams* appeared on the insurance documents Greg received. It was a common name. Greg never put it together.

Jack paid the bill but then asked Greg, "You got a minute to talk? Like, can you take a break? I gotta ask you something."

Greg looked surprised but turned to Norman and said, "Sure, Jack. Keep an eye on Aussie. Aussie, stay." Aussie obeyed, but grudgingly. "Be right back, Norm."

They stepped outside, and Jack glanced down the street to the coffee shop. "Buy you a cup of coffee?" Jack fought the instinct to grit his teeth.

"Sure, what's up?" Greg became slightly suspicious.

"Tell you when we sit down."

With the coffee held between his hands, Jack decided to get right to the point. "Tell me about the gash on your head, Greg."

Greg cocked his head quizzically. *He knows about the accident. Why does he care?*

"I got in an accident. Totally my fault. I was drinking. Really stupid. Now, shit, I'm dealing with lawyers, fines, probation. But I deserve everything that I get, Jack. I almost killed the woman and her kid. I skidded against their car coming home on the bridge. I am still..." Greg paused. "Why do you ask?"

"'Cause my last name is *Adams*. That was my wife," Jack said as he stared into the coffee, never looking up. His hands gripped the coffee cup so hard that it seemed possible that it would implode.

A quiet fell between them. Greg's lips uttered the soft, almost imperceptible sound of "Oh, no."

More quiet.

"Yeah. That *woman's* name...her name is Abby. My little boy is Jake. They're fine. 'Course, we're not so fine. Car's not totaled. It's gonna cost you a pretty penny." Jack stirred his coffee, although it needn't be stirred. He wanted to put another gash across the guy's face, but instead, he found himself gritting his teeth and then nervously trembling.

Greg decided to come clean. He never talked to anyone about the accident—except Norman, who insisted he go to AA and kept pushing him to face it. Face his truth.

"Jack, I think I have said the word *sorry* so many times lately that I just want to slam my head into the mirror. Hell, you probably wanna do that to me right now."

Jack smiled at his coffee and kept stirring. Then, with an unmistakable edge, he looked up from the coffee into the enemy's face and said, "Yeah, that's been on my mind."

The tension between the two had straightened their spines. Perhaps it was coming to the brink of violence that made the two very slowly soften their voices, slowly bend back to the sanctuary of the coffee cups before them. They let out a sigh that seemed to utter the words, *No point in making things worse than they already are.*

Greg now found it equally comforting to stare at his coffee. "It's just...complicated. Shit, Jack, I'm so used to lying to people about my alcoholism that I fooled myself into thinking I could just drink away my demons. I'm sick of myself." Greg paused. He had never mentioned his addiction to a soul—other than Norman.

Greg inhaled a breath of air that stuttered as it made its way from his nose to his lungs. Nerves. He then decided to jump off his cliff. "See, that night I ran into Abby, your wife—well, that was the same night 14 years ago that I lost my wife. And I just get..." Greg found that he could not finish the sentence.

Jack finally looked up. "Drunk. You get drunk."

Greg nodded. "Yeah."

A beat.

Greg coughed up another detail. "The accident happened when I was in 'Nam. I couldn't even..." Greg stopped, hypnotized by the creamy brown color of his now tepid coffee—the color of Raquel's complexion.

Jack felt he knew enough.

Greg just shook his head at the irony of it all. "Here I am, still blaming the kid who killed her. He was stoned...ran a red light...and I go and do the same damn thing." Greg looked away, down Orange Avenue. He used his fingertip to quickly swipe away a tear that formed. "I'm so sorry."

Jack's eyebrows rose as he contemplated what to say. He was still staring at the lukewarm coffee. Another Vietnam vet, like him, broken and angry with a gash in his head. He remembered lots of soldiers with similar gashes that no plastic surgeon could cover up. Not when the wound was so deep.

Jack made up his mind. "Hey, it's just a car, man. You fix 'em up and forget about it. The important thing is that nobody got hurt too bad—except that forehead of yours." Jack felt the trembling stop and his jaw relax a bit.

A sigh escaped from Greg's chest. "Jack, I made a promise that night. I promised I would not be that guy ever again. So I started AA two weeks ago, and I'm gonna do my best. I gotta work things out, you know."

"Oh, yeah, I know." Suddenly, Jack found the need to reach into his pocket and grab his wallet to pay the waitress. But the real reason was to check and see if that business card for Dr. Harold Tillson, M.D. was still in there. It was.

Jack tossed down a five-dollar bill. "You know, that promise you made. Now you've made it to me, too. And all this—the accident and all—it stays between us...if you keep your end." Then Jack softened. "We all got our demons, Greg. Trust me."

They stood up and shook hands. They would speak many times—of tools and nails and hammers, but never of this. Jack never told Abby that it was Greg, the manager of the hardware store, who almost killed her. Greg kept his end of the bargain and became a regular with AA. He would never "overcome" his addiction. He would live with it, knowing it was always there lurking in the shadows. But he never again took another drink.

He owed that to Raquel.

As Greg walked back into the hardware store, he couldn't help but notice that the marquee of the Village Theater read, *Tender Mercies*.

For the second time in a month, someone had shown him exactly that.

Later that night on Orange Avenue, Abby and Jack sat in the Village Theater. She noticed that Jack seemed distant. "Honey, you seem tired."

Jack nodded. "It's just been a long day. You know how Saturdays can go." He feigned interest. "So what's this movie about?"

"Oh, it's your favorite kind. A love story." Abby smiled at him, then leaned into him and kissed him on the cheek. "You like Robert Duvall. He's in it."

"Oh." Jack's mind drifted while Abby nibbled on her popcorn and glanced at her husband.

"You sure nothing's wrong?"

"No. No. I'm just trying to let this day go. Sorry I am being so weird." Jack sat up, grabbed a handful of her popcorn, and smiled at her.

*The guy had suffered enough. We all have.*

Despite their efforts to put the recent events out of their minds, what they were to witness in the ruby red seats of the Village Theater had the two of them wondering. This film was about an alcoholic has-been of a country singer who hits rock bottom and has to face the wreckage of his lonely life. Then he wakes up from a drinking binge at a motel in the middle of Lord-Knows-Where, Texas. The innkeeper, a gal named Rosa Lee, sees the good in this broken down man. She befriends him and all his troubles, his past baggage, his anger—everything.

Abby knew that the man who had hit her car had been wildly drunk. She hoped that he had hit rock bottom. Jack, of course, knew far more than he would tell.

As they headed home to relieve the babysitter, they were quiet—strange for Abby, typical for Jack. But when things were settled and they climbed into bed, Jack said, "This Rosa Lee gal, she reminds me of you, Abby."

"What makes you say that?"

Jack stared at the ceiling. "'Cause that's who you are, Abby. You take people into your heart. Me. The kids. Your students. Even the guy who slammed into your car. That's just you. You always show people tender mercy."

"Well, now, Jackson Adams. Turning poetic, I see." Abby nestled her body closer to him and coquettishly put her fingers on his lips. "How about showing me some 'tender mercy?'"

And he did. It was the first time they had made love since the accident, and it was by far the most passionate they had been in a long while.

# Chapter 9

## *Dr. Harold Tillson, M.D. —1983*

Jack was nervous as he sat waiting in the office of Dr. Harold Tillson, M.D. Jack was self- conscious. *This guy is a shrink. What does that say about me? Maybe if I act like I am waiting for someone else who is in there with the doctor, then people will think there is nothing wrong with me.*

The office wasn't fancy—far from it. The magazine rack was bare except for a three-month-old *Newsweek* and a dog-eared copy of *Country Living*. Every time someone came into the waiting room, Jack found himself slouching down even more. Finally, he grabbed the *Newsweek*. The cover story was "The Puny Superpower." Some guy's hand held a tiny American flag. Jack thought, *Shit. That is all I need to read. I'm sitting in a room for head cases. What am I doing here?*

Just then, the door opened. A tall, lanky, bearded man looked directly at him and said, "Mr. Adams."

Jack rose and approached him.

"Come on back—let's talk," the man said warmly.

When they got into the doctor's small office, scantily decorated with no noticeable long couch, Jack turned to him and said, "Name's Jack."

"Name's Hal. Glad you came in to see me." The men shook hands. The doctor gestured to a comfortable looking chair opposite his far more utilitarian rolling office chair. His desk had only one file on it. Jack took note of the simple decor and clean, casual feel of the room. Not what he had expected.

"So, Jack. I know you went to 'Nam. I was there, too."

Jack was again taken by surprise.

"Yeah, I know. You're wondering why I am the sane one, huh." He chuckled. Jack's lips cracked upward momentarily. But it was far too soon to relax.

"Well, I'm not one of the guys who pulled the triggers. I'm the guy they saw after they did. And I'm not so sure I am all that sane when it is all said and done." Hal looked at Jack and took in his reaction.

For the first time, Jack felt his shoulders soften and his pulse slow. "Should I call you Hal, Doctor?"

"Definitely, Jack. Or else, Captain—just kidding there. So tell me why you are here."

Jack let out a sigh. "Well, I'll give you the short version. Nervous. Sometimes can't sleep. Can't get...can't stop worrying about things."

"Bet you worry about the fact that you are worrying."

Jack found himself uncharacteristically pointing at him. "That's exactly how I feel, Doc. I'm sorry, Hal. I just can't help but call you 'doctor.'"

"No problem. I've been called a lot worse. Jack, if I had a dollar for every man and woman who came through that door and was feeling like you feel, I'd be retired and sitting on the beach drinking a beer."

Jack thought to himself, *Man, I wish I were there right now.*

"Here is the deal, Jack. You have an anxiety issue. Maybe sometimes you even get a little down—depressed. But you are high functioning, and from what I read here in your file from your doctor, you are a successful businessman. I also know that you have some damn good reasons to worry. 'Nam took its toll on you. You would be crazy if you weren't anxious."

Jack finally smiled. The relief registered on both men's faces. Dr. Harold Tillson, M.D. knew he had to win over this proud, tough man. He had to get him to realize that he was simply human. So he got to the heart of the matter. "Jack, you can keep doing what you've been doing, sweating out your nights and trying to tough it out and such. I could give you some damn pamphlets to read about anxiety and such, but..." He paused knowingly.

Jack waited him out.

"You're not much of a talker are you, Jack?"

"Not really, Doc."

"And you probably don't want to take any medicine for your condition, right?"

"Not if I can avoid it."

"So I figured. Okay. You can try to deal with it, Jack, on your own. But there is no lying to your brain. Something—God only knows what—has created a chemical imbalance in you—and here is the most important thing I'm going to tell you: it is very treatable if you work with me."

"Doc, I don't want to take medicine unless I have to."

Dr. Harold Tillson, M.D. beat him to the punch. "You're right. Come back in a week. If you still feel the way you do, then we will start on a very small dose of anti-anxiety medicine—and something to deal with the panic you feel...Oh, I know, Jack. You are already sweating just thinking about it, right?"

Jack felt naked. "Right."

"So come back in a week, okay?"

Silence.

A beat.

"I don't need a week, Doc. I want to start getting better...now." Jack looked down. He did not want Dr. Harold Tillson, M.D. to see the tears welling up in his eyes.

"I understand, Jack. Really, I do."

---

When Jack got home, Abby feigned nonchalance when she asked how the doctor's appointment went. She knew that Jack's stubbornness and fear of showing any weakness would require her to not "make a big deal out of it."

So it was out of character for Jack to reply, "Abby, he was a nice guy. It was good I talked to him. Did you tell me he went to 'Nam? Jeez, he seemed to read my mind. Anyway, we're dealing with it. He said it's treatable, and I told him, 'Let's do it.' So I got these pills I have take for a while, and then we'll see how things go."

Abby merely smiled, keeping her relief from showing.

"I liked the guy. He just made me feel...I don't know...like I wasn't going nuts." He headed for the garage with a bounce in his step.

It would take months before Jack realized what it felt like to live without a monkey on his back.

# Chapter 10

## *Goodfellas —1990*

Norman Barnett's voice boomed into the empty, dark theater. "Hey, Joe, you up there?" It was nine in the morning, when Joe would be doing all his tinkering in the theater. They agreed to have a cup of coffee for a special occasion—Joe's sixty-first birthday.

"Yeah. I'm in the booth, but I'm comin' down—hold on, Norm." Joe's voice echoed back across the theater's walls. Norman waited while his eyes tried to adjust to the darkness from the summer's gorgeous morning light. Joe appeared out of nowhere.

"Hey, Norm."

"Jesus! Joe, you scared the hell outta me. It's so damn dark in here. I can't see a thing."

"It's a movie house, Norm. What'd ya expect?"

"Well, at least have the house lights on, for cryin' out loud, Joe."

"I can see fine."

"That's because you're like an old bat. Come on, let's get coffee."

The two old friends found their way out to the lobby and sauntered down Orange Avenue to the coffee shop. On the way, they admired the early morning vacationers with their beach garb, East Coast pale skin, ubiquitous Hawaiian shirts, and flip-flops.

"The town is hopping, huh, Joe."

"Well, yeah. Theater's been a little slow."

"Well, it's summer. People don't wanna sit and watch a movie so much."

"Tell me about it, Norm."

"You still showing *Dances with Wolves*?"

"Yep. That's part of the problem. Too long for the summer crowd. Great movie, though. My wife loved it. Cried for the last half hour." Joe sneezed abruptly. "I hate summer allergies. We gotta get one of those action movies here soon."

"Ah, those are crap, Joe. What are you gonna show, something like *Die Hard 2?* Forget it. The kids will go to the mall to see that junk." Norman ordered his coffee and a cheese Danish. He did the same for Joe—his treat. They always ordered the same thing. "Now, if you want to get us folks into the theater, you'll show that new movie with Julia Roberts."

"*Pretty Woman.* Whew, man, now that gal's a looker, Norm."

"You got that right. Maybe I'll see that *without* Doris." The two men laughed loudly as old men will do when the subject involves young women. "Oh well, we're just two horny old men, ain't we?"

"Norm, speak for yourself. I'm horny, but I'm younger than you."

They sipped their coffee and leaned back. "Beautiful day for your birthday, Joe. Hey, I got you something." Norman had a small bag he'd been holding. He pulled a dark blue Navy hat out of it.

"What did you get me that for, Norm? You didn't need to do that."

"Shut up and try it on. That old Navy hat is practically disintegrating on your head."

Joe ran his thumb and forefinger through his gray goatee and pulled off his favorite old hat. "Okay, I bet my wife told you to get me this. Sally said she was gonna toss this thing in the trash if I didn't get a new one." He tugged it on, fidgeted with it a bit, bent the beak a bit, and smiled. "Gotta admit, Norm, it's a real nice hat. Thanks. How much did it cost?"

"Will you shut up about how much it cost? It's your birthday." A touch more cream in the coffee for him. "You and Sally going to do something tonight?"

"Yeah. She says it's a surprise."

"Better not be going to the movies."

They burst into laughter. Norm knew the surprise. They were meeting Joe and Doris at the Chart House—Joe loved a good steak.

After a coffee refill, they settled into their routine of "What's new lately?"

"So, what's new?" Joe started off the updates.

"Well, the big news is I'm finally selling the business to Greg."

"It's about time. Greg has really turned things around, hasn't he?" Joe smiled as he put some sugar in his coffee and stirred.

"He's been something else. You know he finished his business degree this spring?"

"Yeah, he told me he was just about done."

"Well, since his folks passed, he has been dealing with their estate, and he and his sisters have pretty much settled things. He's not a rich man, by any means, but that and the money he's made in his investments have got him pretty squared off. I cut him a bit of a deal on the place."

"Well, Norm, I should think so. That guy's kept that hardware store in the black for years now—and dealing with all the competition, too. But your store has always done pretty well."

"True. But Greg gets things that I just don't. All this computer crap. I mean, he's talking about Windows 2.0, and I'm thinking, *what?* We don't have any windows in the store." They both find this hysterical.

"Then he tells me he's invested in this company called Qualcomm. They make semi-conductors—whatever that is—for phones. Jeez, Joe. I just can't keep up with this stuff. Anyway, he says he thinks he is into something that is going to be really big. I sure hope he knows what he's talking about."

"Well, he's a smart guy, Norm." Time to survey the street traffic. "So, you're gonna retire, now, huh? Take Doris to Europe or something?"

"You know my wife. She's got things all planned. Italy is her big thing."

"That's good. About time you got your ass off this island. But I know what you mean about all these computers. Everything is changing in the projection booth, too. I don't need to change a reel anymore—it's all automated. I just get it started and make sure it's rolling right. Frankly, Norm, sometimes it gets so boring that I read a book—or help the kids out with concessions—whatever. I think they keep me on because I'm 'an institution,' I guess."

The bill paid, the two stroll down the sidewalk past all the expensive shops that advertise the "California scene." The subject comes back to Gregory Larson.

"Saw Greg the other day with Aussie up in the balcony."

"Yeah? Just with Aussie? No gal?"

"Not this time. Is he seeing someone?"

"Off and on. One—I kinda liked her—Jennifer, it seems he saw her the longest. I asked him about her. She is quite a bit younger than him. Anyway, he told me that she wants kids and is a control freak."

"Control freak? Isn't that like callin' the kettle black?" Joe mused.

"Yeah. I dunno, Joe. I don't know if he is ever gonna be happy and settle down with someone. He still thinks of Raquel."

"After, what, how many years is it?" Joe stroked his goatee some more.

"Over twenty years, I think. God, he loved her." They avoid some kid on a skateboard. "Did you ever meet her?"

"Yeah, once—a long, long time ago. He took her to the movies here a few times." They arrived at the movie theater's entrance. "She was from Mexico City, right?"

Norm nodded. "So smart. Gonna be a teacher, remember? They were so perfect. The UCLA days. Isn't it crazy how one thing—an accident—just changes a man?"

Joe looked seriously at Norm. "Greg's still sober I take it."

"Hasn't had a drink since the day he hit…well, since he got in that accident on the bridge." Norm stuffed his hands in his pockets; he decided to move the subject away from Greg's accident. "Yeah, store's doing well. 'Course, the regulars keep things going."

"Speaking of regulars, Norm, I gotta call Jack Adams 'bout fixing some things in the theater. He's still using your place as his second office?" Joe's hat is off; he's rubbing his white hair and patting it down.

"Yeah. He is in at least once a week. I'll tell him to drop by." Norman and Joe began their trek back to the Village Theater.

One of the younger kids working there came out to see Joe. "Guess what, Joe?"

Joe looked at Norm. "I dunno, kid. What? They fired me?"

The boy just laughed at him. "No. They can't fire you, Joe. Nobody knows how anything works in here. No." He shook his head. His red vest was clearly a size too big, and his tie was far too loose.

"What then?"

The boy bubbled with the excitement that a teenager has when they have their first job at a movie theater and a new movie comes to town. "Tomorrow we're showing *Goodfellas*."

Joe looked at the kid. "Lord, help us. Scorsese has hit the island. Well, Norm, we won't be taking our wives to that one."

The kid had no idea what Joe was talking about. He asked, "Joe, isn't it like a comedy or something?"

Joe and Norm looked at him with disbelief. Joe said, "Kid, you got a lot to learn about the movies." Then he patted Norm on the back and thanked him for the new Navy hat.

The two of them were, after all, goodfellas.

# Chapter 11

## *Valentine's Day—1994*

In 1994, a life of fishing was at the top of Norman Barnett's bucket list, so he retired and sold Coronado Hardware to Greg Larson. Greg had buried himself in the business for the last several years. His intelligence and ambitiousness served him well, and his sobriety went a long way in helping him deal with people. He finally seemed to have accepted his past—to forgive and forget. However, his love affairs were another matter.

Greg remained athletic and lean. At 46, his hair shaded charcoal gray. His tightly trimmed beard began to turn silver. His hazel eyes were clear and sharp. His only consistent companion was Aussie. Women generally made him feel constrained, even somewhat frightened. The younger women wanted something he would not deliver; the ones his age brought baggage he didn't have the strength or willpower to carry. He found commitment unlikely. He felt a twinge of guilt—or maybe weakness—from this self-discovery, but his freedom to do as he pleased was just too tempting to disavow.

His relationships would come to a dead stop once the idea of having children was placed on the table for discussion. The scenario would follow a logical progression: the adoring woman would usually be about fifteen years younger. Her biological clock would be ticking loudly; she was ready to leave her job, become a mother, and rely on Greg to supply their needs. Despite the fact that Greg made it clear from the outset that children were a non-starter, these lovely women would feel certain that they could change him. The temptation loomed for Greg; after all, their bodies were ripe. Normally, this is when most men Greg's age would succumb.

Greg may have learned to accept and control his alcohol addiction, but he could not—would not—divorce himself from Raquel—as many other men his age had already done with their ex-wife…or wives. Besides, the world of babies was a package deal: soccer teams, homework, and babysitters. That life had passed Greg by.

Understandably, these younger women he dated ran out of patience when Greg refused to budge. So doors slammed, agonizing tears ran, and another relationship would come to an end. Never mind the rationale and damn the justifications—these women made Greg feel like a villain, despite his candor. Greg's redeeming qualities were simple: he was honest to a fault, and he accepted that it was, to some degree, his fault.

---

Greg never wanted to be a father after Raquel's death, but he loved being an uncle. His sisters had kids. All girls. Uncle Greg became their favorite. He helped his sister coach softball. The baseball diamond brought back memories of not just his carefree days, but also those flirtatious conversations with Raquel on the bleachers at UCLA. Raquel would be watching him, her brown hair whipped across her face, shaded by her visor that displayed the flag of Mexico. She would talk to him about her dream to teach elementary school and about how cute her little cousins were.

Sometimes at his nieces' practices, he just stood on the pitching rubber, staring at his baseball mitt and finding himself transported back to Raquel.

*"I want us to have kids, Greg. Not a huge family, but at least three or four,"* Raquel said one day.

*"You do, huh?"* Greg looked up to the sky to see if the rain clouds might cancel practice.

*"Don't you? I mean, you have sisters, right?"*

*"Yeah, they are a pain in the ass sometimes."* Greg laughed, but then winked at Raquel. *"But they probably think I'm really a jerk."*

Then Greg kissed Raquel, pulled away from her to focus on her eyes, and promised her, *"But whatever you want, I want. I love you…and I'll love them."*

*Raquel hugged him, dropped her head on his shoulder, and reminded him of the obvious: "But we have to get through school first."*

Then the rain would fall on his past and present. Softballs would be gathered up, and the girls would moan that their game would be cancelled. Too soon, his nieces went off to college, and Uncle Greg had no team left to coach.

---

On the other end of the estrogen spectrum, the divorced women, a bit closer to his age, desperately needed a man, a substitute father, to step into their world and their children's lives. Greg retreated after a few dates. He learned to be clear from the start with these women because he saw what pain he might inflict, however unintentionally, when the time came to say goodbye. So in being upfront, he found that for the most part, they came to avoid him out of their own sense of self-preservation. He was handsome, but staunchly independent, and they soon realized that a serious relationship with Greg was far too perilous. Over the decade, some tried to coax him from his cocoon, but as they say, word spreads fast on an island.

So those dates amounted to flirtatious appetizers followed by scrumptious dinners. Greg reminded these women that they were merely friends, but more often than not, neither party was willing to pass on dessert, even though both knew the limits of their diet. The last course would be served drizzled with passionate sex. Nevertheless, commitment for Gregory Larson was not on the menu. And again, guilty pleasures often led to hard feelings.

Then there were the nights with no one but Aussie at his feet, warming Greg's toes in front of a fire while he read. He loved historical novels. His latest book blended his two loves, film and truth: *Documentary: A History of the Non-Fiction Film* by Erik Barnouw. The past fascinated him; the documentaries gave it all a Murrowesque quality— drawing him in like a warm fire will do on a damp night near the ocean.

On February 14, 1994, Gregory Larson closed up shop, went home, grabbed a bite to eat, and took a walk down Orange Avenue, all timed to catch the latest movie, *Sleepless in Seattle,* playing at the Village Theater. He had no date tonight except his sidekick, Aussie, even though the movie was considered a "date night" film.

It just so happened that Jack and Abby Adams had the same idea. They needed a little romance to help wash away some of the tension of the last week. They were just a few feet ahead of Greg and Aussie in line when Abby turned around and saw Aussie.

Aussie was a bit of a celebrity on the island, and that made Greg his sidekick. People loved to stop and pet Aussie, and he loved the attention. Greg, not so much. But being the owner of Coronado Hardware made Greg have much more notoriety, something he was trying to get used to. Abby saw Greg and Aussie every so often, and much to Greg's relief, she had never made any connection to the man on the bridge who almost ruined her life. Greg pondered the fact that the scar he had on his forehead remained a reason why he always cooled to most conversations with Abby. *Don't push your luck.*

Abby was a sucker for Aussie. She got down on his level and massaged behind his ears. "You are the cutest dog on the island, you know that?"

Aussie appeared to nod.

Greg quickly glanced at Jack. Jack's poker face revealed nothing, his handshake cordial and friendly.

Greg bent over Aussie and joked, "Well, you know Aussie. He thinks this is *his island.*" The three of them laughed.

"Oh, he's so beautiful. I love his coloring, and three of his four paws are white, Jack." Jack merely nodded. Abby looked up at Greg. "Does he actually sit through the movie?"

"Well, as long as he gets his bone chews. He's kind of a regular here. Joe, the projectionist, and I have an agreement. Usually halfway through the movie, when Joe has time, he takes Aussie for a walk. We sit way up in the balcony."

"Oh, that's nice." With little else in common, the conversation dried up and Abby reached closure. "Well, enjoy the movie, Greg." She waved to them as they entered the theater's lobby. She turned to Jack. "What a cute dog. When the kids are all out of the house, maybe we should get a dog, Jack."

Jack smiled at her. "Well, maybe. A dog's got to be easier to deal with than Carly's mood swings."

Abby gave him an unappreciated look. "Anyway, I'll get the popcorn, you find us a seat." Abby looked back at the man and his dog as they climbed the stairs to the balcony.

Greg sank into his seat and found that his forehead had beads of perspiration dotting a path across it. Being around Abby always caused him some panic. He knew she would never know why, and that was a relief. But Abby always brought back the memory of that night and the face of Nurse Carmen reminding him that "he's a lucky man."

Greg took out the bone chew. "Good boy, Aussie. Now, sit. Here's your bone. Good boy." Greg spent a little more time with Aussie, rubbing him under the collar and getting to the spots Aussie craved.

So once again, the three of them found themselves staring into the silver screen—looking for a silver lining.

---

*Sleepless in Seattle* tugged at the heart of its audience. Abby's favorite actor, Tom Hanks, portrayed a lonely man whose wife had passed away. He simply could not push her out of his mind as he seemingly spoke with her ghost in his living room.

At that exact moment in the film, Greg leaned forward in the balcony. His eyes refused to blink.

Raquel did the same thing to him last night.

*"But, Greg, you need to meet someone else,"* Raquel lectured him as he sipped his coffee, watching another episode of PBS' Frontline.

*"Why?"*

*"Because you're miserable. Look at you, Greg. You're 46, and you just seem to think that no one else will make you happy."* Raquel put her imaginary legs across Greg's lap as she stared at him while he stared at the television.

*"I'm not miserable."*

*"Yes, you are. You just broke up with that latest girl——."*

*"Can we not talk about her, please?"*

*"Why not? She was beautiful. She loved you. Okay, she was a little controlling for my taste…"*

*"A little? Seriously?"*

*"Okay. She's a control freak. So what? And big deal she wanted kids…"* Raquel pressed her case.

*"It is a big deal, Raquel. We had kids…a kid. We lost the baby. I don't want to be that man, trying to create what I had with you…with her. She is not you, Raquel."*

*"I am a figment of your imagination, Greg. I am forever 21. I am a college girl to you. You need a woman."*

*"You are not part of my imagination…you were my wife. I have women I see."*

*"You just won't let them inside you, Greg. That is why you're so miserable."*

*"No. That is why I'm sane. They want things from me that I don't want. I will never want. I had it and I lost it."* And suddenly Raquel just disappeared, leaving only the narrator's voice of the *Frontline* episode to permeate Greg's living room: *"…and so President Clinton's 'Don't ask, don't tell' position brings controversy."*

Aussie shuffled around and wanted another bone to chew on. Greg disengaged himself from Tom Hanks' melancholy…and his own. "Here you go, boy. Quiet, now. Good boy." Aussie's tail kept a slap-slap-slap pace across Greg's boots.

Man's best friend.

---

Cancer.

Is there a more sickening word in the English lexicon? Abby knew that Jack's treatments for Hodgkin's lymphoma were something that the two of them faced with optimism and cynicism—a paradox, perhaps. Their attitudes on how to deal with the disease's physical effects created optimism. However, the reason that Jack suffered from this disease was part of the lie told to the troops in Vietnam, where Agent Orange, a chemical defoliant, was spread over the jungles indiscriminately. Thus, by April of 1993, the Department of Veterans Affairs had received disability claims from 39,419 soldiers who had been exposed to Agent Orange while serving in Vietnam. Jack was one of them. And he was part of the majority who hadn't gotten any compensation. Abby read that only 486 victims received anything from the government or Dow Chemical, the company that claimed that Agent Orange was "harmless to humans." After all, their slogan reminded customers: "Dow: helps you do great things!"

Like having to endure chemo and radiation.

Abby's blood boiled. Jack remained stoic. The chemo treatments were scheduled to start soon. So a night out, a romance between Tom Hanks, whose wife dies from cancer, and Meg Ryan, who is desperately seeking someone to feel passionate about, seemed like a good fit for this evening's entertainment…except for the cancer part. Abby and Jack both winced and shoved that part as far away from the plotline as possible.

Who could not pull for Hanks' and Ryan's characters to meet after so many close calls, to gaze into each other's eyes. How romantic. Abby loved these kinds of movies, in which the future holds so much promise and when love conquers the fates. "Well, I know it was a Hollywood ending, Jack," Abby rattled off as she diagnosed the film, "but it shows what love makes possible."

It was too cold that night to walk anywhere, so they decided to just head to their car and go home. Secretly, Abby hoped the movie would put them both in a mood where making love was also possible. She needed to hold Jack on this Valentine's Day, and she hoped Jack would feel the same.

Strangely, for Jack, the film's "happy ending" carried with it a clear message, one that he felt he had to say to Abby.

Before he turned the key in the ignition, Jack held her hand as they sat in their car. "Abby, I was so scared when the doctor told me about the Hodgkin's, and no matter how treatable it is, when you are only 48 years old—and Tommy a freshman in college, and Carly in high school, and Jake's only, what, thirteen?—well, it freaked me out...and sometimes...I know you know that I am having trouble sleeping...If I didn't have you..." His voice trailed off.

"Jack, we're going to get through this. It's good to talk about it sometimes. But try not to worry, really. Remember what the doctor told you: this is very treatable." Abby held Jack's arm tightly.

Jack started the engine. His gaze, which ricocheted from Abby to the road ahead, finally settled on one spot: Abby's warm, comforting face. "You know how much I love you?"

Abby nodded. She always knew.

Jack undressed that night. Abby looked into the mirror after she had brushed her teeth. She concerned herself momentarily with a wrinkle that had emerged right before her eyes. Jack came up behind her, pressed himself against her, and kissed her neck. Abby closed her eyes. He kissed her again and turned her hips toward him. Abby raised her eyes to his. Jack knew exactly what made Abby melt.

Jack whispered in her ear, "I love to surf, you know."

One of Abby's brown eyebrows rose. "Um, it's a little too dark for that now, Mister."

"No, it's not. It's perfect...for bodysurfing."

"Oh, I see. So that's what you had in mind." He slowly unbuttoned her top until it fell open. He caressed it off her shoulders and onto the floor.

Then they rode their waves together.

# Chapter 12

## *The Doctor's Office—1995*

From the beginning of it all, Jack carried on like he did with much of life. No big deal. Hundreds of thousands of people a year deal with chemo, so can I.

Early in the chemo treatments, Jack stopped at his "second office" to get supplies. He found himself far more tired than usual; feeling dizzy, he grabbed hold of the counter while paying his bill. Greg, somewhat distracted with a quibbling customer, glanced over and noticed Jack's instability.

He made no mention of it when he calculated Jack's tab. Greg couldn't help but notice Jack's body language. Normally erect and sturdy, Jack seemed as if a gust of wind might blow him over. Nonchalantly, Greg asked, "Need a hand with this stuff?"

Jack grunted, then smiled. "Nah, I got it. Thanks anyway." As he walked out, Jack saluted Norman, who found himself still drawn from time to time to his old stomping grounds. "See ya, Norm."

Norman never glanced up from his paperwork. "Later, Jack. Give Abby my best."

"Will do."

Two weeks later, it was a far different conversation between Jack and Norman.

---

Abby Adams scribbled lesson plans. The topic: the Vietnam War. The film: *Dear America—Letters Home from Vietnam.* The film was a staple of her American history course. Abby tried to make the past relevant to her students, and that wasn't hard to do with America again teetering on the brink of another military conflict.

The saber rattling between the United States and Iraq had been ongoing ever since Iraq was forced to admit it had biological weapons. President Clinton was concerned that Iraq would continue to refuse U.N. inspectors access to a number of sites where potential "weapons of mass destruction" were located. Saddam Hussein's obstinacy presented a serious war of words with the West. Thus far, the war remained limited to threats; however, the specter of another war loomed. With all this brewing, Abby Adams knew that history is not just *about* the past; inevitably, the past tumbled into the present.

Abby tried to focus on her lesson plans despite all her worries about Jack. His treatments for the Hodgkin's knocked some of the life out of him. He would recover, get back to his business, try to do more physical labor, start to get stronger, and then the cycle would begin anew. The protocol: repeat for one year, then radiation for six months. Hopefully, he would soon regain strength over the assault on his body.

During this time, Abby's children stepped up. Tom, then twenty-two years old, helped when he could, but college was a three-hour drive away. At least Carly had her driver's license and took her father to his doctor's appointments from time to time. But Abby's children were afraid. Who wouldn't be when their father stepped out of the shower one day to reveal that his hair had fallen out in clumps? Jake thought his dad looked like an alien. Carly started to cry. Abby hushed them up. But it was visual proof that Jack was not the same.

---

"Jesus, Jack. What the hell happened?" Norman Barnett pulled Jack into the small office crammed near the paint supply aisle. This time, there was no hiding Jack's condition. The Padres baseball cap couldn't possibly cover up the fact that all Jack's shaggy hair had vanished, nor could it disguise his haggard appearance.

Greg saw Jack come in and heard Norman's voice raise to a level that surprised him. As Greg peeked around the corner aisle, he saw why. Jack looked terrible. Greg tried not to be obvious, but he felt a kinship to Jack that drew him closer to the office door.

"Well, don't get all worked up, Norm," Jack said, as if he were discussing something as banal as the wrong shade of paint color.

"What do you mean, Jack? You've lost your hair. You going through chemo? You must be. What…why didn't you tell me? For Christ's sake, Jack, I've known you for twenty years! Sit down." Norman tried to lower his voice. Greg remained close enough to hear the conversation but far enough away to be unnoticed.

Jack decided to accept Norman's offer to sit down in one of the two dilapidated chairs. "It's Hodgkin's. It's a very treatable cancer. We're doing the chemo now, then radiation."

"Okay. Well, thank God it is. Did you catch it early?"

"Yeah. I think…I hope so. The docs at Balboa Naval Hospital said they've treated a lot of this stuff—you know, from the Vietnam vets," Jack said. All the while, he was staring at Norman's calendar. Miss March was about as sexy as any Charger cheerleader he could imagine. He hadn't thought too much about sex lately—another causality of all this "treatment."

Norman did not understand what Greg knew immediately.

*Agent Orange. Son of a bitch.*

"Well, listen to me, Jack. If there is anything—I mean *anything*—I can do for you and Abby, don't you even hesitate, okay? I know you're as stubborn as a mule, but don't…" Norman pointed an old, cracked index finger at Jack's face, trying to snap Jack's attention back from the Charger girl push-pinned to the wall.

"Yeah, yeah. Norm, don't worry. We are doing fine." Then with a wry smile, Jack turned to his old friend and told him, "Norm, you need to at least tell Greg to keep the months straight. It's April. You guys can't keep staring at Miss March, here."

It broke the tension. They snorted that laugh that old guys have about beautiful women. "Well, at least you got your sense of humor.

Okay, let's turn the page and see...wow. Look at her, Jack. My God, does the Lord give that much to one gal?"

"Well, depends on if those are real?" Jack posed the question.

"Real. Fake. Who cares? They are there to admire for the entire month."

Greg saw Jack coming to the counter with a few odds and ends. They briefly made eye contact. All he said to Jack was, "Hang in there, Jack."

Somehow, those four words implied an understanding that they both grasped. Jack responded in kind, "I will. Appreciate it, Greg." He stopped, turned, and added, "Really."

*Goddamn, 'Nam.*

---

Abby's lessons could be reduced to autopilot at times. A high school teacher repeats herself five times a day, five days a week. In the faculty lounge, it is referred to as "five shows." Then you head home for the encore. And for many women, home meant cooking, correcting, and cleaning up after everybody.

Abby was lucky. Jack cooked a lot. He cleaned a lot. The kids weren't too messy—except when you opened the door to their bedrooms. Then you were certain a stage-three hurricane had ripped through. But since nature had taken a toll on her husband, even the kids had decided to clean up their act—a little.

In class that morning, Abby found herself in the throes of 1968, with the war at home and overseas. She didn't have to review her notes on these tumultuous years—she had lived them. However, her "sermons" on Vietnam were evenhanded—as much as neutrality could allow—as she flowed through the dubious origin of the war in the Gulf of Tonkin, LBJ's assault on Vietnam, draft dodging, campus protests, Bobby Kennedy's assassination, and the Chicago Democratic

Convention. But for today's discussion, the subject was how the Vietnam War differed from WWII or even Korea.

Abby sat on her stool in front of the class and explained: "When the enemy was not wearing a uniform, or was undistinguishable, or was hidden in the deepest part of a jungle, well, what did the military do?" It was a rhetorical question that she knew twisted right into her description of how defoliants worked. It was normally her sarcastic swipe at the stupidity of anyone who believed that an orange spray could strip the leaves off trees and kill vegetation but not do one iota of harm to a human being who may have inhaled what was billed as "innocuous" vapors. The trouble came when she tried to answer her own question.

"What did the military do?" she repeated. She knew her "lines" by heart. But that made little difference as her voice retreated. Her heart got in the way. She just stopped cold.

Then it happened. Her eyes leaked the truth. The truth ran down her cheeks, which burst into a red blush of anger. The truth made her knock over her notes as she tipped forward from her stool. The truth made her hands cover her face, which was etched with the pain that comes with living with history rather than learning about history.

The quiet of the room signified the respect the students had for their teacher. They could hear each other's breath—particularly when some of the girls' breath rushed inward at the sight of Mrs. Abby Adams folding before them, hinged at the waist.

However, it was a boy named Frank who rescued his esteemed teacher. Wordlessly, he rose. He walked to her desk. He picked up the tissue box. He walked directly to her, offering his apology in the form of soft, pastel-colored paper. Frank kept his head down. Abby looked up. Grabbed at least one, two, three tissues, then a fourth and a fifth. All she could stammer to the classroom of shocked students were the words, "I'm so sorry."

Frank looked directly from her face to the class and back. "So are we, Mrs. Adams."

Of course, their eyes questioned what was happening to their teacher. Abby knew she had to explain herself once she tilted back to a somewhat more composed posture. She asked her students to promise her something that morning. "I know you are concerned. This is just something that I am dealing with. Sometimes history isn't just part of your past, but part of your present. But please don't speak of this to your friends outside of class. I would be embarrassed. I'm fine. It's just an emotional thing for me right now. Okay?"

Heads nodded. Frank, her rescuer, noticed another box of tissues on top of a file drawer. He handed the box to a girl who looked desperately at him. The magic pastel tissue box passed soberly through the room like a communion host does in church.

Abby decided that in the four "shows" that were to follow, she would veer in a direction that had nothing to do with *how* the war was fought. After that class, she faced the mirror in the coat closet and tried to reverse the effects that the truth had taken on her mascara.

Abby never told Jack what happened. It was a secret that she kept— the only thing she never shared with him.

# Chapter 13

## *The Principal's Office—1999*

Principal David Privitt put the phone down and nearly fell into his black leather chair. In front of him on his mahogany desk were all the pictures and little tokens that reminded him of his family, his school, his hometown. Privitt's weary eyes settled on his wife Donna, who had just spoken to him that weekend about retiring from her teaching position early—maybe at fifty-five. She hoped he would retire then too, but he told her he just wasn't ready *yet.*

*Yet. When does that word become a warning sign?* Now all these family photos and a lifetime of mementos that guided him through his years as a teacher and principal of Coronado High School blurred as he uncharacteristically felt his throat tighten and his eyes splash as he blinked. He brought his hands to his face to make sure no one could see. Principal David Privitt felt he could not be seen this vulnerable. He needed to get a hold of his emotions, and he needed to act fast.

He took a deep breath and considered his options. The hospital had already tried her cell phone: it was off, no messages left. He had no intention of calling her classroom phone. He took a deep breath. He wiped the tears away, even though they kept coming to the surface, like a cut that just won't scab over. Eventually, the tears subsided. He waited until his words were formed properly and then asked his secretary to come in.

It was 9:38 a.m.—just twenty minutes before the break for the teachers and students. Teachers would gather in the faculty lounge and grab coffee. Mr. Privitt's secretary, Audrey, would wait near the door that adjoined the lounge to the administration building. Audrey had already contacted the counselor, Lilly Chen. Both Audrey and Lilly had only twenty minutes to prepare themselves. Lilly would go to the classroom to see her students. Audrey would wait and hope that Abby Adams would leave her classroom today and take a coffee break.

Relieved, Audrey saw Abby chatting with her best friend, Karen, as they walked down the corridor. Doing her best to be casual, Audrey stepped up and asked if Abby had a minute—"David needs to see you in his office." Abby was puzzled. *What now? A parent issue? Another District ultimatum to be delivered to teachers about what they should be doing?* Abby noticed how strangely stiff Audrey was.

Karen gave her a discreet eye roll. "Catch up with you at lunch," Karen said as she veered off.

Principal David Privitt stood right next to his door. He could not go to her in her classroom. He needed her here, in the privacy of his office. He peeked out the tiny window in his door. Audrey and Abby were coming. He noticed that his palms were slick. His heart's pace had quickened noticeably as he wondered if the words he had practiced would be the words he would produce. He knew the police were on their way. He had to be the one to tell her, not them. The door opened. Abby stepped in. Audrey did not; she closed the door and raced back to her desk. Then she hid behind her computer and grabbed for the tissues, hoping the other secretaries would not see her. She was not successful.

"Hi, Dave. What's up?" Abby's friendship with her principal went way back to his days when they taught together and hung out, but Abby no sooner finished the question than she knew something was wrong. It was his pained eyes that told her so.

"Abby," Principal David Privitt began, "I have terrible news…"

Abby froze. Her blood pressure had slowly been rising, and now it leaped upward.

"…regarding Jack…"

Privitt extended his hands and softly touched Abby's hands, pulling them toward him.

"Abby, I have been contacted by the hospital. They could not reach you directly. Abby, Jack had a massive heart attack," he stopped a beat to brace for the fall, "and the ER doctor explained to me that Jack died before the paramedics could even arrive." The words came out as he practiced, but he could not prepare for the full consequence they would have on the two of them.

All Abby could utter before she tilted forward and met the body of her principal, who had leaned into her, was, "Oh, God. No."

Principal David Privitt was an average sized man, but at this moment, he willed himself to completely envelop Abby. She was dead weight. Her face fell into the gap between Privitt's blazer and his blue shirt and tie. The small couch was to his right. He wanted to sweep her to it and lower her down to sit, but she was not ready to move.

Principal David Privitt knew that this was the worst day of his working life. He had known Abby Adams for 20 years. He held her—as the entire staff did—in the highest regard. He knew Jack, too. The football games. The events their children shared. The Privitts' twin girls were Tommy's age. He kept thinking, *How do you tell someone their 53-year-old husband is dead?*

Outside the office, Audrey went into action. She looked at Abby's emergency contact list. If Abby wasn't thinking clearly, at least she would have these phone numbers. Lilly, the counselor, had already marched off to Abby's next class. She would tell them a lie. *Mrs. Adams is ill. She needs to see the doctor. Don't be alarmed. If you have schoolwork to do, go ahead. Please do not gossip with other students—Mrs. Adams' privacy is more important. She just got very sick all of a sudden.* Lilly kept her composure. *Tomorrow they would learn the truth.*

Abby's thoughts scattered like little spliced pieces of a film. *Jack looked fine this morning, didn't he? Jack made it through all the chemo, all the radiation. Heart attack—are you kidding me?* Then the cold reality hit. *Oh, my God. What will we do? But there is no "we" anymore—just "me."* All of these thoughts were flashpoints; none remained constant except for the crushing impact of two words: *the kids.*

Privitt eventually guided Abby to the couch. He dislodged her from him so that he could see her face. Abby looked like she was trying to comprehend something told to her in a foreign tongue. He grabbed tissues—as if that could assuage her. Audrey peeked in at this point and slipped into the room. Once she saw Abby, she slid to her knees next to her and embraced her. Audrey wore more makeup than most women in the office, and by now her mascara had smeared down her cheeks.

Minutes later, a police officer stepped into the office. He stood like a statue. "Mrs. Adams…" He was cut off by Privitt.

"Officer, she already knows."

"Oh, I see." The officer returned to the script. "I can escort you to the hospital, if you would prefer." Then he reestablished his position, frozen near the door. His face, however, was shaded with sympathy.

Time had vanished. All four were quiet. Anguish dictated their actions. No one knew how long it took for Abby to speak, but when she did, she gritted her chattering teeth. "I need to see Jack."

Privitt nodded. "Officer, I will take Abby. Thank you, though." He put his blue blazer across her shoulders and helped her to her feet. He opened the door to his office to make an immediate left turn to the parking lot with Abby braced against him, her head down. Privitt saw anxious eyes trained on him; people stood stiffly around the administration office. Perception quickly soaked in. Abby, Principal David Privitt, and the stoic police officer went through the doors into the open air. Then, Audrey stepped out of Privitt's office. Her face had the appearance of Halloween…and each person who saw her knew instantly that their own worst nightmare had just appeared before their very watery eyes.

---

When doctors in blue scrubs approach a family, one has the impulse to shout, "Is he or she alright?" But when that same doctor wears a white lab coat embroidered with their name, one senses that a final judgment has been made. Such a lab coat hung on the petite shoulders of Dr. Susan Howard-Chase. She routinely spoke of death to grieving family members, although it never became anything that she could do without feeling a pit in her stomach. She was thankful for that. So it was with reluctance that she began by sitting next to Abby Adams. She quietly spoke, "Mrs. Adams…"

"Abby." Abby did not blink, despite the tears that pricked her eyes.

"Yes. Of course. Abby, your husband Jack suffered sudden cardiac arrest; his heart is no longer able to pump blood to the rest of the body. Unfortunately, in ninety percent of victims, like your husband…"

"Jack," Abby insisted.

"Yes, I'm so sorry. Jack. Yes. When this happens abruptly and without warning, death occurs. The EMTs explained to me that Jack's co-workers saw him hammering something before he dropped to the ground. It took a few minutes before they realized what had happened, and they called 911. The paramedics came within twenty minutes or so and tried to resuscitate him, but his heart had stopped." Again, she let a breath go and felt the need to explain, though it mattered not. "Jack had a major blockage in his artery, on his left side, leading directly to his heart." The doctor paused to see if this reaffirmation of what had happened to Jack Adams had been fully understood. It had. "I'm so sorry. He is gone."

Abby repeated her mantra: "I need to see Jack."

"Of course."

---

Abby bent over Jack. She held his cold, already graying fingertips.

*Oh, Jack. Jack, how do I go on? What do I do without you? Oh, God, look at you. My Jack.*

Abby's hands formed a mask, which she used to cover her eyes and face. She felt dizzy. Her forehead burst with sweat. Her mind raced. *How will I tell the children?* Abby looked to the ceiling as tears streamed down her cheeks. Anger rushed to the surface. Her jaw clenched.

*I know it killed you. I know. It poisoned you.*

Abby looked down at him. Caressed his forehead. Kissed his drawn cheek. *Jack, I will be so alone. All our plans—they're ruined. We're ruined.* Her hands trembled. *I will always love you, Jack. Always.*

*Oh, God, watch over him. He was my life. Help me, Lord. Please.*

---

Principal David Privitt waited. He would take Abby home. He would ask Audrey and Karen to be there when they arrived. He would call his wife Donna and tell her what had happened. He thought of all this while staring at his reflection in the hospital's restroom mirror. Already, dark circles had etched craters beneath his eyes. That's when he realized that he and Jack Adams were exactly the same age.

# Chapter 14

## *Gregory Larson's Office—1999*

Word spreads like lightning on an island.

It thundered down Orange Avenue and into the shops.

It ricocheted up into the projection room of the recently closed Village Theater, and it threw Joe back against the poster of *Casablanca* on the back wall.

It shot through the percolating coffee shops, where the waitresses gathered and reached for napkins to delicately brush under their eyes, trying to push the tears back where they belonged.

It caromed through the corridors of the high school and sent teachers, secretaries, custodians, and parents reeling; they hunkered down in their classrooms, near Xerox machines, near cleaning carts and wondered about the fate of poor Abby Adams.

It shook the hearts of her students, who worried for their Mrs. Adams and wondered how they should react to her when, or if, she returned.

It crashed into Coronado Hardware with so much impact that Greg immediately grabbed the phone and called Norman. The two of them remained on the line, just talking…as if hanging up was an admission that Jack Adams really was dead.

But the unimaginable was visited on Abby. She tried to remain the eye of the storm, but the winds had torn her heart to shreds. All she could hope for was numbness, but that would not suffice now. For now, she needed to talk to each of her children and tell them that their father was gone.

It did not spare the children: Tom, Carly, and Jake. Each of their reactions was riddled with equal parts shock, pain, and fear—for each other and for their mother.

The numbness would come.

The anger was not far behind.

The will to carry on moved Abby through her routines. *Check them off, Abby*: the memorial; the goodbyes; the people wishing to help her and the children; the fears she held for each of her now adult children. Then the depression; the meds prescribed to her by the sympathetic Dr. Harold Tillson; the half-empty bed; the clothes laced with his scent; the now misleading photographs adorning table tops. Their frozen smiles, which seemed unalterable, now haunted her.

*When can we smile again without the guilt of his absence? Those were the best days; now they are gone forever.*

The list never ended. The business that needed to be sold; the accounts that needed to be addressed; the sympathy cards that just kept coming; the phone calls from potential clients asking for *Jack Adams*, unaware of the stabbing pain that inflicted; the awkwardness of telling people *he's dead*; the unanswerable, unpalatable questions that all began with *why?* The insurance companies and their red tape bullshit that could not dispute the fact that Jack's life insurance was all in order, *thank God*; the galling hospital bills that still kept coming despite the fact that the patient was dead and none of the services rendered mattered; the $1,200 bill that insurance would only partly cover; and the question that loomed over her like dark, ominous clouds: *When will it end…if ever?*

She took a month to brace herself to face her work, her students, her "responsibilities." After that first day back at school, the trauma diminished in minute stages. She still felt like her heart weighed her down each morning, pushing her back under the covers. She willed herself to not look to her right, where Jack would have been. It was the hot water of the shower that made her shed those thoughts and put on a separate identity. Mrs. Abby Adams. Room D-5. She would only remove that mask once she sat behind the wheel of her car, take a deep breath, and drive home.

As the weeks multiplied into months and the months lurched the calendar's pages forward, one incident of goodwill stood out to Abby from the many moments afforded her by those who loved her and Jack.

It occurred three months after Jack's death. Abby came across a ledger—a yellow legal pad—that Jack kept with the word *Norm's* crossed out and replaced by the word *Greg's*. Jack's scribbled notes indicated what he needed, wanted, or had already purchased from Coronado Hardware. Abby would head down Orange Avenue and find out what it all meant, and as she had done too many times to count, deal with all the loose ends of a lifetime of work and diligence.

Greg Larson had not seen Abby since the memorial for Jack, but he and Norman—along with the other owners of the various businesses on Orange Avenue—had met numerous times, with Norman chairing the discussions. They were planning to speak with Abby in a week or so. That timetable changed once Abby walked into Greg's store.

The first to greet her was Aussie. Greg later thought about Aussie's reaction to Abby. Aussie somehow instinctually knew that this was a person who needed his attention. Dogs seem to get that. Aussie got up slowly from his favorite spot near the door and rubbed himself against Abby, never once leaving her side.

The first words were, naturally, awkward…for both of them.

"Hello, Greg."

"Hi, Abby. I know we talked at the memorial for Jack, but, well, you know how much…"

"I know, Greg. I appreciated what you told me then and the flowers you sent." Abby let out a sigh. "You were very kind."

A beat.

A smile came to Abby's face. "God, I love your dog." Then to Aussie, "You are the sweetest thing, aren't you, huh?" She dug in behind his ears, and Aussie seemed to smile back.

Quiet.

"Yeah. I wouldn't know what to do without him." Immediately, Greg realized his thoughtlessness.

"I bet you wouldn't."

A beat.

For some reason, Greg realized that his nervousness toward Abby had dissipated to some extent. He knew that Jack had never spoken to Abby about the accident. Now even the scar on his forehead was an afterthought to Greg. He now understood that Abby's life had turned so dramatically that his past stupidity would not matter to a woman so overcome with the present.

Abby had been enjoying Aussie's soft fur and adoring eyes, but she finally got down to business. "Okay, well, Greg, I came in because I found Jack's notes here," she placed the legal pad on Greg's worn countertop, "and figured we needed to settle up."

Greg looked her in the eye. "Abby, Jack does not owe me anything."

"What? Of course, he does, Greg. It says here that…"

Greg's lies were shrewd. "Abby, stop. First off, he doesn't owe me any money. I never ordered the stuff he needed after he passed away, and the stuff he did need I already sold. Okay? But Abby, remember, whenever you need something—anything—just let me know."

Abby's eyes remained focused on Greg's until she finally looked down at her purse and then at Aussie, who had nosed his way to her hip. "You can't be serious, Greg. You run a business here. I have plenty of money."

"I told you, Abby, you owe me nothing. We are all square."

"But…"

"And there is something else you need to know, Abby. We wanted to come over and do this more formally, but the folks here—all of us shopkeepers, sales people, waitresses, well, lots of folks—we all got together. Norman organized it, so he gets the credit. And we wanted you to know that we have something for you and your son Jacob."

Abby's head seemed to involuntarily shake, as if she was telling him, *No, you can't do this.* But instead, these words poured out: "Greg, you need to tell everyone that we are fine. We don't need help. I am sure everyone has their own problems."

Greg had prepared himself for this line of defense. "It is a thing you can't refuse, Abby. We set up a scholarship fund in Jack's name for Jacob. We know he is going to college, and we all agreed to help him each year. It already has $3,000 in it. We are committed to that amount every year. I know that's not much, but it is a start."

"Are you serious?" Abby stared at Greg with disbelief.

"Just go down two doors to the bank. It is already set up, Abby— it's done."

---

Abby Adams slowly walked to her car in a daze. She passed a trash can, stopped, and took out the yellow legal pad with the word *Greg's* on it. She paused, and with her hand hovering over the opening, she slowly let go. It vanished into the blackness.

Abby replayed that day, that conversation with Greg Larson. It was what lifted her spirits on so many dark days. His gentle offer to her and Jacob provided a bit of blue sky. She thought, *Jack's people—these good souls are the salt of the earth, people who never forget the meaning of kindness.* Sometimes she would walk down Orange Avenue, see the folks there working, and just smile at them. They would nod and smile back. Some hugged her. Some older men tipped their caps to her. *Jack mattered so much to so many.*

And he mattered so much to the one person who missed him the most.

# Part Two:

# "The Restoration"

# Chapter 15

## *Being Erin Brockovich—2000*

Abby's fiftieth birthday fell on a Tuesday during her summer vacation. She was dreading this, not because of the half-century jokes, but because she knew she would be alone. Tom, her oldest, was in San Francisco prepping for the bar after finishing his last year at Hastings Law School. Carly had been told that she might be moving up from Los Angeles to Seattle, where she hoped to be promoted into management at Nordstrom's main office. Abby knew it was quite a jump for a twenty-two year old, but Carly had worked for them through college, and they had had their eyes on her business skills for a while. Jake was with his traveling baseball team in Orange County. The house was so quiet that all Abby could hear was the hum of her laptop as she sat down with coffee to check her email. She put music on just to fill the void; she was not a TV person, except for *Oprah* and the *PBS NewsHour*.

She tried not to count the months since Jack had passed. It was no use. Ten. Everyone said, "Don't decide anything, Abby. You haven't even had a year yet to deal with it all." Abby couldn't help but think, *I wonder what magically happens in the thirteenth month? Do I all of a sudden have an epiphany?*

Abby's best friend at school was Karen O'Malley. She had taught next door to Abby for the last fifteen years. She taught English, and the two often worked together since their subjects were complementary. Even though she was ten years younger, Karen had been Abby's shoulder to lean on. She and her husband Kevin had one son, who was a sophomore at their high school. Abby and Jack had enjoyed dinners with the O'Malleys. The men got along despite some political differences, and the code for each evening was *no excessive talking about school*.

Abby knew Karen was getting together with her today for lunch—at least she had that to look forward to. At 10:30, Karen called and shook Abby's hypnotic gaze from the birds that fed from the handmade wooden houses that Jack had loved making. Her coffee was now cold. Her light housecoat still draped around her. At least she was out of bed. Some mornings were worse—and summer mornings without Jake to feed and routines to follow could be depressing. In the early months, the meds had relieved her panic and anxiety, but now they did little to erase the questions that filtered into every single day's ruminations: *What do I do now that he is gone? Are the best days of my life just memories?*

On the third ring, Abby answered. Karen was in a wonderful mood. "Abby, new plan. Movie first. Later, we go to happy hour. Kevin will meet us."

Abby had not seen a movie since Jack's death. "Oh, okay, Karen. Are you sure that…"

"Abby, stop right there. Yes, I am sure. We will toast your birthday. Your kids are flying in this weekend, right?"

Abby paused. "Yes, I hope so."

"Good. So it is a Birthday Week, and it starts with Woman Power!" Karen had a flair for the dramatic—lots of English teachers did.

"Huh?"

"Have you heard about the new Julia Roberts movie, *Erin Brockovich*? It's supposed to be great. I hear she is going to win an Oscar for it. We can catch the 1:00 show."

"Okay, that sounds great. Too bad we have to go over the bridge to see it. I am still so mad they closed the Village Theater. I loved that place."

"Yes, well, that is also part of what I need to talk to you about. You know about the meeting, right?" Karen could talk fast, sometimes in entire paragraphs. Abby wondered how she could breathe with all the words being expelled at such a rapid rate. "Well, there's a community meeting on Friday night—this Friday—to see if we can do something about it. You've seen the flyers, right?"

"Yes. Well, I would definitely be interested. Of course, I will have to fit it into my busy schedule." A sarcastic sigh followed.

"I will tell you more about it later. I'll pick you up, okay?"

"Karen, thanks so much. I appreciate all you and Kevin…"

"Again. Stop. Abby, I love you. We love you. We are part of the sisterhood. Be over in an hour."

Abby put the phone back on its receiver and dabbed her eyes with the last tissue in the box.

---

Abby lovingly munched away on her buttered popcorn; Karen talked non-stop. They were early for the movie, and they tuned out the ridiculous advertisements that preceded it.

"Oh, God. I missed popcorn. I missed going to the movies. Thanks for talking me into it," Abby said as she spoke over Karen's soliloquy regarding the truth behind the movie and the fact that the real Erin Brockovich had a cameo role in it. Then Karen burst into the news that the Hotel Del had a new happy hour menu up on the pool deck and that Kevin would meet them there later.

Then just as suddenly, there was silence. Karen realized that her cell phone was still on, so she checked her messages. Abby enjoyed the peace and quiet, however brief. She loved Karen, but sometimes she never stopped talking. But Abby wasn't alone, and that's what mattered most to her.

When Karen put her cell away, Abby whispered, "Tom and Carly both called right after you and wished me a happy birthday. Tom didn't even know it was my fiftieth, and Carly sounded stressed over her new job prospects."

"Did Jake at least call? You know boys never remember. My son has no clue. Even my brothers can't remember my birthday. I don't think either of them remember their wives' birthdays."

"No. Jake didn't call. I'll call him later." Abby sighed. *Jack always made it a point of remembering special occasions.* She took a break from the popcorn to suck down her other guilty pleasure—a Coke. Nothing "diet" was on the birthday menu.

The lights dimmed and the film began. Karen was still jabbering, and someone behind them let out a loud "Shh!" Abby winced, and Karen just said to her, "Jeez, we are still in the previews." But quiet was restored.

---

As the film's final credits rolled, Abby was smiling ear to ear. This was definitely her kind of film. A female protagonist fighting for what is right. Noble. Brainy. Sexy. She turned to Karen. "This reminded me of *Norma Rae*, with Sally Field."

"I haven't seen that, but I heard it was great."

"Of course, we'd all like to look like Julia Roberts." Abby reached for her purse.

"I know. But what are you talking about, Abby? You look terrific. You're petite and don't look a day over forty." Karen had taken her cell out and was checking for messages.

"Oh, right. I am 5'3" and my waistline is the result of the 'Grief Diet.'" The truth was that Abby Adams' looks made many men's heads swivel. She did aerobics. Karen had insisted she try yoga, and she liked that, too. She had cut her hair to above shoulder length and had tinted some of the gray out with blonde streaks. Jack used to love her hair longer, but now…*what was the point?*

"Well, I admit, you don't have her boobs," Karen whispered to her as they made the climb down the stairs. "Do you think they're real?"

"Of course they are, Karen. I mean, they have to be."

"Why?"

"Because…because she is Julia Roberts. I saw her on *Oprah*, and they talked about all the 'work' being done, and Julia was against it."

"Yeah, I'd be against it if I looked like her. And Meryl Streep, for God's sake—have you ever seen pictures of her when she was in college? She was a freaking beauty queen."

As they rode back to the island and maneuvered to the bridge, Karen wondered aloud, "Do you think we could ever make that kind of difference? I mean, I know we mean a lot to the kids we teach, or we hope we do…"

"We do mean a lot," Abby insisted.

"Yes, of course, but we are doing something for *them*. Could we do something for the *community* other than recycling or giving stuff to Goodwill?"

"What are you getting at?" Abby flipped down the visor with the lighted mirror embedded in it and reapplied lipstick.

"The meeting on Friday to try to reopen the movie theater is a good example of what I am saying, Abby. Look, you teach history and civics. I teach films as a part of literature. Having this theater restored in our town—it's a big deal. Don't you think?"

"Yes. But I am sure it will take a lot of money. What else do you know about it?"

"I have heard from the grapevine that the businesses on Orange Avenue are lobbying the mayor, who is supportive but pretty tight with money. I know he also hates tax proposals."

"Isn't he a Republican?" Abby was searching for her sunglasses in her purse.

"Yes, but I don't think he is an extremist. He is a moderate, like Kevin."

Abby knew Kevin was a Republican and that sometimes he and Karen argued. But both were reasonable, generally. Kevin was sympathetic to teachers, just not to unions. Karen explained to Kevin that without her union, her pay and benefits would be worse, much worse.

"Some people, Abby," Karen continued, "don't believe in government, period. They want to choke it down and kill it. They don't want regulations on anything to do with energy because they think global warming is a myth. They hate paying taxes and think the government wastes money, but God forbid if you even mention decreasing spending on defense or cutting Social Security..."

Abby started to tune Karen out. Once she got rolling on politics, it would suck the air out of the room—or in this case, the car. Besides, she knew Karen was talking about safe stuff like politics because she was wary of getting to the crux of Abby's turmoil. It wasn't until they arrived at the bar, ordered margaritas, and found a shady place to gaze at the sandy beach that nestled up to the Hotel Del Coronado that Karen finally asked Abby how she was doing.

"How am I doing?" Abby stirred the ice in her drink and knocked some of the salt off the edge where she would sip. "Well, better after I have one of these."

Karen waited her out. The urge to pour out advice was bubbling to her lips, but her good sense told her to cease and desist...for now.

A sigh.

"Everyone tells me not to do anything for at least a year. I've dealt with Jack's physical existence. I know he is gone. His clothes. His stuff. I still can't get near the garage. I see his pictures in every room. I see him before I even grab the milk for coffee because his pictures are all over the fridge. I can't afford to move. The house was *ours*. He's on every wall. In October, it will be one year. I was hoping to maybe retire at fifty-five. He might have sold his business. We planned to travel. Now I can't think about any of that.... How am I? I am numb, Karen."

A longer sip. Chips arrive with salsa. They both let it sink in as they dip into the salsa and try to get the most onto a tortilla chip without dripping. They smile. Their eyes do not.

Abby continued, "It helps to have Jacob around. But he's graduated, and he is still figuring out if he is going to commute to San Diego State or move in with other guys. I told him the money is tight. Thank God for the scholarship fund that Greg Larson and Norman Barnett set up."

"Didn't you tell me that Jake is working this summer at Greg's hardware store? And didn't he get a scholarship to play baseball?"

"First, yes. Greg has been great to Jake. He lets Jake make his hours. Did you know Greg played baseball at UCLA?"

"No. Greg Larson? Really?"

"Yeah, Jake was telling me about it. He blew out his arm but then got drafted. He went to Vietnam a couple years after Jack did."

"How old is Greg?" Karen's tone subtly changed from inquisitive to interested.

"I really don't know. If he went to Vietnam, he has to be, what, fifty-five?"

"How do you know he went to Vietnam?"

"Oh, I think he and Jack used to talk about it. Jack mentioned it a few times."

Karen crunched down on another salty chip. "Oh. He looks younger than fifty-five, don't you think?" One of Karen's eyebrows pulled itself up as if by a marionette string; its meaning became clear.

Abby noticed it. She broke eye contact and focused on selecting a chip—as if the choice mattered. "I guess. Yeah, well, anyway. What was it you asked about Jake?"

Karen realized Abby's shift and had to think about what they had been discussing before the subject of Greg Larson. She reached for more salt to sprinkle on the chips and then remembered, "Scholarship?"

"Oh. No. Jake has been encouraged by his coach and an assistant at SDSU to walk on and see if he makes the team. He thinks he has a shot. He told me that the coach, Jim Dietz, is open to local kids trying out. And get this—rumor has it that Tony Gwynn may be the coach next year."

"Really? Wow. Okay, so when Jake leaves, then what?"

"God if I know, Karen." Abby finished her margarita and knew she needed to eat something before she ordered another. "I just take it one day at a time."

"Are you going anywhere this summer?"

"No. My mom's visiting for a week or so."

"That's good."

"Yeah. Well, I am glad she feels well enough to travel. We'll catch some movies." Abby flagged down the waiter and asked for the happy hour snack menu.

"Kevin should get here soon. Abby, listen. If I knew someone you could see…you know, someone to get a cup of coffee with…meet …would you be open to it? I know it's soon, but…"

Abby smiled and reached out for Karen's hand. "I know that's what you were getting at. I don't know, Karen. Let me think about it."

Then she sat up and looked Karen in the eyes. "I will tell you this. If I do get involved with someone, he will have to be a person who understands what I have gone through—and probably has gone through it himself. I just don't know if I can be with someone to whom I have to explain how I feel about Jack. I need someone who doesn't feel sorry for me. I don't need sympathy, Karen. But I do need empathy."

Minutes later, Kevin appeared. "Ladies, if you follow me, we have a nice table inside. I understand that one of you has a special occasion to celebrate, and I am the lucky man who gets to have two beautiful women to enjoy this sunset with."

Abby and Karen stood and embraced him.

Abby fought the tightness in her throat that came every time someone reminded her of Jack.

# Chapter 16

## *A Community Organizer—2000*

Greg Larson never imagined he would be a "community organizer," but he found himself at coffee with Norm and Joe. They had convinced the mayor, Marty Nils, and three representatives from the Hotel Del Coronado, the Coronado Restaurant Association, and the Coronado Community Development Agency to meet them for a preliminary conversation to see if they could muster support, public and private, to re-open the movie theater, which was closed going on two years. As Joe put it, "The Village Theater is part of the history of the island—and besides, I'm too damn old to drive over the bridge to see a movie."

Of course, money was the primary issue. Could money be raised through a parcel tax? Did the community even support the idea? Could the theater be self-sufficient? What independent theater franchise could be convinced to set up shop?

Greg had considered this far more than Norm or Joe, who were more invested emotionally. However, Greg's metamorphosis to self-educated small businessman and savvy investor made his contribution to the meeting essential. Naturally, he had done his homework.

"Well, I know everyone here remembers Jack Adams," Greg began. "Jack and I had quite a few chats about the theater when he came into the store. He said something I never will forget. He told me that with the size of the theater, it could easily be redesigned into a mid-sized main theater and two mini-theaters, holding maybe thirty seats each. My thought was that it would allow the theater to show three films at once. One of them could be an older, classic film; another mini-theater could show a more artsy, modern film; and the main theater could show the big ticket film of the time."

Heads nodded. Go on. Everyone had a stake in seeing more folks on Orange Avenue.

Greg continued. "One of the local architects, Peter Sawyer, volunteered some time to pencil something out using that plan. I have contacted two of the local smaller art theater franchises, and both showed some interest in operating the theater, if—and this is a big if—the community can raise money to restore the theater. One of them sent a rep over, and Joe showed her around. The theater would need to be restructured with soundproofing, new seats, screens, projection booths, and a much better sound system. Then there is the issue of the whole Art Deco look of the place. The good news is that we have a lot of artists on the island who would help spruce it up considerably. Of course, I would make a substantial donation in terms of hardware and paint, and I have contacts with contractors."

All heads still nodded. Then the mayor, Marty Nils, spoke.

"Well, as for a parcel tax, Greg—I don't see that flying. People are not in favor of taxes in general, but they might be when it comes to schools. A movie theater, even if it is a historical landmark, as you feel, is just a non-starter. That's not to say I cannot push a few funds your way. The most important thing for me is getting the theater back on Orange Avenue and removing those damn boards from the windows. I mean, it's in the center of the business section. It's an eyesore now. So count me in as a supporter. But a tax…not happening."

Maya Solis, representing the restaurants, was sly but supportive. "Of course, we could provide some funds. One-time start-up funding. We agree with the purpose—keeping people on the island. Go to dinner and a movie. But the funding would require networking the businesses."

Perhaps the most influential of all the people at this meeting was the distinguished man with the silver beard, the President of the Coronado Community Development Agency, Javier Ramos. He followed her lead: "We can do that. We also have influence with the military base—lots of deep pockets have retired here. We see community building as part of our mission as well. So I think we can get local real estate folks to pony up." Greg knew Ramos was a key player. If it was going to take a million dollars to get this done, Ramos was the one with the most contacts and the most sway with the oldest and wealthiest members of this island community. Greg was encouraged by Ramos' enthusiasm.

The hotel representative, Simone Foster-Park, was more cynical. She sighed and then offered this: "Of course, we have a history with Hollywood—the filming of *Some Like It Hot* and such. The Hotel Del would make a contribution, and we could influence others, too. However, how much is needed and how much we can support are numbers we are not seeing, and we must have firm figures before we can make any serious commitment. My chief concern is the viability of a theater when there is so much competition in downtown San Diego, especially now that the bridge is paid for. And since there is no longer a toll, people here will want to head to the Gaslamp District. Now that the Padres have broken ground on the new baseball stadium, that area will be booming in a year or so. I just don't know if a small movie theater can survive on this island."

Greg thought these concerns were all important, none more so than the hotels' support and skepticism. "Well, that's why Friday's community meeting is important. Let's see who shows up and in what numbers. That may tell us if people care as much as we do."

The nodding continued.

Greg knew it was a long shot, but Norm and Joe were as excited as hell.

# Chapter 17

## *It Takes a Village —2000*

Abby's Fridays were usually when she crashed from a week's work, but summer made every day a weekend—at least for a month or so. So on Friday, Abby picked up Karen, and they went to the Coronado Public Library for the evening meeting concerning the renovation of the Village Theater. The encouraging thing was that as they arrived, they discovered that the parking lot was overflowing and that people were already gathering at the front door.

When they entered, they spotted Norman Barnett up front with Greg Larson. To the left of the entrance was old Joe, the theater's longtime projectionist whom everyone knew; he held the leash of Greg's dog, Aussie. Abby couldn't help herself. While Karen grabbed two seats, Abby knelt before Aussie and stroked him. "Hey, Joe, quite a turnout, huh?"

Joe was all smiles. "Yes, it is. I'm a little surprised. Guess those flyers did the trick and got folks talkin' about it."

"Well, everyone misses the old theater, Joe."

"Sure looks like it." His suspenders held up his pants about as loosely as he held the leash. His Navy hat was now a decade old and broken in just right.

"Okay, Aussie," Abby cooed, "you be a good boy. Joe, let me know if you need me to take over."

"Will do, Abby. Will do."

The meeting started with introductions of some of the major players from Greg's first meeting. Norman Barnett handled the master of ceremonies duty, but soon he turned things over to Greg for some of the specific plans.

Greg had spotted Abby as she came in and had smiled when he saw that she was giving some attention to Aussie. He was nervous about being in front of a crowd this large. "There must be 80 people here, don't you think, Simone?" Simone found it in her nature to be conservative—or, to use a word she preferred, realistic. The Hotel Del's representative had often heard of "big plans" for this and that, only to see them fizzle. It would take more than a crowd of film lovers to raise what she had calculated as at least $1.5 million to restore the theater—and that was contingent on an expense that could be much more difficult to arrive at: they still needed to buy the land.

"Well, Greg, you're on," she whispered.

As Greg approached the microphone, his nerves reached into his throat. He started haltingly, but Aussie barked upon hearing Greg's voice amplified, and that brought forward a laugh from the crowd and a smile of relief from his owner. "I know you are on board with this project, Aussie. Now let me explain it to the rest of the folks here." More chuckles.

As Greg explained the restoration project and introduced the team of volunteers, people listened intently. The idea of splitting the theater into two smaller sections for classic films or more artsy films got a warm reaction. There were a few who felt that this plan would take away from the larger theater, but Greg reminded them that in the current climate, they needed to draw folks with more than one choice. For the most part, smiles emanated from the group.

Once money came up, things changed dramatically. The mayor reassured everyone that he was not going to promote a tax to raise the funds. That was a relief for most people, but it begged the question: how much would the project cost, and where would the money come from?

Greg and Peter Sawyer, the architect who had done some preliminary designs, faced the questions head on. "Depending on how much we want to restore the theater to its original Art Deco 40s design and such," explained Peter, "we are looking at between two and three million—but if we did it more bare bones—one-and-a-half million."

Simone raised her eyebrows. *At least they are being realistic.*

But the word *million* had some reeling. There was a quiet rumble heard among the crowd. "That's a lot more than I thought. Did he say *million?* What does he mean, *Art Deco?*"

Hearing these questions caroming around her, Abby looked at Karen, and they both shared the same thought: *Houston, we have a problem.* Abby looked up at Greg, wondering if he had anticipated this.

Greg proceeded to explain some of the issues: purchasing the property, demolition and reconstruction, sound systems and such. This was unfamiliar territory for Greg. He was certainly no expert in real estate, but he had been tutored by several developers over the years. They had all insisted that he be the face of the project. So Greg tried his best to quell the concerns echoing toward him. He wanted to at least get the broad ideas out to everyone, but he could see that smiles were fading and being replaced with frowns. His voice seemed too hollow. He glanced at Abby for a moment. She was sitting up, focused on him. *Well, at least someone is rooting for me.* With a small sense of relief, he turned the microphone over to Peter.

Rather than calling upon the memory of the older crowd—and most were over forty— Peter showed a PowerPoint that included the theater's opening in 1947, the original mural designs on the walls, and the Art Deco lobby in its better days. Then he showed the crowd some of the less flattering photos that he and Joe had taken recently: the torn screen, chairs in disrepair, the worn-out carpet, broken concession stands. Both men heard reactions ranging from *"Oh, what a shame"* to *"Oh, what a mess."*

Peter Sawyer's rendition of what the theater could look like came up next: the revitalized *VILLAGE* sign, the repainted murals of Coronado Island and the city of San Diego, the redesigned Art Deco lobby. The crowd seemed to grasp the notion that the Village Theater could return to the historical landmark that it had once been. The presentation went a long way toward convincing them that the whole idea was grand and worthy of the island's attention.

But then there was the money.

Greg introduced Coronado Community Development Agency President Javier Ramos, who made the biggest splash. He told the audience that this would be a solid investment for the island—an incentive to keep people there. Otherwise, their tourism dollars would travel over the bridge to downtown San Diego. Dinner and a movie. Families staying at the hotels could just walk over and see one of three films. The Village Theater could once again be the centerpiece of Orange Avenue, nestled amongst bookstores, shops, and restaurants, not to mention the Hotel Del Coronado at the end of the boulevard. It would be the final piece of the puzzle. "Pockets are deep and fundraisers are planned," Ramos claimed. He was confident.

Greg was glad Ramos was so upbeat; he helped turn the tide quite a bit. When asked for a show of hands for general support, a sea of hands slowly rose. A question and answer period followed. Most negative questions were versions of "Specifically, where will you get all that money?" More positive people were curious about how long the project would take.

Abby remembered Jack speaking to her about the theater. He had mentioned the idea of breaking it into three sections but had said, "It'll never happen, Abby. Costs too much…and there is too much competition." His cynical pragmatism sometimes contrasted with his romantic notions that began with *what if…?* Now Abby was staring up at a man who seemed to share that concept of what could be. Would the community pull together? Would they be willing to help pony up the cost? Could they see the value of it all—the beauty in Peter Sawyer's designs?

She could feel more resistance from those who sat in the back of the room than those who sat in the front. Maybe that's the way it always is, she reasoned, just like the kids who sat in the back of her classroom, arms folded with a look that says, "I don't believe in you until you prove yourself, lady."

For this reason, Abby raised her hand to speak. She stood up. Now it was Greg who leaned forward in his chair. "Everyone, I don't have a question. I just want to say two things. First, I loved that theater, and I love what these folks are trying to do. And whether we can get this thing done or not, they deserve a round of applause." Abby looked directly at those with the hardest faces. They grudgingly softened and clapped. The ovation rose to a moderate climax and then subsided, signaling the close of the meeting. Hands were shaken, names taken, promises made, business cards exchanged. And hope sprang eternal.

Greg felt himself being pulled toward the back of the room. He tried to scurry past some well-wishers without being rude. He knew it was not Aussie's wagging tail and impatience that drew him. He knew exactly why he kept his eyes on the back of the room.

Karen turned to Abby and said, "We'd better scoot if we are going to get out of here. The parking lot is going to be a zoo. Besides, we have a coffee date."

Abby frowned. She didn't mind staying. Frankly, all this had fired her up. For the first time in a long while, Abby felt that this was something she could be involved in—something other than school and students and even her children. She acquiesced and allowed Karen to nudge her toward the door. She glanced at Joe, who was still holding on to a now-excited Aussie, and told him, "Joe, I think this is great. Please, tell Greg Larson he did a terrific job." Then she glanced toward the front of the room. But Greg had disappeared.

"Will do, Abby. Will do." Joe tipped his cap to her and then rubbed his white goatee.

By the time Greg made it back to Joe and Aussie, Abby was turning down Orange Avenue, listening to Karen's nonstop explanation of how this "theater project" sounded great, but the cost just seemed *blah, blah, blah*. Abby's mind was not on the cost—not in the slightest.

# Chapter 18

## *The Walk On —2000*

Abby was not home more than five minutes when Jake came bursting through the door. "Mom, you are not gonna freakin' believe it! Mom, where are you?"

Abby jumped in the kitchen when she heard his voice. "Don't tell me you wrecked the car..." Abby's face instantly transformed when she saw Jake's smile as wide as a giant half-watermelon slice. "What? Jacob, what? Don't keep me in suspense."

"Mom, okay, first thing is: I MADE THE TEAM. I freakin' made the team—as a WALK ON, MOM. Can you believe it?" Jake was so excited that he was literally jumping up and down as if on a trampoline. "But that's not all, Mom. Mom, get this: you know who stepped up and put in a good word for me—no, you would never guess." He was relishing the suspense.

Abby looked at him and calmly said, "Tony Gwynn?"

Jake was stunned. His mother, who knew so little about baseball that she did not know a balk from a walk, had just blown the air clear out of his balloon. "What! How could you possibly know that?"

"Because, Jacob, you mentioned that he was going to be the Assistant Coach this year. You know, Mister, I *do* listen to you. If you could just listen to *me* every once in a while..."

"Okay, Mom, okay. Isn't this awesome? Coach Dietz said I would maybe get some spot play in blowouts, maybe doubleheaders. I would travel with the team, and Coach Gwynn—you know what he said to me?"

"You made the team?"

"No...after I made the team."

"What?"

"He said I'm a scrapper."

Abby looked at him, fairly confident that *scrapper* was a compliment.

"A scrapper! Mom, isn't that cool?"

"Yes, Jake. And does this mean they are offering you a scholarship?"

"No. But one of the guys on the team told me that he also walked on and that if Coach kept you and you produced, you had a good chance of a scholarship next year—maybe even a full one."

Abby opened her arms, inviting her man-child to embrace her. "Oh, Jake. I am very proud of you. I am even more proud that you were accepted on your grades, though." Abby noticed Jake's eyes rolling. "Have you told Tom or Carly yet? You should call them."

Jake could not sit down. He regaled his older brother and sister; both were suitably excited despite being uncomfortably stressed at work. Abby decided to treat him to a steak dinner. Jake showered and changed. As he was walking out the door, he remembered something. "Shoot, Mom. I promised Mr. Larson that I would work tomorrow— or was it Wednesday? Mom, I can't work there now. I mean, between school and baseball and..." Abby cut him off.

"Jacob, Greg Larson will understand. You are a part-timer. I am sure he will be very happy for you. You can call him tomorrow."

"Right." Jacob then did something that he did not do often; actually, he had not done it with a smile on his face since before his father died. He kissed his mother. "Mom, I wish that Dad..." His throat tightened and his jaw with it.

"I know, Jacob. I know. Somewhere up there is one very proud father." Abby knew that if she thought about Jack for a second longer, she would tear up, so as quickly as possible, she punched Jake in the arm and surprised him for the second time in an hour with an old baseball adage.

"Besides, what do they say? There's no crying in baseball."

Jake's good fortune had the effect of directing Abby down Orange Avenue the following week and into Coronado Hardware, where Aussie greeted her. But strangely, he was limping. "Oh, Aussie, what's the matter? Do you have something in your paw?" Abby knelt down next to him; he nuzzled her and then plopped down right on her knee.

"I am afraid it's hip dysplasia—anyway, that's what the vet called it. He has bad arthritis, and his vision is gone in one eye—going in the other, Abby." Greg came over to the two of them and squatted down. "He is well past his prime."

"Oh, no, Greg. How old is he?"

"He's at least 18. I got him at a rescue when he was about eight months or so. Hard to know for sure. He is my third shepherd, though."

"Oh?" Abby kept her fingers in Aussie's fur, behind his ears.

"Yeah. My first two were named Aussie."

"Original."

"Yeah, I know. I'm kinda boring…at least with names."

"Well," Abby said as she began to rise up, "we all love you, Aussie."

A beat.

Greg rose with Abby. "Greg, I know Jake called you about the Aztecs and making the team."

Greg grinned. "Yeah, I'm so happy for the kid. It's tough to make it as a walk on. You have to have something that catches the coach's eye—nobody walked on at UCLA."

"UCLA? Oh, right. Jake told me you played baseball in college. I can't remember if he mentioned UCLA. Oh, that's right, he did. Well, anyway, I just wanted to personally thank you for letting him work here this summer. He really liked it, and he learned a lot. And since Jack came here all the time…well, you know." Abby found herself going the wrong way on a one-way street.

"Hey, it was a pleasure having Jake here. He wasn't a slacker, Abby. He worked his tail off. It will be fun to follow how he does at State." Greg could not help but notice how easy it was to talk to Abby but how difficult it was to get past anything that was just "news." And when Jack's name came up, both of them seemed as if they were shocked backward from each other, like they were repelling down a cliff.

Abby managed to rebound off the wall. "Well, he was never allowed to be a slacker."

A beat.

She continued, "Anyway, the other thing I wanted to tell you was that I was really impressed with how you and the others spoke to everyone at the meeting a few weeks ago. It seemed that people were very supportive. I can't imagine how much work it is going to take to get the theater back into shape, but please keep me in mind as a volunteer."

"Well, thank you, Abby. I will. I think the Community Development Agency here is going to be the key to fundraising. They have some folks already committed financially, and a few ideas are in the works to get more people involved. But you'll be the first to know what we are up to."

"How many years will this take, you think?"

"That depends on money, stubbornness, bureaucracy…you name it. Best guess—five at least."

"Let's hope it's sooner rather than later. Five years seems like a long time. That's the same time frame I've been thinking about for retirement." Abby surprised herself by blurting out something personal. "Oh, please, don't say anything to anyone. I am just hoping it will be then. Who knows, really?"

Suddenly, she had the urge to leave. Even though she knew she was being abrupt, she couldn't help herself. "I have to be going, though. I have a meeting at school for department chairs—school hasn't even started and we are having meetings. Crazy, huh?"

Greg nodded. "Well, take care. I will let you know what comes up about the theater." As he said this, he noticed that Abby was walking backward to the door.

"Please do." Abby left. As she took the fifth step from the door, she realized that she hadn't said goodbye to either Greg or Aussie.

And she didn't have that meeting until tomorrow.

# Chapter 19

## *Aussie—2001*

Abby's phone would not leave her alone—not that she wanted to be left completely alone. She just had trouble dealing with people who seemed bound and determined to find her a man "to share her life with," as they would say to her. It seemed that as soon as the New Year's celebrations ended, people assumed that she would just have a change of heart and feel that "enough time" had passed since Jack's death. However, the calendar had nothing to do with the timetable for Abby's soul to heal.

Karen, the primary instigator, gently complained, "You are too young to be just—just, well, just not seeing anyone. You can't bury yourself in work, or calling your kids, or going to Jake's baseball games."

"But I like all those things. And I did go have a drink with Bill and the other guy, what's his name?" Abby was walking into the kitchen to get a yogurt with her cell phone tucked to her ear this Saturday morning.

"Ed."

"Right. Like I told you, Karen, neither of those guys is my type. We talked about it, remember?"

"Well, your specifications are rather limited, Abby."

"I'm in no hurry. I like my life. I still miss Jack. Besides, there is nothing there when I talk to them. And they don't understand what it is like to lose someone who was your soul mate. They nod their heads, but I know, Karen. I know. And I don't want to get involved with someone just to get…involved. It's way too soon."

Abby appreciated Karen's concern, but she was simply "not settled," as Abby put it. But she wondered if she would ever be *settled*.

Tom's phone call was the one she was not expecting, although she did hold out hope he would call soon. She missed him. Tom had been an attorney going on two years, and Abby knew that he was dating a girl in San Francisco. Tom could be a cool customer when it came to telling his mother about his love life. Nina was his latest girlfriend, but Abby had never really met any of the girls he dated once he left for the Bay Area. They were "just friends," he told her. Obviously, Nina was far more than a friend. Tom couldn't contain his enthusiasm when he told her, "We are flying down for the weekend to see you, Mom. Nina really wants to meet you." Abby, naturally, was hopeful where this may lead.

When Jack died, she and Tom did most of the legwork in terms of all the medical bills, insurance, investments—all that comes along with a death certificate. She missed the day-to-day contact she had with him for those two weeks. The conversations the two had during that time drew them together in a manner that they had never before experienced. Tom developed into his father's mold: pragmatic, stoic, and diligent. She could lean on him.

For Tom, his mother had transitioned from someone he needed to someone who needed him. Fortunately, he had some of the early demands of the legal world behind him—some, but the life of a young attorney was precarious; like the salmon swimming upstream, the bear is always ready to snatch him up. Passing the bar was a huge relief; getting hired at a smaller firm was a godsend; managing his workload was a juggling act; not screwing up something big was nerve-wracking; but meeting Nina…that was his salvation.

Nina was a paralegal, but she was considering opening her own small business or buying into a partnership in a franchise. She had worked her way through college as a yoga instructor, and she and her partners were serious about owning their own studio. Yoga was beginning to really catch on, particularly on the West Coast. Being a paralegal, she felt, could be rewarding but exhausting—and unlike being a lawyer, it didn't come with the paycheck and perks that attorneys enjoyed.

Nina was a dark beauty. She would materialize with long black hair, olive skin, and a twenty-four-year-old body that was very well trained and toned. Her family had emigrated from Italy. Her father was in the wine business; her mother was in sales. Their home in the Napa Valley didn't convey opulence, but rather European eclecticism. It helped that Nina was out of college and on her own, even if she had notions of financial risk and reward. Bianca, their oldest, was married and settled and had already provided two delightful grandchildren. Nina's world would be the subject of conversation over the next few days, when she would meet Abby.

Abby could tell simply from the tone of Tom's voice that Nina was someone very special. The excitement of having Nina meet his mother percolated his usually blasé voice. *It will be an interesting weekend,* Abby thought, especially when Tom told her, "Mom, Nina and I are staying one night—at the Hotel Del Coronado."

Those three words told Abby more than anything else he'd said.

---

Greg thought about calling Abby for several weeks that January. Ostensibly, he wanted to have her spread the word about the summer fundraiser, and he wanted to tell her that Peter Sawyer, the architect, thought perhaps the high school could be involved in the theater's restoration. Peter's son attended the high school, so he was involved in the school's fundraising and was on its Foundation Committee. He had run the idea by Greg but wondered if teachers would support it. Knowing Greg's friendship with Jack Adams and, as he assumed, Abby, Peter asked Greg, "Could you see if this would be something that maybe a civics class could do? Maybe the students could pass out fundraising flyers door to door or do some phone banking? Doesn't Abby Adams teach senior civics?" So the ball was in Greg's court. He said he would contact her. That was two weeks ago.

He still pictured her backing out the door of his store. Had he said something wrong? Had he been too inquisitive? Had he simply let his guard down and allowed a glimmering hope to break the surface of his routine composure? He flipped open his cell phone. Greg looked at it and remembered the very first time he called Raquel—how nervous he had been, how worried he was that he would jumble his words and intentions. He hadn't been concerned about calling any woman since. Mostly, women called him. He stopped and realized how silly this all was. *I am just going to ask her a question and see if she thinks Peter's idea is a good one. After all, she said she wanted to help—to volunteer. No big deal.*

But it was. Why?

He knew Aussie was part of it.

One week ago, he had put Aussie down. His devoted Australian shepherd would not eat. He could not walk. He could not see in one eye, and soon the other would dim. He lay there with that pathetic eye gazing up at him, head glued to the floor. The eye communicated all Greg needed to know but was trying to avoid. Aussie's eyes offered one vacant thought: *I've had enough.*

All the emotions that Greg had bottled up for decades—emotions that he had buried with booze—had rushed to his face. The veterinarian could see that Greg was distraught. Greg couldn't speak. He gasped out several words as he placed Aussie on the vet's table. Tears poured down his face so fast that his shoulder's sleeve simply could not keep up with the flow. He held onto his best friend as the vet placed the needle into Aussie's fur. Aussie was not shaking like he usually did when he came to the vet's office. Greg was the one shaking.

When it was over, he sat on the truck's tailgate and tried to vacuum up all the emotions that had spilled out so painfully. But Aussie's limp body had blown all Greg's pent-up emotions into his eyes, like layers of dust. What would it take for it to all settle?

For the first time since the day of the car accident, Greg's mind gravitated toward a single powerful thought: have a drink. But when his phone abruptly rang, he flipped it open, and Norman Barnett's voice came booming out.

"For God's sake, Greg, why didn't you tell me you were putting Aussie down? They just called me from the store. They could tell you were upset, and they put two and two together and—well, it didn't take a rocket scientist to figure out where you were going. I just called the vet. Are you okay?"

Greg smiled through his tears. "Yeah, Norm. I just can't talk right now."

"Okay, look, meet me right now at the coffee place, okay? No bullshit, Greg. I will be there in five minutes. Okay?"

A beat.

"Okay? Are you there, Greg?"

"Okay, Norm." Greg was about to snap the cell closed, but try as he might, he just could not get the word *thanks* out of his mouth. He heard the line go dead.

*Coffee. Well, at least it's something.* He stared at his phone and thought of calling the store. He pushed "Contacts," and the name that appeared at the top of the alphabetical list gave him pause.

*Abby Adams.*

---

He hoped he could just leave a message. Something impersonal. Maybe Jacob would answer—that worried him. He could make small talk and then ask if his mom was home. Jake would wonder why Greg Larson was calling his mom. Maybe this whole thing was a dumb idea.

"Hello?" Her voice.

Greg hesitated a moment. "Um, hello, Abby?"

"Yes, who is this?"

She did not recognize his voice. How could she? But he knew hers instantly. "Greg Larson. I hope this isn't a bad time to call."

"No. Of course not. Hi, Greg. Sorry I didn't realize it was you. The dishwasher is going, and it makes a racket." Abby felt she needed to explain why his voice was unfamiliar. The dishwasher remained silent.

"Oh. Yeah, same with mine. I gotta get a new one, but I keep putting it off." Small, small talk. "Anyway, I called because something has come up with the whole theater restoration project, and I wanted to ask for your help...or at least your opinion about an idea that Peter Sawyer came up with. You know him?"

"Oh, sure. He is at school a lot. My friend Karen has his son in English." Abby started biting her nails. *Why am I doing this?*

"Good. Well, there is that—and then there is the summer fundraiser at the park that I wanted to ask you about. Like, whether or not we could advertise it at the school. Maybe students could pass out flyers. I don't know exactly—we are still brainstorming things." Greg found that he was just talking without direction—something he rarely did.

"Oh. Okay. Of course, we should talk. Look, I've got to go to the post office—maybe we could meet later at the coffee shop on Orange? I mean, does that work for you? If not, we could just talk on the phone." Abby glanced toward the photos on the refrigerator. It was an old habit. Talk on the phone. Sit on the barstool in the kitchen. Lean against the pillar, turn toward the fridge, and chat away. But as she said the word *phone*, her eyes fixed on a photo of Jack and her in Hawaii years ago. It was the oldest picture on the fridge. Jack looked so fit and young. Her hair was long and in a ponytail. Sunglasses were propped up on her head.

She lost herself for several seconds. She thought he said something about three o'clock.

"I'm sorry, Greg. Um, that damn dishwasher. Can you repeat...?"

"I said, 'Three o'clock is fine'—so I will see you then. It shouldn't take long." Greg began to feel the relief that comes with the denouement of confrontation.

"Great. See you then. Bye, Greg." Abby quickly pushed "End" on the phone. She closed her eyes, realizing that she had just asked a man to meet her for coffee. She would not reopen her eyes until she knew she was not looking at any pictures on the white refrigerator.

Abby got off the stool, turned on the dishwasher, walked back to her bedroom, and turned to her closet. This time, for the first time in a long time, she wondered what to wear.

Greg tossed the cell phone down, and for the first time in a long time, wondered what it would be like walking into the coffee shop alone.

---

All the waitresses knew about Aussie. They had already expressed their sympathies. Greg sat at Aussie's favorite outdoor table, nursing his coffee. He looked down at his feet, where Aussie had always sat, attentively watching all the passersby. Now Greg was doing the same. Strangely, he was not as anxious as he had been on the phone. He kept saying to himself that this was about the restoration. That mantra kept the butterflies at bay.

It was a sunny day, unusual for February when it was foggy and damp on the island. Abby wore jeans and a canary yellow button-down shirt with the sleeves rolled up three-quarters of the way. She held a denim jacket on her forearm. She thought, *The last thing I need to look like is some frumpy schoolteacher.* Abby looked anything but.

After Greg stood up to thank her for meeting him and Abby placed her jacket on the extra seat, the waitress told her that her café mocha was on the house. She insisted. Abby turned to Greg and said, "I wish people would stop doing that. It makes me feel like I need some sort of help."

Greg smiled and nodded. He understood. People just did that on an island. Then Abby looked down for Aussie. It was a reflex everyone seemed to have whenever they talked to Greg.

She knew. She looked up at Greg, and her face blushed with sympathy. "Oh, Greg. You had to put Aussie down, right? When did it happen?"

Greg glanced at her, then down. With a wry look, he said, "I wish people would stop doing that. It makes me feel like I need some sort of help." Then he smiled—but they both knew it was an act.

A beat.

"I'm so sorry, Greg." Abby hesitated and offered, "But, well, let's not talk about it, then."

"No, it's okay. It had to happen, Abby. He was so miserable. It was something I had to do—I just didn't have any idea how difficult it would be." They found that there were often spaces of silence in their conversations, as if both needed a beat to spot the direction they were going, and if they didn't pause, they might wander off a cliff and fall helplessly into something that felt too personal, perhaps too honest. "I've been looking around at rescue homes and shelters for another shepherd. I've got a lead on one."

"Do you want a puppy? They can be a handful."

"Not my first choice. I am just set in my ways a little. So I will look for another Aussie."

"I bet you'll name it 'Aussie,' right?"

"Maybe. We'll see what turns up. Anyway, I wanted to ask you about the theater plans."

The conversation leapfrogged from one topic to the next. Greg explained the plan of having "Classics in the Park," a summer film series to raise money for the restoration. Would the school be interested in supporting this? Would students be interested in attending? Eventually, it got around to Peter's suggestion of a civics project.

Abby watched as Greg carefully jumped from ledge to ledge. She sensed his unease. Was it because Aussie was gone? Was it her presence? Was he just worried about the restoration? But the more he talked, the more he smiled. His hands became more animated. When it was her turn, she explained, "Greg, the summer idea is great. Those of us in the English and History Departments can see what we can do—perhaps suggest a film for the series—something we teach, like *Romeo and Juliet* or *Casablanca*. But the civics project is something that I've been thinking about. The night you guys presented to the community, I was thinking that the students could be involved in fundraising, canvassing homes with information, or even helping with small things like painting. This is going to take how long, Greg?"

"At least three to five years, so we could do things in stages. I should also mention that the Hotel Del is willing to host a Village Theater Gala—that's what they are calling it—in the fall to get folks with deep pockets and philanthropists from the city to make significant contributions."

"Oh, well, that sounds exciting. A fancy event—black tie, I take it?" Abby sipped her café mocha.

"That's the plan. The little people like us will probably be priced out of it." Greg smiled.

"Oh, you can't *not* go, Greg. You are the organizer." Abby found that she was slowly beginning to feel more relaxed talking with him, chatting away about the business of the restoration. "Greg, as for the civics project, it would be something we would have to work on this semester and roll out next year. Right now, I'm planning the Vietnam War unit in my US History class. My kids are reading excerpts from *The Things They Carried…*"

"Really? I loved that book. I've read all of O'Brien's novels."

"Well, we can't just teach them the facts and the battles—you have to get into the hearts and minds of the soldiers."

"Of course. That's how they learn from the past." Greg found himself leaning forward, even more so than when he had been discussing the restoration. He also noticed that Abby had nudged closer.

"Greg," Abby found herself speaking without considering the implications, "Jack told me you served in Vietnam."

"Right. I did. A year or so after Jack." Greg felt the conversation's turn, like a gust of wind that moved napkins and such on a table. His footing on the ledge was giving way.

Abby's teaching gene had kicked in before her personal firewall could deflect the question. "Would you ever be willing to talk to my classes about it—your service, the war—whatever you think you would want to tell them?" Before Greg could react, Abby blurted out, "Wait. I'm sorry. I shouldn't even be asking you this. I know all that is very personal—Jack would never, ever talk to my students. Sorry I brought it up—it's just the teacher in me." Abby found herself trying to mitigate the damage and regain her balance.

Greg steadied himself and cut into the apology. "No, no, Abby. It's fine that you asked. Really. Don't apologize. It's just that I have never been asked…I've never even thought about talking about the war." He decided to go a step further. "I did with Jack—but even then, not much."

Abby was sliding away, even as Greg leaned in. "No, really, Greg—I don't want to stir up bad memories—especially now, with Aussie and all." Abby wished she had just not brought up the subject.

"Hey, kids need to know that war is no stupid video game, Abby. I'll think about it and let you know in a day or so—will that be okay?" Greg was not finished. "But I want to ask you something—and you can say no to this. Next week, I am going to the Helen Woodward Animal Center—they have an Australian shepherd there for me to see. Would you be willing to drive up with me and check it out? You loved Aussie, and I trust your dog sense." Greg realized he was bartering, and he hoped he had not overplayed his hand.

Abby leaned back. Greg took that as a *no*.

Abby knew this was something extraordinary; she also knew that she was the one calling the shots. He had taken a risk, but she had control. He asked her softly; she liked that. It was time for her to make a decision.

"Well. *Quid pro quo*, huh? I tell you what, Greg. If you come to my class, I will help you find your shepherd." Abby found herself presenting a sly smile.

Greg reached his hand across the table and offered, "Deal."

Abby delicately held his hand and echoed, "Deal."

After a little more talk of the décor of the theater, Abby glanced at her watch. *Where had the time gone?* Then she remembered that Tom and Nina were due in tomorrow morning, and she had to get things ready at the house. She had lost track of the hour. "Greg, I have Tom and his girlfriend coming in tomorrow. I have to go get things ready. Anyway, I am glad we talked. Oh, and I'm really sorry about Aussie." Abby stood up and backed away from the table in a similar but far less frantic manner than she had at the hardware store. Again, the real world had just leaked back into her conscience. She hoped Greg didn't perceive her abrupt departure as rude.

Greg told her that he was fine, that he was glad they had talked, and that he hoped she would enjoy her weekend. When she was out of view, he looked to the place Aussie would have occupied and said softly, "Yeah, I know she is pretty." Then his eyes followed Abby down Orange Avenue. "No, I am not gonna back out."

# Chapter 20

## *Molly—2001*

Abby was nervous, and she knew exactly why. The Grand Bargain she had offered had its first installment due. Greg had called her and explained that the Helen Woodward Animal Center had informed him of its newest arrival: an Australian shepherd. The family that had her needed to move, and the one-year-old dog wasn't part of the plans for a family of five.

On the phone, Greg gave Abby an out. "Seriously, Abby, you don't have to come with me. I will still speak to your class. I know you are busy," Greg conceded. Then, worried that he sounded too much like he didn't want her company, he quickly added, "But if you would like to take the ride up there..."

Abby felt the need to stop him, partly because he seemed to be flustered and partly because she too was anxious. Slicing into his uncertainty would put him out of his misery. Besides, she knew her answer. "Greg, don't be silly. Of course I have time. I love dogs. Really."

And so it was agreed. He would *pick her up at ten o'clock*. Those words pinged around Abby's mind from the moment she snuggled into bed Friday night and throughout her Saturday morning routine. *He is picking me up*. A man had not said that to her since Jack first took her to the movies in 1971. Then she was Abby DiFranco. Now she was Abby Adams, *widow*.

Meeting for coffee was one thing—but this was different. Should she invite him in? Should they make small talk first? Would they run out of things to say on the trip up there? Would neighbors see him pull up? See them walk out together? Would word get around as it does on an island? *"It's not an island, Abby. It's a peninsula."* Jack's voice echoed back from the refrigerator door's photo collage. If Greg came in, he would see all the pictures of her and Jack. *They are everywhere; the house oozes of the two of us.*

Abby brushed her teeth. *Perfume? No. Makeup? Definitely.* She talked to herself as she looked in the mirror and carefully applied eyeliner. The rhetorical questions finally got to her as she turned off the blow dryer and leaned forward into the countertop. *Oh, my God, Abby! Will you listen to yourself? You sound like a...like a person who was married to the man of her dreams and...I don't know what to do now—with a man who...*

*Who? That, of course, was the question. Who is what? What is Gregory Larson to me? Is he a friend, a confidant? No. We are friends, yes. But do I want more out of this? Does he? Of course he does. Doesn't he? This can't be about "picking a new shepherd," is it? Why am I going, anyway?*

Abby found the barstool and the coffee cup still awaiting her arrival. She put her hands over her eyes and let the coffee go cold. She had already overcome the what-to-wear jitters. She had cleaned the kitchen counter three times. Then she remembered something: as she was using a dishtowel to make sure the counter was spotless, she realized that her arm had rotated over the same spot for over a minute. That was when it hit her: *Pleasantville.* She had just rented the film last weekend and had watched it alone on her sofa, slowly eating popcorn and remembering how she and Jack had seen it several years ago. *The man who flips the burgers, the same man who becomes the artist—he keeps wiping the counter, waiting, waiting, waiting for his assistant Bud to come into the shop. He is frozen in time.*

*God. So am I.*

Then the doorbell rang. It was five minutes to ten. *He is here.*

When she opened the door, he was on the porch a few steps away, his back to her. Then he turned, and they looked at each other. "Sorry, I'm a little early." Greg said this as he turned, but the word *early* came from his lips just as he looked past the screen door into Abby's face.

A beat.

It was something about the way he looked at her, as if he had seen her before but had never admitted to himself how beautiful she was and how truly drawn to her he was. It was something about the way she looked at him, as if she had seen him before but had never admitted to herself how handsome he was and how truly drawn to him she was. It took them both several seconds to speak; their eyes refused to blink.

Abby was having, as she would say later, an out of body experience. *Pleasantville. The same man, the owner of the burger place—damn it, what was his name? Bill! Bill Johnson. He comes to the door of the woman in the movie, Bud's mom—Betty...and their eyes meet and something just hits them both...a realization that something powerful was drawing them together.*

She looked at him, trying to wipe the scene from her mind's eye, but it wouldn't wash away quickly enough. So for a second, she was mute. Greg broke the silence.

Abby saw his words, but her ears did not hear them: something like, "*I don't mean to rush you...*"

Then, as if the film sped up to real time, Abby woke up, shook her head faintly, and smiled. "No, no, Greg. I'm sorry—I was just distracted...too many things to juggle..."

"Are you sure that...?"

"Oh, no. I mean, yes. I'm all ready, Greg. Let me just get my sweater—kinda windy, huh?" Abby retreated to the kitchen, leaving Greg on the porch, where he stayed awkwardly, but with a sense of relief.

Abby sprung to the door, turned the key to lock it, and let out a very quiet sigh. "Okay, let's go see your new shepherd, Greg."

As they approached the car, Greg realized what he needed to do—a simple thing, really. But it is the simple things that are often the most telling.

He opened the car door for her.

---

Greg's peripheral vision took Abby in. Black capris, black button-down shirt, beige scarf, and black flats—casual and elegant. He noticed that she wore some makeup—just enough to indicate that she was being seen. For his part, Greg wore blue jeans, a black mock turtleneck, and a dark green flannel shirt, unbuttoned with the sleeves rolled up. He was far more dressed up than he usually was—and no baseball cap either. After all, he didn't want the shepherd to be afraid; dogs were sensitive to a person's face—sometimes hats confused them.

After they crossed the Coronado Bay Bridge and headed north to Rancho Santa Fe, the conversation veered from the dog's change of address, Abby's work week, and updates on the restoration of the Village Theater to more personal topics. Greg asked Abby if she had had a nice time with Tom and his girlfriend several weeks ago.

Abby was surprised that Greg remembered. "Oh, yes. It was great to see him and meet Nina." Abby took a second and then made her decision. "After all, it isn't every day that your first child gets engaged!" Abby let herself unreservedly break into a smile. She had told Karen, Kevin, and a few other friends. She had admonished Carly on the phone for not being more forthcoming with Tom's secret. She took note of the fact that Jacob saw this as an opportunity to celebrate. But telling Gregory Larson—for some reason, that made her heart race. She didn't need to tell him, but she wanted to.

"Is that something you expected? I mean, did you have any idea Tom was that serious about, um..." Greg was angry that he did not remember her name.

"Nina," Abby interjected. "No, not at all. I mean, Tom is so closed-lipped about all the girls he dates; I had only the faintest notion that something was different. Did I tell you they stayed at the Del?"

"No. Really?"

"Yes. That was the first clue. But honestly, he makes more money now, and I just figured that he was trying to impress her—or that maybe Nina was special—but I had no idea how special." Abby adjusted the vent so that the cool air hit her face. Greg noticed and turned the AC on low.

"Thanks. Whew. I got a little flushed there, huh? Anyway, I have to tell you, Greg, Nina is lovely. And Tom is head over heels—and I think she is, too. They were very cute together."

Abby paused.

"They told me before telling Nina's parents. I'm not sure why, really. Maybe Tom was just worried about me and what I would think, being...you know...alone."

A beat.

Greg glanced in the rear view window to check the traffic. Abby quickly looked to make sure her cell phone was in the purse.

"Well, when's the wedding?" Greg broke the silence with the appropriate enthusiasm. He surmised why Tom and Nina had spoken to Abby first. The phrase *"you know...alone"* meant only one thing: Jack would not be there to see them get married. Abby would face this milestone alone. Greg figured that the couple had discussed their engagement and that they knew Abby would feel the loss of Jack most acutely.

"Well, it is tentatively set for December." The air from the vent quelled a feeling of perspiration on her brow. "I am very happy for them. It's exciting."

"Ah, a Christmas wedding. Great. Well, what was Nina like, if you don't mind me asking?"

Abby's monologue carried them all the way to Rancho Santa Fe. It was a relief for her to speak about someone other than herself. Her description was interrupted only humorously by Greg on cue:

"A yoga instructor? Ah, now I know what Tom is up to..."

"The wine business in Napa? Tom's in-laws are going to be fun to visit..."

Abby's description of Nina and her family ended just as they pulled into the parking lot. "...they have not decided for sure where the wedding will be, but I know they really want it to be in San Francisco; they just don't want to tell me that yet. But it just makes sense."

Throughout, Greg listened intently. It was just what he needed. She was surprising him with her openness, and he was not thinking about Aussie or what a new shepherd would mean to him. He already knew there would be one change; this shepherd was going to be different—because *her name was Molly.*

---

Take most of Aussie's physical traits, twist them into reverse, and you got Molly. Whereas Aussie was a large shepherd, Molly was more petite. Aussie was black with dark brown patches and thin white lines from the crown of his head to around his muzzle. White fur flowed under his chin and crested on his breast. Molly was white and light gray. She had assorted black spots, but the auburn flecks that highlighted her eyes made both Greg and Abby melt—that and the fact that one of her ears tended to stick straight up.

"Oh my goodness, Greg—she is adorable!" Abby gushed, fighting the desire to move too close to Molly too quickly. Unlike Aussie, Molly was shy and understandably afraid to warm up to Greg and Abby. Greg got down on his knees and very slowly allowed Molly to compose herself and creep a bit closer, letting her nose scan this stranger. She was obviously frightened by all that had happened to her in the last three days: a trip to a foreign place, the smells of other animals, the enclosure she was kept in. All of this was nothing like her backyard had been, with three romping children she had loved to herd and two adults who had taken her for euphoric walks, few and far between as they had been.

Glenda, the keeper who had known Greg for years through all his volunteerism at the center, understood Greg's love for Aussie and his affection for shepherds. She had been contacted by the family weeks ago; even she was astonished by Molly's beautiful coat and charm. Glenda knew that if Greg was not right for Molly, this shepherd would still have many "suitors." Glenda looked up at Abby, whose presence somewhat surprised her since Greg had never mentioned a woman in his life, let alone escorted one. "I see you also love shepherds, Abby."

"Well, yes. I mean, I loved Aussie—everyone did. After all, he was part of the charm of Greg's store." The two women smiled and then laughed a bit.

Greg had not said a word to them; he was softly engaging Molly with his voice, then allowing her to smell his hands, then his knees. He moved cautiously to pet her flank and neck, then behind her ears. Greg smiled when he realized that this too was her favorite place to be stroked. Molly now sat and allowed her tail to brush the floor. Her gaze fell to the other person new to her. On cue, Abby slowly approached and followed Greg's lead. Molly seemed to sense something about Abby, inching closer to her, head down and eyes up until she was close to Abby's kneecap.

"Oh, Greg, look at her. She is so soft and sweet." Abby loved the two chocolate brown patches around her eyes. "What do you think?"

Greg looked at Glenda, then at Abby, and said, "I think she is a keeper."

"Greg," Abby said in an admonishing tone, "you can't call her 'Aussie.' She is all girl—she is a Molly. You know that, don't you?" Abby cringed when she said it—afraid she came on too strong. But the feeling lasted only a second or two because to her relief and Glenda's, Greg replied, "Of course. She is a Molly."

Then Greg looked down at his newest shepherd and smiled. "Good golly, Miss Molly."

They all laughed. But for Greg, it was a subtle but important admission of what he needed in his life.

On the drive home, Abby chatted about how her mother's trip was delayed because her father had to have cataract surgery but that she would be visiting in two weeks. Abby admitted that despite all the years away from her folks, she still missed them. In the summer, she would be flying out for a week or so to see them in their New Jersey home, which they had lived in since the '50s. Greg glanced between Abby and Molly, who was sitting in the backseat of his Honda CRV, peeking out the window from time to time. Greg told Abby of his parents' passing and of his two sisters. Then he added, "It is a blessing that your mom can come out to see you. You know, there are times when I just wish for a day I could sit in my parents' living room and just talk to them. Just talk. Tell them about their grandchildren and what my sisters and I are up to, you know?"

Abby nodded. "Yep. My mom is great because she just takes things as they are. She is not nosey or judgmental. I'm very lucky." Abby looked around at Molly and softly pet her backside; Molly shifted around and licked Abby's fingers. "Molly has taken to us faster than I thought, considering all the change."

"Shepherds are like that. Once they get a feel for someone, they trust them. Aussie was like that with everyone who had a kind nature. Now, if a customer was a jerk, then he was on full alert to protect me." Greg's chuckled.

As they approached the Coronado Bay Bridge, Abby asked how the restoration was going, and Greg summarized: "Not badly at all. We finally purchased the place from the previous owners—I am glad to be done with that. And a bit more money is coming in. We are lining up contractors to demolish the walls. Peter said that every restoration is very symbolic. The way he explained it was: 'You have to break down walls to reconfigure, remodel, and renovate.' He says you have to leave the best memories and create new ones."

Abby gazed out the side window. *Pleasantville. Her mind flashed to the ending: the characters ask each other about their future now that they see the world differently—in color. They admit that they don't know what is going to happen next in their lives. Then they laugh at the folly of man's stubborn desire to find the 'perfect life.' The hero of the film, a mere teenager, puts it all into perspective for them: life is unpredictable and wonderful.*

"Yeah. It's very symbolic." Abby hesitated, then turned to him and asked, "Greg, have you ever seen the film *Pleasantville?*"

Greg looked at her. "Yes. I loved that movie. That is the one where the characters change color when they…they gain…"

"Perspective." Abby, always the teacher, finished his thought.

"Yes. Thanks. Exactly." Greg smiled at her.

Abby smiled at him.

They held it for one moment longer than usual.

Then Abby said, "I think *Pleasantville* should be one of the films that the Village Theater shows from time to time, you know."

Greg nodded. He realized for the first time in many years that he was seeing a woman in her true colors.

# Chapter 21

## *Abby's Classroom—2001*

*Quid pro quo.*

That is how former Private Gregory Larson found himself in front of Abby Adams' United States American History class. Abby, like Greg, had given him an out, but he just couldn't say no to her—and he didn't really want to. He had always liked teenagers, although he hadn't been in a high school classroom since...high school. Those were the innocent times, playing baseball and knowing that nothing seemed all that serious, even as the world around him was marching to the drums of war and protesting Jim Crow laws. But now he didn't know what to expect. Abby told him not to worry: "Just tell what happened to you, Greg. Talk about how you felt about the war, and maybe what you think you—or America—learned from it."

No big deal.

Abby introduced Mr. Gregory Larson to her class. He sat on a stool in front of some 35 students who were juniors. It was early May—time for history classes to be studying the 1960s—and Greg personified that era. Abby sat to his left. She asked Greg to explain how he became involved in the "Vietnam conflict." After clearing his throat and telling the students not to expect too much from a hardware store owner compared to their articulate teacher (he received the smiles he had hoped for), Greg began:

"Out of high school, I got a scholarship to pitch for UCLA. I was lucky enough to be able to throw a baseball really hard—being left-handed helped, too. (A few more smiles allowed Greg to relax somewhat.) But my luck ran out when I blew out my arm during my second year there. I was so bummed out—well, to be honest, depressed—that I just didn't do very well in school. I know I shouldn't have been a ballplayer first and a student second...or even third. That is one thing I regret—just not taking school seriously. I paid a big price."

Greg found that he was a bit breathless. Nerves, he figured. Abby interjected something about the draft, and he nodded and continued. "So anyway, I lost my student deferment, and the really dumb thing was that I wanted to enlist in the Navy, but I waited too long, and before I knew it, the Army got a hold of me. That is where they needed the most troops—infantry. The Army didn't much care about a pitching elbow. But then I got lucky again." *That's not how I felt.*

Greg sipped from a bottle of water Abby had given him. "Boy, I don't know how you teachers do it—all this talking. Yeah, so…I was lucky, and the artillery division wanted to train me here, and I figured that was a good thing, for obvious reasons, you know; better to be on that end of an M101 howitzer than the other."

The students were quiet, and all eyes were on him—except for those of a Hispanic girl. She had her head down; she was not writing—more like doodling. Greg had a strange, familiar feeling about her. He knew that she was listening because she did look up if he paused, but only for a second. "I was in 'Nam in '69, when the war was expanding…" Greg spoke of what it was like there and how scared he was, and Abby interjected a few historical timelines. Finally, and offhandedly, Greg remarked, "I came home after being there for four months." *Why did I just say that?*

Greg reached for his water bottle once again, and Abby took that as a cue to open things up for questions. One hand flew up the moment she made the invitation.

"So you were only in Vietnam for four months? Mrs. Adams said that the soldiers were there for a year if they got drafted?" This petite girl in the front row to his left transformed a declarative sentence into a probing question. She wore black jeans that were ripped at the thighs and a Linkin Park T-shirt. She seemed confident and smart, but not conceited; she just wanted to get the facts straight.

"Yeah. That's a long story, but true—most guys were there a year. I should add that I came back and finished my year…here, in the States." Greg looked for a less inquisitive questioner, but the Linkin Park girl pressed on. *What have I gotten myself into?*

"What's the long story? Were you, like, wounded or something?"

"No. No. Although that battle was, like Mrs. Adams said, one of the bloodiest. That's why they called it 'Hamburger Hill.' I was lucky—since I was aiming artillery, I wasn't on the frontlines." *Maybe that will be enough.*

The Linkin Park girl just looked at him; he hadn't really answered her question.

Greg looked down for a moment. Abby wanted to rush in and redirect the conversation to the war's purpose or its outcome. She didn't know what Greg's answer might be, but she sensed something secretive and foreboding. She started, "Guys, we ought to…" but Greg looked up. He felt that shaking that always accompanies fear. He wanted to tell the class about Raquel's tragic death: the glass-shattering, metal-crushing, blood-splattering truth, but instead he said, "There was a death in the—in my—family, so I got sent home for a while. You know, I was the oldest, and well, um…I had to make the funeral arrangements. Then the Army sent me orders to go back and train new recruits at the artillery school. So the rest of my year was done, and I was discharged."

The Hispanic girl's eyes met his. *She knows I am not telling the whole truth.* The girl noticed the water in the bottle rippling as his hand shook. Then her gaze turned from his hand to the back of the student's head who sat in front of her.

There was an awkward silence in the room. Abby felt her body heat rising. *What isn't he saying?* She wanted to right the ship. So she rescued him by asking what lessons he had learned from the Vietnam War.

"Look, I didn't come here to upset you guys. I told you what happened to me because the truth is that people die in wars and people die at home. There are consequences for the actions we all take. If you vote for war, count on thousands of deaths—not just soldiers, but civilians, too. The military calls it 'collateral damage.' You know what I am talking about." Greg paused. "Well, that's what I learned when I was in 'Nam."

Greg quickly swallowed more water, for the fire was hot. "And for all you guys—and girls—sorry, didn't mean to sound sexist— sometimes your battles are...inside you, you know? The pressure you feel to...to do things that are—that you think are—cool or wild. Sometimes they are part of growing up, but..." Again he stopped for a moment. "But there's a line that you have to know about. If you cross it, bad things happen and people get hurt...even killed. And it really happens. They really do die."

He almost told these kids that he became a drunk—that he came within a guardrail on a bridge of driving their devoted teacher to her certain death. The memory formed on his lips, and then it slid back down his throat where it belonged. He realized that his own disease was not part and parcel of this warning to students.

He thought about how some lessons go relatively unscathed, by the grace of God, and must never be repeated...unless one was a fool.

The room was quiet for a time. Once he reached closure, his hands stopped trembling. Calmness settled into his voice, allowing the students to absorb what he had said, like paint soaking into a canvas. Abby understood that Greg had never planned on saying some of this, but he did want to create a true image of his war. Abby thought that Greg, like Jack, had made his peace with the war. She was wrong. The landscape of his battlefield remained a mystery to her.

After a moment, the Hispanic girl, with her jet-black hair braided to the side, stopped her doodling and blurted out without looking up from the page, "So was Vietnam worth it?"

Greg looked at her and wondered why she had not looked up. "I'm sorry. May I ask your name?" His intent was to see her face; he half expected her to say "Raquel." She reminded him of her. He also had a suspicion.

She finally surrendered and looked up at him. She was striking. Her large oval eyes conveyed a pain that she was unwilling to show others, so as quickly as possible, she met his gaze and softly pronounced, "Grace."

Greg sensed that this girl, too, had lost someone, and she was now calculating the damage done by what value came of it. Greg had to make a decision.

"Thank you, Grace. No. I'm sorry. No. Some vets think that the way America fought that war was all wrong. They feel that if you're going to fight a war, then fight to win—don't just play for a tie. Me—I had some problems with the war, but I didn't know then what I learned later. For example, the way we even got involved in it—the whole Gulf of Tonkin deal—I mean, don't lie to the American people about who shot first. I'm sure Mrs. Adams will tell you more about that, so listen to her. The bigger thing with me was why we were there in the first place. The poor people we supposedly fought for were just farmers, and we destroyed their land. The leaders of South Vietnam were not communists, true—but their leaders were pretty corrupt. I guess you have to know exactly why you're fighting—and who or what you're fighting for. You gotta know some truths, and we didn't know those things—not well enough. Maybe it's not the way they write about it in your history books, and maybe others who were there wouldn't agree with me. But I just think it was a waste of life, you know? Thousands and thousands of lives."

*And then there was Raquel and the baby.*

Greg looked at Abby. "That is the biggest lesson I learned."

He carefully checked back on Grace. That's when he saw the tear hit the page, followed by another. She quickly pulled the sleeve of her hoodie over her palm and snatched away the tears, wiping away the evidence that had smeared the ink on her notebook page.

Abby was aware of this play-within-a-play. She would talk with Grace later, when time had at least scabbed over her wound.

Abby smiled at Greg, proud that he had found the strength to talk about his experiences. Her eyes conveyed a message that translated into an urgent plea: we need to talk...later. Greg looked at Abby and nodded.

A bell rang. Students brushed by Greg and Abby, who stood together in front of the room. The girl in the Linkin Park T-shirt stopped momentarily and said to Greg, "Thanks for telling us the truth."

"Thanks for asking me to," Greg replied. *The truth. How ironic. If only Abby knew.*

But former Private Gregory Larson's education had just begun.

# Chapter 22

## *Greg's House—2001*

"Yes, Mom. Of course, I will be waiting at the gate on Sunday. Flight 212. Remember, 2 p.m. my time is 5 p.m. yours, so you will be tired and getting hungry. Right. Of course, we will go out to eat. No, you 'can't just cook something'...yes, yes. Tell Daddy I love him. Okay? Love you. Bye."

Abby had not put the phone down for more than a minute when it rang again. *Oh, Mother!*

"Hello, Mom, what did you forget?"

"Abby?"

Immediately, she was slightly embarrassed. "Oh, my goodness. Greg. I'm so sorry; I was on the phone with my mom for an hour, and I thought she still needed to tell me something."

"I know. I was trying to reach you yesterday, but the line was busy—and today—I'm sure you have a lot to talk about. Isn't she due in Sunday?" Greg was smiling for two reasons: Abby recognized his voice, even if the dishwasher was going, and he had finally broken through all the anxiety of calling Abby. His voice was plop-down-on-the-couch comfortable. They had chatted several times in the two weeks that had followed Greg's speech to her high school students.

"Yes. Oh, gosh, I know why you are calling, Greg. I'm just so...so overwhelmed lately: my mom, my last batch of papers for the year, figuring out next year's schedule at school. I'm sorry." Greg just let her go. "Anyway, yes, Saturday night is fine. Are you sure you want to cook?"

Greg just grinned. "Yes—it's simple. Besides, Molly misses you. She is looking up at me right now."

"One ear up, one ear down, right?" Abby turned to the refrigerator and then quickly pivoted away.

"Yep. About six-ish?"

"Great, but what can I bring—a bottle of wine?"

"Um, no." Greg was a little caught off guard. "Really, I'm fine."

"Dessert, then?" Abby glanced at her calendar. She had two days to get ready for her mom and this…this dinner date? *Is that what it is?* Her back remained parallel to the refrigerator door and the gallery magnetized to it.

"Okay, ruin my waistline. I'm gonna let you go; you sound busy."

"Oh, no. Well, yes, but it is nice to talk to an adult and not talk about school."

So they did talk. And she did plop down on the couch. As did he.

---

Molly barked and rushed over to Abby as Abby opened the white gate into Greg's small front yard. Molly had a ball in her mouth, and she dropped it at Abby's feet. But Abby decided that sitting on the porch steps and plowing through Molly's white and gray fur was more to both of their likings.

"You know you love it here, don't you? Don't you?" Abby cooed as Molly did everything she could to get closer to Abby. This wasn't the first time the two had bonded; various trips to Greg's store, a latte at the coffee shop, and a stroll on the beach were some of the meeting points for the two of them…three of them, really.

"I see Miss Molly has made herself comfortable," Greg remarked as he stepped through the propped open, brick red front door. Like many houses on the island, Greg's was a cottage, more or less: white with dark green trim, built in the late 1940s. Its front porch with two rocking chairs made for perfect viewing of a sunset from spring until late summer.

"Yes, she is your welcoming committee." Abby got up and handed a brown bag labeled "Francesca's Bakery" to him. "Don't worry. It's a light French pastry—well, two of them. I couldn't decide."

"Perfect. Let me give you the not-so-grand tour." Greg ushered Abby into the living room, which was set off by a rich wood floor, Mission style couches and chairs, and cream-colored walls that displayed Greg's preference for landscapes. The fireplace was flagstone, the mantel a dark brown beam that hosted pictures of what Abby assumed were Greg's sisters and nieces and nephews. She took it all in as if it was a wing of a museum—the Gregory Larson Wing. She didn't want to be nosey, but Greg was forthcoming.

"That's my older sister, Sara, and Mike with their two girls, Sophie and Lauren. I coached them in softball for years. Now they're both in college." Greg pointed to the smaller picture. "That's Melanie— divorced, no kids. We don't see her too often. She lives in Oregon with her partner, Marie." Greg paused. "It took Melanie a long time to figure out—or maybe *accept* is a better word—her sexuality. We try to get together every few years." Greg waited for Abby to absorb the family album.

"And then there is Michelle and her second husband, Derek—no kids either. Michelle is a travel agent, Derek a very successful dentist. I should say he *was* a dentist; he just sold his practice and retired. The two of them travel everywhere—as a matter of fact, they are somewhere in New Zealand as we speak."

Abby nodded. "Wow. Travel. That is on my bucket list. I've never left the States, except for a trip to Vancouver once. Oh, and there is Aussie and you—hmm, your hair was quite a bit darker then."

"Oh, well, if you want to see darker hair—check this out." He pointed to a small, framed picture that had clearly faded with the decades. "That's the first Aussie and some guy you probably don't recognize." Abby crouched down and picked the picture up to look closely. She made no remark.

A beat.

"Well, that is the Larson living room. Kitchen is back here, and the bedrooms are down this way. Everything is kinda miniaturized, you know. Fifteen hundred square feet will do that."

"Well, my house isn't much bigger, Greg. Anyway, I like your taste." She noticed the books on the bookshelves. "As I suspected, a nonfiction fan. Lots of David McCullough."

"Yeah, that's me. One of the few fiction writers I read is John Grisham—he seems to be a blend of both styles."

Befitting a hardware store owner, the kitchen and dining room were rustic. Greg led Abby out to the small back porch, where he had his state-of-the-art grill and two forest green Adirondack chairs. "Can I offer you some iced tea with lemon and a plate of brie and baguettes?"

Abby thought to herself: *no wine, interesting.* "Oh, that would be great. I have to admit I'm hungry. Karen and I went for a long walk this morning, and I didn't want to eat too much at lunch. Did I tell you about Jake's game the other day?"

"The doubleheader against Cal Berkeley...no, but I thought he might get to start in the second game. How'd he do?"

"Well, they are up there in Berkeley, and he calls me to tell me it is really cold and windy and—get this—he goes 2 for 3 with a double and a stolen base...and they won the game he played in. They lost the first one."

"Wow, really? Cal has always had a good baseball program. I remember playing them, but it is really cold in April."

And with Molly right between them, the afternoon disappeared into early evening. And just as slowly, the more mundane topics of conversation disappeared, leaving them rocking on the front porch as the sun set. Abby had run out of superlatives about the shrimp and scallop skewers, and Greg couldn't think of anything else to ask about Abby's children or her job or the upcoming wedding in December.

They had reached this point before, only to look at their watches and fidget or have some excuse that required a departure. There was no excuse now to exit because coffee was brewing and Francesca's pastry waited in the dining room.

"Milk?"

"Just a touch." Abby cut the pastries in half.

"Looks delicious." Greg's rectangular maple table seated four. He sat opposite Abby. When she sat down, she shifted forward and broke the unspoken code.

"Greg, tell me something," Abby ventured carefully. "That day in class…talking about the war…when the students asked you why you came home early. There was something else, wasn't there? What was it?"

Greg blew into his coffee mug. Suddenly, his mind raced back to that day that he and Jack had sat in the coffee shop, Jack staring into his coffee just as Greg was now.

"You notice everything, don't you?" Greg said gently. "Your students love you, you know. You see inside their hearts…what they're saying and what they're *not* saying."

"I have my moments," Abby said. "Greg, what was it?" Abby knew she was pushing him to the point of no return.

He felt that old nervousness that made his teeth chatter and his body feel cold, although it was quite warm in the house. "Why I came home early," he restated, clearing his throat a little. "Well, I was married. Her name was Raquel. There were a lot of blessings in my life, but if you had to name just one, Raquel was…was it, really. Raquel and the baby. So I go to 'Nam, and I see all the death and carnage there, and I'm thinking, at least I have Raquel. And then," he paused, gritting his teeth, "they were killed." *I got it out. Damn it, I wish I could stop shaking.*

"What?" Abby's jaw dropped. Her hand flew to her mouth as the air sucked inward. Before she could regain that breath, Greg added, "She was killed in a car accident by someone your students' age. He was stoned. He ran a red light."

A beat.

"So I buried myself—drinking, you know? I drank before the war— started when I blew out my pitching arm and got depressed. Then I drank in 'Nam. But after the accident...well, I didn't stop drinking until..." He just waved off the years that followed and then looked down at his coffee cup. "Until I hit rock bottom. Norman—you know, the store's owner—he took me to AA, and that was the end of it. Eighteen years sober."

*And I'm still not telling her the truth.*

They sat for a while. Abby saw the trembling. She felt badly for him and wanted to soothe him, but how?

"I'm sorry if I brought up a subject that is hard for you to talk about. Believe me, I understand. Can I ask—you said 'the baby.' How old...?" Abby's question was intercepted just as she began to realize that there was no name associated with this child.

"Raquel was about four months pregnant."

Abby's voice poured out over the coffee cup. "Oh, my God." She felt her body heat rising. Flushed, her throat tightened.

A beat.

"It's okay, really. Abby, I want to talk about things other than what-we-have-done-lately. It's just that we both have been through a lot, and it's been hard times. Me, well, I've kept things inside for so long that getting them out is just..."

"I know. I know." Abby cleared her throat. She tried to put this man's life puzzle together. Some key pieces suddenly presented themselves, like the fact that he did not serve wine with dinner, but she suspected that others were hiding just out of sight—out of mind.

Abby noticed that neither of them had even looked at the pastries. "Hey, let's take a break and enjoy dessert." And she offered up the plate for Greg to pick his two halves.

"That day I spoke to your kids—they were great." Greg took a bite of the Danish.

"You made quite an impression."

"What about that girl, Grace?" *Greg thought of Raquel.*

"We talked. She has a number of uncles and cousins serving in the Army and Navy. She told me that years ago, her uncle—her godfather, actually—was killed in Desert Storm. Then another cousin was severely injured in a helicopter crash. That happened when the school year began. I knew something serious had happened because she kept missing class, so I spoke to her counselor. I just never knew the extent of it. But you were right to tell her how you felt about the war—she could handle it."

"Abby, it wasn't just that she was upset." Greg hesitated. Did he want to wade back into the water that Abby had so carefully allowed to recede? "The thing is that she reminded me of Raquel. See, Raquel was Mexican—same black hair, same big, brown, oval eyes. We met at UCLA. I mean, we were just eighteen. She was killed when she was twenty-one, and Grace just reminded me of her."

There were always pauses when they spoke to each other, but none longer than this one. So much to take in, so much left to divulge. So many questions raced through both of their minds.

Abby decided to do something that she had not done before. She reached across the table and placed her hand on his. Her fingers fell into the gaps between his, and he tightened his fist softly to welcome her in.

Greg looked up. Her face emitted empathy. Loss was contagious. He looked down at her hand. It was his move. *Is it too soon?*

"Where do you want this to go, Abby?"

Abby squeezed his hand. She had spent the morning debating this very question with Karen on their walk, yet the answer was still elusive.

"I don't know. I do know that I care about you, Greg. Very much. Can that be enough…for now?" Abby's question indicated that she had control, but she also understood the meaning behind Greg's question: he was more prepared than she was. *How patient is he?*

Abby realized that he rotated his hand such that their hands now embraced each other rather than protecting one another. "Can I tell you something?"

Greg lips formed a sly smile. "Please do. I've been doing all the talking."

Abby took a breath. "Okay, the refrigerator. It's covered with pictures...of Jack...of us both. All the memories. Every day, every meal—it just stares out at me. My house, Greg. My house is what Jack and I built together. I just don't know what to do yet. What I want...who I want to be with. I don't know when I will be ready to really, really move forward..." Abby began to tear up. Greg squeezed her hand, then released it so that he could bring her a tissue.

Abby delicately wiped beneath her eyes. Then she explained to him, "I don't want to spend the rest of my life living in the past, you know, and feeling sorry for myself and thinking about how nothing happened the way we planned." The tissue was balled up in her left hand; the flush of tears had subsided, thankfully. "I don't want to think that the best years of my life are over and now I just have to settle for living my life through my children...or my students." Abby took a deep breath and then released what was balled up inside. "I'm still angry about it all. I am so angry about what they did to Jack—to me."

A beat.

Abby voice hardened: "You know about Jack's cancer. You know that there was a good chance that came from the defoliant they used..."

"Yes. I knew that, Abby. Jack didn't tell me, but Norm and I talked." Greg conceded.

"So I'm still just...just angry."

A beat.

"But I can't live this way. I can't live in the darkness, Greg. I have to let go." Abby looked away from Greg. Her eyes swept across the room to the fireplace, to the mantel with its pictures, but she allowed her right hand to fall back into Greg's.

Greg recognized the anguish and the anger that he too lived with. He felt guilty for succumbing to it for two decades. He lived vicariously through his sister's kids, his dogs, his customers, engaging women only when physical desire demanded, never once opening up to any of them.

"Abby, believe me when I say this to you. You have come so far. I wish I could have moved forward and let my past go. I just never trusted anyone enough. They just didn't understand—or maybe I just didn't want to change...I don't know."

A beat.

Abby's eyes left the mantel and returned to meet his. "Do you have a picture of her—of Raquel?"

Greg realized what had drawn Abby's attention. Pictures. Pictures haunted them both. Abby kept hers in plain view; Greg kept his in a storage chest that contained the remnants of his life with Raquel and photographs that had begun their yellowish transformation. He had not looked inside the storage chest in several years...or was it decades?

"Yes, I do. I will bring you one. It's my favorite."

Abby nodded.

Greg returned with a five-by-seven-inch picture of Raquel wearing a powder blue UCLA T-shirt and Levi shorts that had been cut off in the fashion of the '70s. She was barefoot. Her legs were tanned. She was sitting on an outcropping of rocks near the beach. The wind blew her long black hair. She was laughing.

"Oh, Greg, she was beautiful." Abby let out a sigh.

"Yes, she was."

Abby put the picture on the table and looked at Greg. "We can't replace them, you know."

"I know. I don't want to. I don't want you to. They're part of us; they've made us who we are today." Greg stood up from his chair, pulling Abby with him, hand in hand. She allowed him to draw her to him. She tucked her head beneath his chin. She felt his heart beating as fast as hers.

"I need—I need more time, Greg." *I do want him. Why am I fighting myself? Am I just being sensible? Or stubborn? Oh, I am just not used to this. I need time to think.*

"I know. We both do. I've been a loner forever." *I do want her. She's afraid. Am I telling her the truth? Do I need more time?*

Abby stepped back, realizing that Molly was staring at them. "Well, you have Molly. Look at her. One ear up, one ear down."

"Story of my life." Greg smiled.

"I'm going to go now, Greg. Okay? 'Cause if I stay, I don't know if I can stop from crying, and I don't want to cry…with you." Abby broke eye contact. Greg let her go. Abby looked for her purse, found it, walked to the front door, and knelt down to caress Molly. When she stood, with Greg a foot away, she made a decision. She needed time to digest all that had happened on a night when emotions were so raw that they could easily bleed through any bandage.

# Chapter 23

## *Heart Talks—2001*

Abby's mother and father, Helen and Fred DiFranco, lived modestly and loved generously. They were an odd couple. He was a master mechanic and loved cars. She was a librarian and loved books. He was an Eisenhower man. She was a Kennedy fan. Fred served in the Army at the end of the Korean War while Helen served hot turkey sandwiches at Harry's Diner. Although both attended Catholic services, he longed for the Latin mass, while she preferred the modern sermon. However, both loved their Yankees, even if they had to leave New Jersey to see them. Both loved to travel and learn more about a world in which they were aging gracefully. Neither had ever missed a chance to vote, and both always missed their daughter Abby.

Fred's eyes were a problem. So was his hip, not to mention his hands, which bore the strain and stains of forty years under the hood. So at least twice a year, Helen ventured out to California to see Abby by herself while Fred played as much golf as his body could take. Abby's brother and sisters had him over for dinner most of the time, or he had his buddies over for pizza and poker, so Helen knew he wasn't going to starve anytime soon.

When Helen saw Abby, they embraced. Since Jack's death, each joyful welcome and hug seemed to last just a little longer, as if time and death could be fended off by being closer physically as well as emotionally. Their conversations became less small talk and more of what Helen called "heart talk."

She held the book she was reading entitled *Me: Stories of My Life* by Katharine Hepburn. "Oh, I finished the book as the plane touched down, Abby. It is wonderful. She is one of my heroes," Helen said as they waited for luggage to be unceremoniously slammed onto its merry-go-round. "Now I want to rent some of her movies and eat popcorn with you and catch up on everything, including Tom's fiancé, Nina, and the wedding!" She gazed out the glass-paneled walls of the San Diego airport. "Oh, the sun! It feels wonderful. It is still too cold back home—I know it's the first week of May, but it just hasn't warmed up yet." Luggage in hand, off they went to Abby's to unpack, change, and have an early Sunday dinner out.

But just as they got home, the phone rang. It was Carly.

---

"Really? A promotion. That is wonderful, Abby!"

"She's flying down here from Seattle for business this week," Abby gushed.

"Will she have some time to visit?" Helen replied as she hung up her last few blouses in the closet.

"Well, Nordstrom is having a western regional meeting, and her boss wants her to come with. But she asked if she could stay longer and be with us next weekend. So she won't need to fly home until next Sunday." The timing was perfect since this was Abby's spring break from school. Of course, everything that had happened the night before with Greg was still emitting a pulse that would not stop, but she tried to not allow it to consume her. Having her mother and daughter with her this week would give her a chance to simply *be*. She had no papers to grade this week, no appointments to keep, and no meetings with Gregory Larson to bite her nails over. *Was that a good thing?*

While her mother was getting settled, Abby jumped on her computer and emailed Greg. *Shouldn't I at least call? Of course I will...later.*

**"My Mom's here, safe and sound. Grabbing dinner. Won't be as good as yours. Lovely evening with you. I'll call tomorrow, okay? Abby."** She clicked SEND.

**"You've got mail."** Greg smiled at his computer's America Online icon. He typed, **"Good to hear. Thinking of you. Greg."** *Is that all I should say?*

Greg realized he had hovered around his phone and computer all morning. *Was this a good thing?* Greg normally spent Sunday morning reading the newspaper, walking Molly, and eventually going for a bike ride on the Silver Strand. Sunday was the one day that the store opened later, closed early, and was left to his manager, Pedro, to handle. It had taken a long time before Greg had the confidence to allow others to run the store. Now he sat around, not knowing what to do with himself. *This isn't the way my Sundays go. I don't just sit around, waiting to hear from someone, do I?* He could not ignore the fact that Abby's face was there when he closed his eyes.

That evening, he didn't sleep well at all. The roll call of misgivings rattled around his brain until sometime around four in the morning. *Should I have told her the truth about how I smashed into her on the bridge? What will happen if I do? What will she think of me if I tell her now? And what if this whole affair is all a fool's errand? Can she let go of Jack? If so, how long will it take? It's taken me decades to deal with Raquel. And did I really? I'm never going to be Jack, and she's never going to be Raquel. Maybe I just never gave anyone a chance to love me. Was that it? Or is it that I like my life the way it is? Why can't we just be together? How committed do I want to be? What do I really want?*

*Or am I just a chicken shit? Just a scared old man afraid of what I have to face?*

Greg ripped off the covers and felt the sweat that had gathered around his neck. He looked at Molly, who immediately rose up, hoping a walk was in the cards. "Come on, girl. We gotta get out of here. How about the beach, huh?"

Molly's tail moved at the speed of light even though it was pitch dark.

Greg thought, *Man's best friend. Maybe my only friend.*

"So Tom and Nina have moved the wedding back to after New Year's?" Abby's mother Helen settled onto the couch with a blanket around her legs and her tea on the table.

"Yes. They have just received so many replies that Christmas has too many conflicts. It will work for me, although I'll need to take a few days off work." Abby sat on the opposite side of the couch, legs crossed under her, feeling soft and relaxed. Being with her mother was simple: Helen made no demands, rarely criticized, and gave advice infrequently—only when she sensed it was asked for. She was there in a supporting role. Abby was her leading actress.

They had already covered topics ranging from Jacob's baseball and college aspirations to Carly's business acumen to Abby's twenty-sixth year of teaching. Abby spoke of the joy that came with her avocation as well as how much it took out of her as she found herself in her fifties.

"I know you are exhausted, Abby. I don't know how teachers do it. The good ones are saints."

"Sometimes I just get home and crash on this couch, Mom. I am so tired, I don't feel like eating."

"Well, that's not good. We will do something about that next week when you go back. I'll make some of your favorites." Helen smiled softly, but her eyes betrayed her true concerns for her daughter. There were things she wanted to ask her, but she felt that if she waited Abby out, those issues would bubble to the surface. "Heart talks" were always mostly about timing and patience. Helen didn't have to wait too long.

"You're probably worried about me." Abby looked up from her teacup.

"*Worried* is a strong word. I just want you to be happy, and I hope you're at peace with…with Jack and all the changes. I have noticed that you've lost weight." Helen tilted her head in such a way that Abby could tell this was not a diet of which she approved.

"Oh, a little. But I am happy, Mom. It's just that I have some things I have to sort through."

"Do you miss having Jacob here?" Helen asked, knowing what her real concern was.

"I do. It gets very quiet here without him making a racket. My phone doesn't ring much."

"Oh?"

"Except all the dumb sales people who naturally call at dinner. Sometimes they wake me up and get me off the couch. I feel like ripping the phone out of the wall when that happens, but I never know if it's the kids. I tell them to call me on my cell phone—so I should know better."

A beat.

"But I have things I need to figure out, going forward." *Am I ready to tell her about him?*

"Ah. Finances? It must be hard to do everything by yourself." Helen was being coy.

"No. It's not really money, so much. Of course, you and dad have been great with helping Carly and Jake out." *Should I change the subject?*

"It's what we do. Grandparents love spending money on their grandchildren. But something tells me they are not part of your—how did you put it—'sorting out process.'" Helen sipped her tea.

"No." *Oh, God. Here I go. Talking to Karen is one thing. What will my mother think? How much should I tell her?*

Abby took the plunge. "Mom, I have been seeing someone. His name is Greg. Gregory Larson."

With little interruption, Abby spilled out the story of two lonely people: a widow and a widower. One who has lived alone (albeit with his dog) for decades and one who has lived alone for a year and a half…though it felt much longer. He was just three years older than she. Leaving out some worrisome details, Abby covered the basics: what Greg did for a living, what he looked like, what he liked to do, and how often they saw each other. Helen's occasional reactions were always warm and her smile genuine.

"Abby, I am happy for you, though you never mentioned how you met him."

*Ah, that's part of the issue.* "Well, that's the strange part. He and Jack were friends. I mean, not best friends, but they knew each other for years through their businesses. And, you know, an island makes everyone closer. Well, anyway, that's a little weird for me."

"Why?" Helen couldn't help herself.

"Oh, Mom…" Abby let out a sigh that seemed to empty her lungs of all the air and tension they held. "I don't know. We have history. Maybe if he was a perfect stranger it would be different." She grabbed onto a thought as she nibbled a cookie. "And then there is the fact that we both are—I don't know just how to put this…"

"You don't have to 'put it' any way other than the way it is, honey."

"Sometimes I think we are just tragic figures. We are just meant to be alone. I don't know if he wants to change his ways. I don't know if I want to be so involved with another man…so soon. Besides, I still see Jack here," Abby pointed to her heart, "and I don't want to forget him, nor do I want Greg to be him. They are so different, but they are cut from the same cloth in a way."

"How so?"

"They both went to Vietnam, Mom. They both have baggage that came from being there."

Helen knew the damage inflicted on Jack. "Greg has baggage?"

"Well, yes."

Helen felt that Abby was holding back and knew that whatever it was, it had to come out now.

*I'm committed. Here comes the darkness.* "Mom, it's terrible. When he was in Vietnam, his wife was pregnant, and she and the baby died in a car crash. He's never recovered, really. I am just finding out about this now. And his life just spiraled downhill after that." Another sigh of anguish. She put down her teacup.

"I don't know, Mom. I am scared." Abby put her hands on either side of her forehead, as if holding all this inside could make her brain explode. The first tears formed and bubbled over the surface of Abby's brown eyes.

Helen took all this in. It was far more complicated than she had assumed. She had wondered if Abby had begun to see other men. She had fretted that Abby was lonely or that she was burying herself in work to avoid facing a life without Jack. And she had been concerned that her daughter would never find someone she could love to the same degree that she had loved Jack. Now, Helen understood part of Abby's fear.

"He's complicated, Abby. So are you. Life is very difficult sometimes. But remember this: you must embrace life and enjoy it."

Abby nodded as she searched in her sweater pocket for a tissue she knew was hiding there.

Helen considered her options and finally raised the issue to the point of no return. "Abby, you have feelings for him. Are you afraid you are falling in love with him?"

Abby looked up at her mom and nodded. Without any words, they drew each other to the middle ground of the couch and embraced. Abby melted in her mother's arms. Helen felt the weight of Abby's burdens, not just with Greg, but with being alone with so much responsibility.

The house creaked as the wind from the ocean stirred. The quiet was broken by a soft *ping* that emanated from Abby's computer. *You've got mail.* Abby knew it was Greg. She hadn't called like she said she would yesterday, and on cue, he entered the conversation in the way one did in the new millennium.

She decided to ignore it. The sound couldn't have meant anything to her mother—and she probably didn't hear it anyway.

"I told him that I am not ready for a relationship—a serious one—yet. And I don't know when I will be ready. I won't blame him if he loses patience with me. I also know that he is very independent—well, so am I—and I just don't know if he can change. I mean, he has been a bachelor forever, Mom. And I've been a mom and a wife for my whole adult life. How do we even fit together?"

Helen knew she was being asked for the first time for her opinion. She knew she didn't have all the facts yet. But she did know her daughter.

"Honey, all I can tell you is that I know how special you are. And if he knows it, he will wait for you. And if he doesn't know it, he isn't worthy of your love."

"You haven't asked me how he feels about me." Abby put her tissue away.

"No. I haven't. But my guess is that he may already be in love with you. But perhaps he's having the same misgivings you are."

Abby pulled away from Helen and marveled at the wisdom etched into her mother's face.

"We all have doubts, Abby. I had my doubts about your father. It comes with giving yourself to someone and trusting them with your heart." Helen settled back and sipped her lukewarm tea.

Abby rose from the couch. "Mom, let me warm up your tea."

"Oh, that would be nice. And by the way, that sound I heard—wasn't that your computer?"

Abby was surprised. "Oh, yeah. It does that when I've got mail."

Helen smiled. "Perhaps you might want to see who it is—and answer him."

"I told my mom about you today, Greg. I'm sorry I didn't call. But I have been thinking about you. It's late. Can I call you at work tomorrow? I think my mom would like to meet you. I would like it, too. How is next Sunday for brunch?" Then she clicked SEND.

"It's a date. Glad I haven't scared you off. I'd love to meet her. I've been thinking about you, too. Call anytime."

For several minutes, each stared at the blinking curser that sent their words into the invisible world of the Internet.

# Chapter 24

## *Three Musketeers—2001*

Like many girls, Carly had times when growing up meant feeling down. She was very smart, so boys were put off. She was aggressive, so girls thought she was bitchy. But college changed her outlook and made her feel comfortable in her own skin. Boys could still be the bane of her existence, but she kept things on a "just friends" plane—that is, until her junior year. His name was Brock. He was cute, fun, and her first heartbreak. Abby hated to see that happen to her daughter, but at the same time, she knew Carly couldn't keep up all her defenses. Now that Carly was in an unfamiliar town where it rained 180 days a year, Abby hoped that the Seattle gloom didn't set in on Carly's world.

Abby thought that Carly looked the part of a professional woman when she picked her up at the hotel; however, in the space of an hour, Carly transformed back into a twenty-four-year-old "jeans and T-shirt" girl. Her hair was the longest Abby had seen it in years—light brown with highlights of blonde cascading down past her shoulders.

Abby hadn't seen Carly since the summer; Helen hadn't seen her in over a year. All of them had a lot to chat about, but Carly's love life was the featured subject of dinner on Saturday.

"Well, Seattle is very cool, but it's going to take some getting used to. Actually, my goal is to get back to California. The rain is just something they take for granted like we do the sunshine. Besides, I really don't know anyone other than people at work. It's hard moving to a new city and not knowing a soul. I'm not saying I'm lonely, because I'm so busy but…" Carly looked up at both perceptive mothers. "Okay, I admit it—I am kinda lonely."

*Lonely. Check.*

"Then there are the guys I meet. They fall into three categories: miserably married, bitterly divorced, and gorgeously gay. The married and divorced jerks hit on me, and the gay guys are so cute but, naturally, uninterested. Ugh. Very frustrating. But I've only been there six months. The women I work with are really nice. Anyway, Seattle is a really fun town, and there are a lot of great bars and, of course, coffee shops. I did meet some nice guys who are friends with my fashion design team. They are kinda computer geeks, hoping to catch on to Microsoft up there." Carly stopped and noticed she hadn't taken a bite of her spinach stuffed ravioli.

"Well, give it time, Carly," Abby found herself saying.

*Give it time, Abby.*

Helen gently dispensed kudos to Carly's judgment as she sipped her cabernet sauvignon. "You are wise to keep those divorced men far away, dear. And the married ones, well, I rather think they will be divorced soon, too."

"But I love, love, love what I am doing. I love the way the company treats us. Nordstrom is all about doing things the right way, so I've finally found my match, you know, Mom." A rare break in the conversation. Carly was hungry.

As Abby played with her oversized meatball, Carly's description of her not-in-love life swirled around like spaghetti on a fork and spoon.

*I've finally found my match. Well, he's not bitterly divorced, he's not miserably married, and he is definitely not gay. He is a very handsome 54-year-old man.*

"So, Mom, are your girlfriends trying to set you up with anyone?" Carly's words seemed to come from somewhere other than right across the table.

"Huh, what? Oh, well, you know, Carly, I am still just trying to get things settled." Abby glanced at Helen, a perfect poker player who showed no sign that all the cards had already been played and that she held all the aces. Helen feigned only the slightest interest, indicating to Carly that she wanted Abby to move on with her life. Abby once again appreciated the fact that her mother understood the code of silence—at least until invited.

"I am sure your friend Karen has been thinking of who to set you up with. And, Mom, let me tell you, you've lost weight. And you look fabulous. I love your hair shorter, and that style is so cute on you…" Carly just kept going, moving from Abby's looks to her fashion choices. Abby merely smiled; Helen slightly nodded; and the wine slowly disappeared.

Abby never took the bait. But as they left the restaurant, Abby took Carly's arm and whispered to her, "Sweetheart, I love you. Don't worry about me, okay? When I am ready, I'll know."

*God, at least one of those things is true.*

"I know, Mom. I love you so much." They held hands and walked down the street. Carly reached for her grandmother's hand. They were the Three Musketeers.

---

Sunday was busy. Driving Carly to the airport with a promise to visit her soon dried the tears. Brunch with her mother and Gregory Larson was far more relaxed than she had expected. He was warm. Charming would be a better word, but it was not a façade. He was exactly as advertised. And her mother's eyes peeled through the casual conversation—as one does an onion—searching for the man's core. Helen DiFranco was an expert at watching people and never giving a hint that she was gleaning information. It was a subtle art.

So when the evening came and Abby was faced with school the next day, she sat back on the couch and tried to put everything into perspective before she asked her mother the all-important question.

"So what did you think of Greg?"

Helen knew that Abby wanted her advice on navigating her way with Mr. Gregory Larson. She also sensed that Greg lived a life so fundamentally alone that he would be foolish to think that he could easily adjust to life with Abby—or any other woman. And then there was Jack, who loomed over both Abby and Greg, like a statue to be revered but that never leaves one's vision.

Helen also knew of Greg's skeletons. Abby told her that Greg was a recovering alcoholic, and she explained the depth of his despair. All this reflected well on his character, Helen felt. He seemed to be a man of conviction, of substance, and he was a survivor. He had spirit. She loved all the conversation on the restoration of the theater and its progress; his leadership, which he downplayed, was particularly attractive. His kindness was evident. He seemed gentle.

All of this came to Helen's mind as she sat reading a magazine—or pretending to—while Abby got ready for school the next day. So by the time Abby raised the question, Helen had made her decision: say less, but say more.

"Abby, before I tell you what I think, let me tell you a little about Katharine Hepburn and Spencer Tracy. I just finished her autobiography. I know it seems off the point, but there is something about them you need to know. It is sad—really almost tragic—how they lived their lives. Tracy wouldn't divorce his wife, but he didn't even live with her for decades. Hepburn only loved Tracy and no other. They maintained separate homes. They kept it a secret for almost their entire adult lives. Of course, keeping a secret in Hollywood was next to impossible. Everyone knew the truth, but they were never seen in public. She didn't move into his home until she had to care for him as he was dying. She never even attended his funeral. She never spoke about their love for one another until after his wife died. When I finished the book, it saddened me to think that they could never be honest. The world they lived in back then wouldn't allow it, I suppose. They could never fully live the life they wanted."

Helen reached for her teacup and took a sip. Her eyes, however, never left Abby's.

"Abby, thank goodness times have changed. When you do find someone, you have to be honest and courageous."

Abby waited her mother out. Helen had not given her verdict.

"Abby, he is very handsome and charming. Very. There is not much to not like about him," Helen began.

"But." Abby edged toward her mother as she moved to the middle of the couch, that sacred ground between a mother's judgment and a daughter's need for guidance.

"Go slowly. Abby, just don't let fear dictate your happiness."

Abby knew her mother had more to say. But in truth, Helen had said all that needed to be said.

---

Abby stared at the computer screen. It said: You've got mail.

**"Loved meeting your mother. Loved seeing you. Sorry your vacation is over. Let's talk soon."**

Abby typed, **"She really liked you, Greg. I loved seeing you, too. Yes, we do need to talk."** She stopped typing. She thought of so many things she could write, but the curser blinked like a stop sign.

# Chapter 25

## *"When I Fall in Love"—2001*

It was a warm, breezy summer morning. Before Abby's eyes opened, she knew her world had changed dramatically. For one thing, she felt Molly's wet nose bumping against her hand, which dangled off the bed. For another, she felt herself cocooned within sheets and pillows unfamiliar yet thoroughly comfortable. Her eyes opened, and above her was a foreign ceiling. Twisting, she reached for him. He was not there, but the sheets were still warm. Then she smelled the strong aroma of coffee. She smiled.

Her mind raced backwards. The mind moves faster than the ticking of a clock. Two months had passed since her mother had left. A week in New Jersey visiting family had been wonderful but strangely empty. Greg was waiting for her return at the airport. Most people merely pull up at the curb and scoop up the arriving party, luggage and all. Greg waited inside. He had flowers. Abby's pace quickened as she moved toward him, and then suddenly, they embraced like people do in sappy movies. Onlookers must have thought they were long separated lovers.

They immediately grabbed a bite to eat. Their bodies were so close that it seemed their foreheads would touch as they whispered to each other.

Greg drove to his house, and the moment they stepped into the foyer, with Molly celebrating Abby's return, Abby gave herself to him—heart and soul. Abby had made up her mind. The time was now; there was no turning back. She wanted him, and his patience with her was rewarded.

Abby let herself go. She had not been with any man other than Jack. Greg was gentle with her. He understood. She allowed the years of loneliness to fan her desire for him. But it wasn't just physical yearning; it was Gregory Larson, the human being. Who he was. How he had changed. What he meant to her, to others. And how he had restored himself despite all his tragedy and weakness. Most importantly, how much he cared for her on a daily basis and how willing he was to sacrifice his needs for hers. All this drove them to his bedroom and the sultry, ocean-scented air. The darkness devoured them. Their eyes took note of every movement, every touch, and every breath until they collapsed.

---

"So what happened with Greg this weekend?" Karen gushed. They were sitting in the bleachers at San Diego State University, watching Jake play a charity baseball game between the current Aztecs and a team of alumni who played high school ball in San Diego and went on to the major leagues. But the big draw was Ted Williams, who sat in the stands and generously signed autographs for children. The event was a major fundraiser for the team. Jake had been talking nonstop about it for months.

Abby and Karen cheered when Jake was announced as the second baseman, wearing number 4. Jake had made the team as a walk on and now had a partial scholarship. He knew that he was going to have to earn playing time, but today was a day for fun and laughter; serious baseball was not on the minds of anyone—though none of the SDSU players wanted to embarrass themselves or the invited guests. Jake looked up to the stands and tipped his cap to his mom.

"Isn't he cute?" Abby smiled as she stood taking his picture—one of many she would take on this day: the twentieth of August, 2001.

"Who? Jake or Greg?" Karen was confused and frustrated. She didn't need to know *everything* about the newest developments in the Abby and Greg saga, but she hoped for the highlights.

Abby looked through the lens. "Both." She laughed. So did Karen.

As the first two innings played out, Abby revealed to Karen how much she had missed Greg when she had traveled back east to visit her parents. "We called each other every day, Karen. I found myself waiting for his call. And then there were times I called him during his dinner time because he told me he hated eating alone."

"That's weird for a guy who has been alone for thirty years. Don't you think?" Karen applied sunscreen to her neck, but added, "I'm not saying he's weird; it's just…"

"No, no, I get it. I am sure he has had lots of other women or friends in his life, Karen. And he told me he is comfortable with being alone, too. But dinner is when he hates not having someone to talk to. Anyway, he told me he missed me. It was sweet, you know—not sappy, just sweet."

"Okay, I get it. So you came to what conclusion after all these minutes on the phone?"

Abby said, "Karen, I decided to allow myself to fall in love with him. God, I made that sound like, like I was buying a car or something. That's not how I felt. It came from my heart, but it came because I wanted him. You know what I mean?"

"Yes. Of course I do." Karen looked at Abby, and the two simply understood the subtext.

The entire time Abby poured out her feelings, Karen listened carefully. She was cautiously joyful. Of course, she wanted her dearest friend to find love, but she also knew that the two of them had led lives that were in some ways polar opposites. Karen wondered what would happen when the wave of romance receded from its crest and the reality of their disparate daily lives rolled in. But she kept those thoughts to herself and enjoyed the account of it all.

"When we had dinner at Peohe's, the sunset was stunning. The bay and the city sparkled, Karen. It was just a perfect evening." Then Abby realized that Jake was coming up to bat. She stood and cheered; Karen was up a moment after.

"Go, Jake! Show 'em what you got, number 4!" Abby shrilled. When Jake grounded to the shortstop, Abby was only slightly disappointed. "Good hit, Jake!" she said, but her volume was significantly reduced.

Karen wanted to know more about that evening, but before she could get her question out, Abby volunteered, "Oh, that was the other thing we did, Karen. On a lark, we went to the Hotel Del and just decided to walk around, you know? Just for fun. Maybe have a drink. The tourists are still packing the place, but downstairs in the lounge they had a singer playing the piano—actually it was a trio, come to think of it."

Karen sipped her Coke and couldn't care less if it was a combo, a duet, or a full orchestra. Whatever. Karen cut into Abby's monologue: "Wait, wait, Abby. Was this before or after you slept with him?"

"Oh, after. Anyway, where was I?"

"Piano, drinks…"

"Right…and the best part was that I told Greg that one of my favorite songs was that old Nat King Cole song called 'When I Fall in Love.' You know the one?"

"Duh, Abby. Yes. That was the song they played in *Sleepless in Seattle*, remember?" Karen sucked on her straw, paused, and managed to talk at the same time.

"Oh, that's right! I forgot that. I love that movie. Anyway, Greg goes up to the guy on the piano and asks him to play it…and guess what?"

"Let me guess," Karen feigned disappointment, "he never heard of it."

Abby gave Karen a look, a playful one that said, *Don't mess with me; I'm telling a romantic story.* "So they played it. It was perfect. That song just speaks to exactly how I feel right now, Karen." Abby softly repeated the song's message: "'When I fall in love, it will be completely.'" Abby sighed. "And I haven't felt this way…since Jack, you know."

Karen reached for Abby's arm and brought the two of them together. "I know, Abby. I know." They tilted their heads together.

They quietly watched the next inning go by. Then Karen said, "Well, when do I get to meet him—you know, with you? I mean, I don't want to invent some reason to go to his store and ask him for a hammer or something."

Abby looked at her watch. "As a matter of fact, he should be here in about twenty minutes. I told him about the game, and he rearranged his schedule at the store to get here. He told me he would be down the left field line, behind the short fence, out in the area where there is grass. Over there," she pointed, "with Molly."

At the appointed time, Greg and Molly appeared. Abby and Karen left their seats and walked down to greet him. Greg hadn't met Karen before, but he understood the sisterhood.

"Karen, this is Greg Larson and Molly. Isn't she adorable?"

Karen and Greg held each other's hand for a few seconds longer than typical while they added their I've-heard-so-much-about-you's. Karen waited until Greg seemed distracted by the game, then whispered into Abby's ear, "They are *both* adorable, you lucky girl." Abby almost blushed. Her eyes widened as if to reply, *I know!*

Small talk of people they mutually knew was the order of business as the business of baseball came to an end. Karen told Abby she needed to go, but Abby told her not to worry—she would ride home with Greg. At that, Karen merely smiled.

The picture-taking took over after that: Jake with this baseball player and that. A photo of him and his coaches. The one with Ted Williams was the most important to Jake. The one with his mother was the most important to Abby. What made it even more special for Abby was the person taking the picture: Jake's former employer and Abby's newfound love.

---

"Jacob, I want to tell you something, and I hope you…understand." Abby was serving up Jake's favorite meal: filet mignon and a baked potato with everything on it. Jake had already cut into the steak and was chewing voraciously.

"Yeah, Mom, what? Oh, this is awesome, Mom. Really. So what's up?"

She loved to watch him eat. He and Tom both had the same contented look when they ate—the same one that Jack had had whenever he had enjoyed a good meal. Seeing Jacob—any of the kids, really—always brought her back to Jack, even when doing so was not what she had in mind. But Abby pressed forward. "Jake, I want you to know that I am seeing Greg Larson. I haven't told your brother or sister yet, but I will soon."

Jake looked up from his potato, which he was filling to the brim with butter, sour cream, and chives. Abby watched his face carefully. Jake stopped. He sighed, and then a faint smile appeared. He looked down and restocked the potato. Just like his father, Jake found that speaking from the heart meant avoiding eye contact with his mom.

"I had a feeling about that, Mom. At the ball game and all...and before. Kinda the way you talked about him. Are you, like, getting really involved?" He finished decorating his potato, but did not take a bite.

"Yes. I mean, well, yes. We are getting more serious, but we are just getting to know each other, too."

"When did you start seeing him? I mean, like, when I was working there?"

"No, of course not. Your father had just...no. Jake, we started dating at the beginning of this summer." Abby's steak and potato remained untouched on her plate.

"Jake, I miss your father. We all do. It has been two years..."

Quiet.

Jake still had not taken a bite. He missed his father badly, but he thought of his mother's loneliness. Then he put his knife and fork down, took his mother's hand, and finally glanced up. "Mom, I wish Dad could see me playing for State. I wish he could just...just play catch with me again." He sighed. He again broke eye contact. "But he can't. You're all I got, Mom. And I want you to be happy. So if Mr. Larson makes you happy, then I'm happy. But he's not Dad. He's a really nice man, Mr. Larson is…"

"Jacob, his name is Greg. He will never be Dad. I will never ask him to be anything other than what he is, and I will never ask you to think of him in any other way. But I do want you to know that I care for him. A great deal, Jacob."

With that, dinner commenced. Jake chewed much slower. He didn't ask what the verb *seeing* meant exactly, much to Abby's relief. Carly would surely not allow her to avoid the subject of intimacy. Thankfully, Abby's pulse also slowed.

"Jake, please don't tell your brother or sister, okay? I will tell them later this week."

"Okay, Mom." And just like that, he began to devour his dinner.

Abby had stepped out onto the ice. It was slippery, but at least she hadn't fallen through.

---

Greg was a man of few close friends but many acquaintances. His best friends had always been his dogs; there had been a running one-way "dialogue" with Aussie. Indeed, it had been a strange method of self-discovery. Now, however, the tables had turned. Molly seemed to see things through Abby's point of view, or at least Greg imagined it to be so. Molly was attracted to Abby like a magnet, following her every step. Just the mention of the name *Abby* brought Molly to her feet, tail wagging furiously as she raced to the front door to see if she was coming. So discussing his reservations about the speed with which things were progressing with Abby was a non-starter with Molly. As far as Molly was concerned, Abby was already part of the family.

Greg's misgivings gnawed at him. They seemed silly at first, but they made him realize the different course his life had taken compared to

Abby's. Meeting Abby's mother months ago seemed pleasant enough. Helen was sweet, wise, and far more in tune with the world than either of his parents had been. But then, there had been no expectations because, after all, he and Abby had just been friends. *Funny,* Greg thought, *how sex changes everything. It always does.*

However, meeting Jake at his baseball game had been awkward. Greg knew that Abby hadn't told any of her children about their relationship yet. Abby was going to come over later tonight and tell him how Jake had reacted to his mother's "involvement" with him. But even Abby's behavior around him with Karen showed a subtle transformation in her. The way she touched his shoulder, the looks she exchanged with Karen, and something about the way she simply spoke to him had an air of intimacy that Greg enjoyed. But for some unknown reason, he was unsure of his next step.

*Have I moved too fast?* Certainly this was what he had wanted. He was clear about his feelings for Abby. Those feelings were intensified now that they were lovers. But thirty years of independence and the instinct to not rush into a commitment were part of his DNA. *Am I just being stupid? This will pass as soon as I just get used to having Abby in my life, right? But to what extent am I committing myself?* Greg found himself putting too much coffee into the filter. *Damn, what am I doing? Pay attention, Greg.*

Greg wondered how Jake would accept his mother's news. But even more daunting for Greg was how he would feel when around Jake. They had always had a friendly relationship. They were baseball buddies; they could talk about the Dodger-Padres rivalry, the College World Series, and all the controversy about steroids. But how would it be between them now?

When Abby arrived after talking to Jake, Greg did not let these worries be a part of their conversation, except to acknowledge that Abby had handled the situation well and that Jake seemed to be "okay" with the changes that "Mr. Larson" seemed to cause.

Abby stirred her decaf coffee. "I just think I need to be honest and give each of the kids—kids! Will you listen to me? They're adults! Anyway, what was I saying?"

"Being honest," Greg reminded her. *Honest. When do I even start to be truthful with her? When do I tell her what I did? Who I am?*

"Right. Anyway, I think they will all be happy for us. It may take time. Carly isn't the one I'm worried about. It's Tom who's more protective of me, you know?" Abby noticed that Greg was quieter than usual.

A beat.

"You seem awfully quiet, Greg. Is something bothering you?" Abby brought her coffee cup to her lips and blew.

"No, not really." *Honest, Greg. I'm the drunk, Abby! I'm the man on the bridge who crashed into your life.* But Gregory Larson said none of what he was contemplating. Instead he merely philosophized: "It's going to take time for all of us to adjust, you know. I mean, you and I have a lot to learn about each other. And our lives...how should I say it?" *How, indeed? What will she think?*

"Just say it, Greg. I'm a big girl. I know you have never been deeply involved with someone—other than Raquel. You've never raised kids." Abby placed her coffee cup down carefully.

Greg leaned back. *I can't tell her...not yet.* "We are at the core very much kindred souls, Abby. Jeez, listen to me. I sound like one of those teacher friends of yours." He smiled broadly. Abby's lips parted with the smallest trace of amusement. "But, well, let me put it the way a hardware store owner would: we are gluing two things together that fit pretty well, you know? It's just that it takes time for the glue to set and the two pieces to hold." Greg took his turn blowing on his coffee, which he raised to his lips. *Whew. At least that was a start.*

Abby took his hand. "That, my dear, is a metaphor. You're not fooling me, Mr. Larson, with your folksy talk. But listen, I know you're right. I do. We have all the time in the world. Let's go slowly."

Greg looked carefully into Abby's eyes, trying to make sure she understood that his apprehension was not to be confused with aversion. But he knew he twisted the truth because that distinction blurred in his own mind. *Damn it. Trust her.*

He stood and turned to his stereo. Nat King Cole's magical "When I Fall in Love" filled the living room.

Greg heard lyrics that were forewarning.

> *In a restless world like this is*
> *Love is ended before it's begun*
> *And too many moonlight kisses*
> *Seem to cool in the warmth of the sun*

But what Abby heard was foreshadowing.

> *And the moment I can feel that you feel that way, too*
> *Is when I fall in love with you.*

# Chapter 26

## *September 11th —2001*

*Abby, answer your phone.*

"Greg, are you watching?" Abby's voice was shaking as she picked up her cell.

"Abby, hold on, okay...right there, sir. Aisle 5. Yes." Greg moved to his office. "Are you still there, Abby?"

"Yes. Greg, it's horrible." Abby was sitting at her desk in her classroom. She was between class periods.

"I know. We have the TV on here. Have you heard from your parents?"

"No. I tried to call, but it won't go through. The second tower has been hit, and I think the Pentagon, too. Greg, they flew planes into the Towers! My God..."

"Abby, listen. If you hear from your folks—that they are alright— please let me know, okay?"

"Okay."

Greg walked back and forth in his tiny office. "Are you okay? How are you handling things at school with your students?"

"Greg, they are scared. They keep hearing rumors and things about us being attacked. My kids are looking at me and asking why this is happening. I don't know what more to tell them. Hold on...what, Karen? Karen's in here...No. Are you sure?...Okay. Greg, Karen says there was another plane that was hijacked, and it has crashed somewhere in Pennsylvania."

"Yes. They're reporting that now. No news about survivors yet. Abby..."

"Greg, I gotta go. The bell just rang. I'll call at lunch. Can you meet me at my house today at 3:30?"

"Of course."

"Good. I just don't feel like going to an empty house. I'll call Jake later. Gotta go. Love you. Bye."

"Love you." Greg heard the click as the words were coming from his mouth. It was an instinct—*Love you. She's the first person I thought of. She's the person I can't lose.*

---

Greg brought over a pizza. Molly was wonderfully untroubled by what was to become the most devastating attack on America since Pearl Harbor. At least back then it was warships being bombed by planes. Today, commercial planes packed with innocent passengers were the bombs, tearing into skyscrapers with thousands of people unaware of their impending death.

Abby and Greg watched aghast as the Twin Towers melted into an incredible gray cloud. Everything that once was just disappeared into dust and fire.

Then it all dissolved into the blackness of the New York City evening.

Off and on, each of them reached for their phones.

Both of Greg's sisters called him. He couldn't remember the last time he spoke to each of them on the same day. Weeks ago, he had told them about Abby. They knew she had family back in New Jersey. They told Greg that she was in their thoughts.

Abby finally reached her parents. They were fine, but they could see the smoke from across the river. The city was consumed by it. Tom called and told his mother that his law firm had offices in those buildings. No one knew anything yet. Carly had a similar reaction. She had a friend working in an office building a block away from the Twin Towers, but no word had reached her. Jake was up in Los Angeles visiting high school friends at UCLA. They were all watching their televisions.

Abby and Greg sat as close together as possible on the couch. The only thing separating them was a box of tissues that Abby used to dab her eyes. Molly curled up below them, covering their feet. There was little to say and too much to watch.

Just weeks ago, they had told each other that they had "all the time in the world" to grow into each other's lives. Suddenly, the unspoken message resonated from the CNN NewsCenter:

It can all change in the blink of an eye.

---

The time that fell between September 11, 2001 and the Thanksgiving that followed was the latest manifestation of the Dickens line, "It was the best of times, it was the worst of times." American sorrow juxtaposed with American patriotism. Acts of heroism were ubiquitous, but it did not soothe the nation's deep wounds. The carnage, the toxic fumes, the fear, the desire for revenge—all of it was draped over "a city that never sleeps."

For Greg and Abby, like most Americans, it was a time to grit their teeth and do their jobs, contribute what they could, and eventually, on Thanksgiving Day, pray for the souls of the departed. They realized, as many did, that no ocean could ever protect them from harm. They felt, as many did, a twinge of guilt that they had been spared when so many had lost so much. Thanksgiving couldn't possibly be the same.

Abby decided that she and Jacob would fly to San Francisco and meet Carly there for Thanksgiving so that Tom and Nina could host the holiday meal. With all of them together, they could also work out some last-minute details of the wedding in January. Greg would be visiting his sister Sara. She and her husband, Mike, had recently moved to Carlsbad, some forty minutes from Greg. To his surprise, his other sister, Melanie, was flying down with her partner, Marie. At the last minute, Michelle and Derek decided to fly in from Scottsdale where they had retired. Their travel bug had been quashed since 9.11, but when Michelle heard that everyone was getting together, she and Derek packed their bags. Greg knew that 9.11 had shaken them all up and had made them feel the necessity of being together.

Abby was disappointed that Greg would not be with her, but she completely understood. Greg, on the other hand, was relieved. The anxiety of meeting all her children—of being perceived as either an interloper or their future stepfather—was still very troubling to Greg. Regardless of how Abby's children felt, the "family commitment" made him nervous. There was no middle ground.

Greg knew that there was something else plaguing him that he was afraid to face. Something that he knew he had to come to grips with before he could move forward.

*What triggered it?* Greg wondered. His mind dwelt on the vulnerability that came with 9.11, the flashing red lights of ambulances, the wall of pictures of the missing or presumed dead, the emergency rooms filled with battered, crippled survivors pulled from the rubble, that awareness that there is no time like the present. Was this what compelled Greg to face the memory that haunted him? Maybe.

But in his heart, he knew the truth—*it was their voices.* The recordings of the last words spoken into cell phones on planes destined for destruction. The men and women who cried to their loved ones that they would forever keep them in their hearts. The recordings were ubiquitous. CNN and every television network played them over and over again, always warning the listener of the frightful message being delivered invisibly from the seat of an airplane to an unsuspecting, helpless loved one. Those were the voices that haunted Gregory Larson, forcing him to admit that he could no longer ignore his phone call.

*I just stared at it and then put it away. I drank when its ring was piercing. The more I drank, the less I heard, until it was barely audible. But it was always there. The years of ignoring it made it simply not resonate. It became part of the chatter, the static, the banal sounds that muffled my ears so that nothing really rang true.*

*But now, since 9.11, I can't ignore the voice that has been calling to me for thirty years.*

It rang even louder when both his sisters asked the all too predictable but innocent question: "So, when did you two meet?"

Gregory Larson knew that he had to go back into his past before he could be at peace.

---

It began during the week preceding Thanksgiving. Greg and Abby had dinner at her house. The subject of family naturally came with the entrée.

"I wish I could meet your sisters, Greg. How long has it been since all of you got together?"

Greg sliced through the chicken. *Maybe now is the time to tell her.* "Hmm. Well, I was talking to Sara about that. I think it was when her youngest, Lauren, graduated from college. That was two years ago, I think. As a matter of fact, the time before that was when Sophie graduated. It seems that her kids are what pull us together."

"Kids will do that." Abby looked up from the asparagus and smiled at him.

"Yeah. I guess so." Greg swallowed slowly. *But maybe they are what keep us apart.*

"I wish you could be with mine. Carly and Tom are more than a little curious about this new man in my life. I think Jake's descriptions are pretty vague." Abby spoke with no hesitancy.

Greg began to feel that old sensation. *At what point do you tell your secrets? What price does it entail? The longer I wait, the more difficult it becomes. And what if she feels I have been deceitful—then what? Am I worthy of her love? If not, will I feel a pain that I have not felt in thirty years?*

He began by putting down his fork and knife. "Abby, I haven't told you the truth."

"What do you mean?" Abby noted his hands, empty of utensils and beginning to tremble ever so minutely.

"Abby, there is something about me that we have to—I have to—get past." He could not suppress the chattering of his teeth no matter how hard he clenched his jaw.

Abby wanted to be sympathetic, but she was too confused and nervous. "What's the matter, Greg? Tell me."

*Deep breath. Just say it.*

"Abby, the night you got in the accident on the bridge. That was me. I was the man on the bridge. I was the drunk who almost killed you and Jacob. I am the one who slammed into you and came within a guardrail of ending everything. Me, Abby. Me."

*There's no stopping now.*

He pointed to his forehead. "This is the scar. I see it every morning. Every day, I wanted to tell you that it was me. But I couldn't. I couldn't because I was afraid of what you would think, of what you would ask yourself: 'How could he know me all these years and never tell me?'"

*Now what? She seems stunned. Do I finish the story? Do I bring up Jack?*

A beat.

Greg looked Abby right in the eyes. "Jack knew. He figured it out. We talked—I knew how he felt. He wanted to kill me. The accident on the bridge—that was rock bottom for an alcoholic like me."

*It's almost done.*

"And I am the one you want to take with you to meet your kids?"

Abby was stunned. What she knew about him was distorted, like in a fun house. But no one was laughing. She had questions, but the lump in her throat was growing. The only word she could release was, "Why?"

"Why? Why did I get drunk that night...lots of nights...years of nights?" Greg looked away momentarily.

*Raquel. I have to talk about Raquel.*

"I drank so much that night because I was trying to put myself out of my misery. Raquel died fourteen years to the day that I passed out on the bridge and crashed into your life. That's why. It's not an excuse at all. I was a drunk who couldn't deal with…with losing her. I was so pathetic that I…" Greg had to stop and gather himself.

*The car is skidding, the guardrail gnashing.*

Abby remained silent. Tears were flicked from her cheeks; she wanted to remain eye to eye with the man she had fallen in love with, a man whose secret she now shared.

A beat.

"Abby, if it wasn't for you, I would have been over the rail and into the bay. Maybe that was what I wanted. I've carried that guilt—that loathing—ever since. And then when I met you, I wanted to bury myself far away from you because I felt I didn't deserve your attention. I felt so unworthy of you. You never knew that you were the person who saved me from my demons." Greg skidded to a halt.

*It's over. The past is now the present. Then why do I still hear the phone ringing?*

Abby found her mind racing back to the bridge. To the screeching of tires. To the gnashing of metal on metal. To her panic. To Jacob's crying. To the flashing police lights. To the sirens of the ambulance. To the hospital room. To the phone call to Jack. To the frightened sound of his voice. To the voice of Carmen, the nurse. To the embrace with Tommy and Carly and Jack and little Jake in the waiting room.

"Greg, I don't know what to say. I'm sorry. I'm just trying to…to just clear my head of that night. I haven't allowed myself to go back there. You'll have to let me just…"

Greg understood. *How long does it take for the regrets of the past to become less painful? What will she think of me now? How can our relationship ever compare to what she had with Jack?*

Abby pushed herself from the table. As she rose, Molly, who had moved closer to her chair, rose to meet her. She walked into the kitchen and blew her nose. Greg could hear the unmistakable sound of tissues being pulled out of their cardboard box. One. Two. Three. Finally, after the fourth, Abby returned.

Greg stood.

"You told me once, Greg, that we needed time to understand each other. You were right. I am relieved you told me what happened. I know it wasn't easy. For you. For me. I can't say that I understand you, but I do understand loss. You need to know my secret."

A beat.

"I think of Jack every day. Even when I am with you. I try to compartmentalize my thoughts when I hold you, kiss you...but sometimes I can't. I just can't. I know what I just said hurts you."

Greg could not conceal the damage. *I am not the only one with secrets. Jack was her love. Will always be the love of her life. And I will always be his understudy.*

Abby sighed and looked down at Molly. "You have told me some things that I have to think about. One day, I will be able to deal with this, but not tonight."

Greg was silent. *I haven't told her everything. I haven't told her about the phone that keeps ringing. It's Raquel's call to me. 9.11. And I haven't the strength to answer her call.*

Abby looked up at him. She knew he had beaten himself up. The bruises were obvious. She also knew that he took the blows she delivered without seeming to flinch. But they landed. Hard.

"Whatever happens to us, Greg, I want you to know something very important. You are a survivor. You are. We are. You probably think I should be angry with you. I'm not angry. I don't know what I am feeling right now, but anger is not it. I feel like I need to breathe...and one more thing: no matter what happens to us, I love you and admire you, even if you feel you don't deserve it."

Greg merely nodded his head.

*Thank you for that, Abby.*

*But the phone is ringing louder than ever.*

# Chapter 27

## *The Wedding Date—2001*

The wedding invitation was Greg's moment of truth. Abby had made yet another decision in a long series of decisions. This one seemed simple enough—she wanted Greg to come to Tom's wedding in San Francisco.

Abby viewed it as inevitable.

Greg viewed it as inescapable.

On a crisp December afternoon while they were walking on the beach, the wind blowing across their faces, Abby raised the subject of Greg buying his plane ticket.

When Greg gave his answer, Abby's face fell. "What do you mean you're 'not sure you can get away?'"

He listed what she thought were lame excuses: the store, the dog, the timing, his family, her family…anything that came to mind, except the truth.

She waited him out. Then she told him what she thought. "All of this is bullshit, Greg. Please, please just tell me the truth about how you are feeling. What is really bothering you?"

A beat.

"Okay. I hope you understand. There are two things." *Big breath.* "The expectations, Abby. Your children. Your family. They are going to look at me and expect something."

"Like what?" Abby was shaking her head, trying to decipher the message as if it was in some cryptic code.

"Like…like, I am there because you want me to be a part of the family."

"Well, I do." Abby's face flushed as her exasperation rose. She walked over to some boulders that formed the reef near the Hotel Del and sat down.

Sitting next to her, Greg continued, "And…that I am making a commitment that I am going to marry you…and before we can move forward, I have some things I need to resolve—I'll get to that in a minute. I guess part of it is that I don't want to be Jack's replacement, not at the wedding of his son."

"Nobody's asking you to be Jack. I certainly am not. And as for marriage, Greg, is this what happens when you face commitment? Are you committed, Greg? Because I am."

A beat.

"Abby…"

"What, Greg? Make up your mind. Are you going with me to the wedding or not? I am not talking about us getting married. I am talking about me giving away my son and you accompanying me. Why? Because I love you."

"I love you, too."

"Fine. That's easy to say, Greg. But saying it and acting on it are two different things."

"I know that." A constant ringing in the back of his mind made it difficult for Greg to focus on what he was trying to say.

"Really? Really, Greg? 'Cause I have not asked you to do anything. Now I am, and you are folding…why, because of my family?"

"No, damn it, Abby. No." Greg took her hand. "Because when I go to a wedding with you…when I do, it's going to be because I am going to marry you—it's going to be our wedding."

"What are you saying, Greg? Are you telling me you want to marry me?" Abby was now thoroughly confused.

"I'm saying that that is what I want. What I hope you want. Look, I feel like it's been five months since we've been intimate, and you've made me realize what I have missed in my life. But, Abby, I've got to sort some things out still, things I've…"

"Like what? I'm trying to understand you, Greg. But you're making me crazy."

"I know. It's just…my past."

"Your past?"

"Raquel."

"Raquel? Greg, I don't mean to sound patronizing, but God, that was over thirty years ago. Are you serious?"

"Yes." That was all he said.

Abby was determined to not get any angrier than she already was. She didn't want to cry. She didn't want to push him or make him go to the wedding out of guilt. She didn't want to chastise him any more than she already had. She didn't want to talk about marriage because she was simply not in the mood to talk about anything that important. She wanted to understand why a man as strong-willed and caring as Gregory Larson could not get that she just wanted him to escort her and be with her when her first born was married. So because she didn't want to regret saying so many things that were on her mind, she chose to say nothing. Her actions would speak volumes.

Abby let go of his hand and put on her sweater. She stood. She walked right past Molly without touching her. Right up the beach to the hotel bar. She sat and ordered a drink. The message was abundantly clear: don't follow me.

She called Karen to pick her up. She felt like getting drunk, but she was too old for that. So she just had a good cry with her best friend.

---

The next day, Karen tried her best to make things right. She and Kevin had had two dinner dates with Greg and Abby and found Greg to be a wonderful match for Abby. Kind. Thoughtful. Affectionate. Karen felt so happy for her best friend.

After talking to Abby and seeing how hurt she was, she found herself wandering into Coronado Hardware.

"Hi, Greg."

It took Greg a split second to realize that this was not a customer, but a friend—Abby's best friend. "Oh, Karen, it's nice to see you. Is there something I can help you with?"

"Greg, can we talk—privately?" Karen looked around at the men who were talking about power tools and other subjects alien to an English teacher.

"Yes, yes, of course. Please, follow me." Molly was sitting in his cramped office, and the two of them managed to squeeze in with her. Their voices were low and somber.

"You know, I just feel terrible about things with you and Abby. She'd be upset if she knew I came and talked to you. But I just felt that I needed to say something to you." Karen stopped and judged how he was reacting. He was calm.

She continued. "Greg, she is hurt and confused. She loves you, but she can't understand you."

"Karen, you're right. I sometimes don't understand myself."

Karen couldn't help but crack a soft smile. "Anyway, I just wanted you to know that she is kinda down and, well, I may as well be blunt—she's closer to me than my sisters, so I am wondering what you're thinking. I mean, she said you have talked about getting married, but you are so vague about it, she doesn't know what to think." The smile was gone. She was close to putting on her war paint.

"I know how close you two are. And I know I let her down. Look, Karen, here is what I told her: when I finally meet all her family—when that happens—it will be because I am fully committed and I want us to get married. That's how I feel. And I love Abby. Karen, I have been by myself for thirty years, and for the first time since, well, since a long time ago, I finally feel like I hate being alone. I want to be with her. She's just gotta give me time."

"Time for what?" Karen's frustration made her press him more than she expected.

Greg heard the ringing. It was unmistakable. He had to tell someone. Karen's insistence and earnestness made it such that he could leak out some of the angst he was trying desperately to control. So he turned his gaze to Karen. "The reason I'm not going with Abby to the wedding is more than just her family, Karen. It's something in my past that I just have to accept. It's about Raquel's death, about what I have never done for her."

For the first time, Karen knew he was exposing part of his soul. He was confessing his guilt. She remained silent.

Greg stopped short of telling Karen his sins. Instead, he told her why Abby brought him to this juncture. "I've just never met anyone like Abby, who has meant so much and—she doesn't really know this, but Abby has made me face memories I buried a long time ago. But I promise you—I have made a start."

Karen looked at him the way a teacher looks at a student to ascertain if he or she is telling the truth. Her eyes bored through any signs of nervousness and regret and sought an answer to the question: is he to be trusted?

"Okay," Karen sighed, "Okay. But remember something, Greg, and remember it well. A person like Abby Adams comes along once in a blue moon. You miss your chance to lasso that moon, and you never get that chance again."

Greg smiled as he understood this English teacher's allusion; she was referring to that great love scene between George Bailey and Mary in *It's a Wonderful Life* in which Jimmy Stewart tells Donna Reed he will lasso the moon for her if need be to show his love for her. Then he replied with a soft voice, "I will make sure that when that moon rises, Karen, I will have my lasso ready. I will. I promise."

Karen looked at him sternly, but her face melted with sympathy for a man who harbored some guilt about what he had done—or rather, what he had refused to do. She instinctively knew that this was a man who carried pain with him as routinely as she carried her purse. Karen wasn't sure what to say to him, but it was apparent to her that Gregory Larson had had anything but a wonderful life.

---

As Karen was leaving Greg's hardware store, Abby's phone rang. It was her mother, Helen. Abby just melted. She told her mother the story of a man she just could not understand. A man who hurt her. A man who wanted her to wait for him to get his shit together. "Damn it, Mom. It's not like I am asking the man to marry me. I want him to get on a friggin' plane and meet my children and you guys—dad—the people close to me. Is that so difficult?"

Helen's interruptions were small and limited to a few *I see's* and *Hmm's*. Then she asked a question that Abby did not expect.

"If a man can't commit to you—if he hasn't committed to anyone in thirty years—then maybe, Abby, he has something he hasn't been able to face about himself, about his past. Have you ever asked him about that night, the night his wife died?"

Abby stopped and stared at the cell phone for a second. "What are you saying, Mom? I know what happened. She was killed; she was pregnant. He was in Vietnam. He became an alcoholic. I don't think that is his issue, Mom. He is all uptight and freaked out about my children and you guys…" Suddenly, Abby stopped mid-sentence. She shook off her anger and was splashed with a word that Greg uttered days ago: *Raquel.*

"Abby, are you there?" Helen wondered, since the line had abruptly gone silent.

"Um, yes, Mom. I just remembered something Greg said. I was so upset when he said it that I didn't think about what it really meant." Abby drifted off.

Helen heard in Abby's voice the same thought she had had. She decided to make sure that her daughter knew that she, too, was on to something: "I think Greg has demons, Abby. Those demons run deeper than you may ever know. I'm not saying that he is unworthy of you or that he doesn't love you, but I am wondering if there are things that he needs to work out about himself and his past." That was as much as Helen could infer from Greg's behavior. She decided to give her daughter one last warning: "He may be a cool customer on the outside, but inside, the things that have been haunting him—the reasons he has never committed to anyone—those things take time to work through." Helen paused. "If they can be resolved at all."

# Chapter 28

## *The Storage Chest—2002*

It was Christmas Eve, when many people were making plans to be with their family and perhaps attend church services; when parents were putting the final touches on the wrapping of gifts for their children; when Christmas carolers were strolling down Orange Avenue, entertaining tourists and locals alike with songs that manifested the holiday spirit; when menorah candles were at various stages of illumination; when not a creature was stirring, not even a mouse—it was on that evening that Gregory Larson and Molly walked on the beach. The sound of the waves muted the ringing in his ears. He knew what he had done. And he knew that he had to decide which world he would occupy.

The Ghost of his Christmas Past was to visit him on this night.

As he walked along the edge of the water, he thought of Peter Sawyer's plan to restore the theater and how that project was part of his own restoration. "You have to tear things down in a restoration, but not destroy the original beauty. It is delicate work, but you just have to be careful and know ahead of time what must be kept—for the history, for posterity…for the memories, Greg."

Greg thought about how one by one, the seats in the old Movie Palace had been removed. As more money flowed in, walls were constructed to allow the theater to house three movie screens. The Village Theater was now bare walls, but the murals, the artistry—that was still to come. It would take time. Peter had told Greg earlier that month, "It's easy to tear things down, but not so easy to transform things into a work of art. There is always something that seems to hold up a project like this—something unexpected."

The ringing of a distant phone kept piercing Greg's consciousness as he walked along the beach, then up his street and into the yard of his cottage home. He stood for a moment and wished that he had never said anything to Abby about not going to the wedding. He wished that he were with her on Christmas Eve. But the phone just kept ringing. He knew what had to be done.

Greg walked into his house. He brushed the sand off Molly's feet and fur. Then he crossed the living room and went into his bedroom. He stared at the bed that he and Abby shared. He thought of how softly she breathed at night. How she always fell asleep before he did. How peaceful she looked. He thought of the contour of her figure pressed against his as they slept close together those first nights. Then he looked across the room to the dark brown storage chest.

He had owned this chest longer than any other object, except maybe his baseball glove. It had two buckles that snapped it shut on the sides and a larger one in the middle that could be locked, but that was quite unnecessary.

He had opened the chest on the night that Abby had asked to see Raquel's picture. It was right there on top. Years ago, he had put the picture away because it was too painful. What was under it was far worse. He opened the latches, cleared the buckle from the middle loop, and lifted the lid. The smell of the past rose up and saturated him. He looked into the chest and saw her picture again. He held it and, like a reflex, took his sleeve and wiped away the dust, even though there was none to speak of.

*Here I am, Greg. I've been calling and calling, waiting for you to answer.*

*Don't stop now, Greg. Pick up the phone.*

He delicately placed the picture on the floor. There were five or six other pictures—all of them faded, encapsulated in that yellowish color that becomes of things born decades ago. Raquel and Greg sunning on the beach. Raquel posing at UCLA in front of Royce Hall. Greg standing on the pitcher's mound. Both of them laughing, drunk at a party. He pushed thirty years of memories aside.

Then there was the black cloth that served as a barrier to the deeper memories. This he had not removed since the day he put it there. *Keep going. I am here. Answer me.* He had kept very little of hers. But there were two dog-eared books that she had loved: *To Kill a Mockingbird* and *One*

*Hundred Years of Solitude.* He picked them up and gently leafed through them. Her handwriting was in the margins. He let his fingers lightly graze over her words. He imagined what Raquel looked like, studying these books and their powerful themes. She would become so serious; in those moments, she was in sharp contrast to the glowing, effervescent girl pictured in those frames. He gently put the books next to the pictures.

Then he saw her powder blue UCLA T-shirt, which had been folded precisely for thirty years. He simply sat there and stared at it— for how long he did not know. His emotions washed over him. He finally picked it up, like he was holding a lily pad, fretting that it would slip through his fingers—or worse yet, tear apart. He managed to maneuver his shoulder's sleeve closer to his face so that he could wipe away the tears, but it was pointless—they fell unabated between the *U* and the *C*, spotting Raquel's shirt, making the baby blue instantly darker as the cerulean spots spread.

*Don't worry. Keep going. Answer me.*

He smiled as he found her stuffed Bruin. It had always been on her bed during her freshman year. Next to it was the small photo album that contained pictures of her parents and family, all taken near their home in Mexico. He continued his journey deeper into the chest: her visor with the Mexican flag and her silver cross. His fingers found the tiny vial of her favorite perfume. He was sure it could not have any remaining scent. His fingers delicately squeezed the round top and turned. He heard a single soft snap as it rotated. He assumed her fragrance had been snuffed out by the latches that held his storage chest's lid tightly shuttered from the light of day. He brought the vial to his nose. To his amazement, he realized that the soft, lovely, rose-like scent of Raquel's perfume was not completely lost to the decades. The perfume was so intoxicating that he found himself under the illusion that she was somehow with him.

Greg slowly touched each object and allowed the memories to run deep and clear. He was unaware that dusk had settled in. When

Raquel's scent finally dissipated into a trace, he stood for a moment and turned on the light by his bedside.

He then descended to the bottom of the chest. There, beneath a black cotton scarf was the manila envelope. He knew what was inside.

When he tipped the envelope down, the letter fell out and onto his lap. It sat there like an anachronism—a relic that would be replaced by a cell phone in the decades to follow. He stared at it. The letter was the type that was mailed to the troops back then. Light blue paper, fairly thin. In the upper corner was Raquel's name—their apartment's address. It was supposed to be delivered to Private Gregory Larson.

It didn't have a postage stamp.

It did have something on it that Greg stared at—a single deep red spot of her blood. Greg's eyes widened. That was the one thing he had not remembered.

The letter was unopened. The moment that former Private Gregory Larson carefully broke the seal on the letter's envelope and unfolded it, the ringing finally stopped.

It was a single sheet of paper. Light blue, so thin that he handled it carefully. Unfolding it, he was somewhat concerned that it would break apart in his hands. He read her words—words that he knew would make his anguish come flooding back.

*My Dearest Greg,*

*All I can do is pray for you every day. Each time I get your letters, I'm so relieved. But my letter is not about worries and war. This time it's about joy. Greg, you are going to be a father! Yes, that's right, a daddy! I am pregnant. I'm past the third month—I waited to tell you because I was a little scared. But the doctor says the baby is doing fine. Don't worry about me. I'm so happy and healthy. I have not told my parents yet. I wanted you to be the first to know. So when you write back, I will tell them (unless I just can't wait! I'm so excited!). Maybe if you can, think of what name you would like for a boy or a girl. My aunt and uncle here in the States will be here in LA if I need them, and I probably will. But remember, don't worry about me. I love you. I love you so much.*

*You have to be careful, Greg. <u>Promise me you will be careful!</u>*

*The baby will be beautiful. When you come home to us, we will be waiting for you. We will be a family. I'm getting close to finishing my teaching credential, and you will be home. Then we will start our new life.*

*I love you, Greg. So please, please be safe, my love.*

*Your Raquel*

The letter lay at his side, next to the silver cross, the stuffed Bruin doll, and the well-worn novel *One Hundred Years of Solitude.*

Gregory Larson sat stunned. Thirty-three years ago, she pleaded for him to stay safe. The irony did not escape him—nor did the acknowledgement of what he had to do next.

---

When a plane leaves San Diego heading to the Bay Area, it heads west over the ocean. And before tilting to the north, one can see the Coronado Bay Bridge, which links the downtown to the island. Abby looked down from her window seat on this January morning and saw the exact spot on that bridge where their lives had crashed into each other. She stared at that spot until it vanished from view and was replaced by ocean and sky.

When Karen had told Abby that she had met with Greg after their argument on the beach, Abby had pretended to be upset with her. Nevertheless, Karen's insight into Greg's refusal to go to the wedding was telling. Karen explained that the problem wasn't just Greg's meeting the family, awkwardly standing in for Jack, or his hesitancy to commit to their relationship. Karen sensed that Greg's first wife, Raquel, was at the center of his storm; her death remained unfinished business for some reason. Yet Karen's attitude toward Greg was what seemed most remarkable.

"Abby, I was angry at first, then mystified, and by the time he finished, I just felt sorry for him. But I also knew that he was fighting for you."

"What do you mean? Fighting his past—his memories of Raquel and what happened some thirty years ago?" Abby asked.

"The struggle has to do with what he hasn't done, I think. Not what he did. That's my guess, Abby. But I got the feeling that whatever it was, he was determined to go there—he was going there for you." With that, Karen decided a word of caution was required. "But he has baggage, Abby. So be careful."

"I know, Karen. I know. We all do." Abby kissed Karen on the cheek, and Karen wished her a wonderful trip up north to see her first born become a husband to a lovely wife. "I can't thank you enough, Karen."

"I love you, Abby. I just want you to be happy."

As she accepted the Coke and peanuts offered by the flight attendant, Abby wondered if she was doing the right thing by not again confronting Greg about what he was going through. She concluded that her mother was right. It seemed that whatever secrets Greg held were his and only his to reconcile. He would have to figure out his issues on his own. But she would make sure that she would not expose her heart any more than she already had. Her walls needed to be raised. These were her defenses. But as she slowly nibbled on her salty snack and sipped her sugary drink, she knew that this morning had turned her stubbornness to sympathy.

As the plane's engines droned on, Abby reflected on the weeks between her fight with Greg and this day. During that time, they slowly accepted their fate—like adults. They acted the part of respectful friends, as if neither wanted to venture too close to the fires that burned around them. They were afraid that saying anything might only make matters worse. They sensed that the time and the place were not aligned. Only on one other occasion did Greg repeat that he needed more time to "work things out"; consequently, Abby merely gazed at him and wordlessly delivered a somewhat passive-aggressive message that fell somewhere between "Okay, I'm really trying to understand, Greg" and "Whatever, Greg, let's just not go there."

So they worked together diligently on the theater's restoration. They discussed what her students could do as volunteers to help out with some of the basics. They kept their distance despite their desire to do just the opposite.

Before Christmas, they would meet and sip coffee, but they would quickly grow despondent as their stubborn natures butted heads. Greg couldn't bring himself to reveal the existence of Raquel's unopened letter. Abby couldn't speak of the invitation and the wedding plans. They exchanged Christmas wishes and small tokens of affection, and they even sometimes laughed. But Abby remained cautious and Greg ambiguous about his Christmas plans. They were both miserable. It was the worst Christmas either could recall, but neither would admit it.

Abby offered her empty plastic cup to the flight attendant as the pilot explained that the flight into San Francisco was beginning its descent. The weather, he told them, was far more brisk than the balmy climate of San Diego. Abby took out Greg's letter. She had received it this morning; it had been wedged in her front door. She placed her reading glasses on her nose.

---

Greg decided that Raquel's letter and all the other contents of the storage chest would take time for him to sift through. He thought about just running to Abby's house and pouring out the story, but he didn't want pity. It had taken so long for him to finally go to the depths of his past—to the folded, blood-splattered, desperate call for him to be safe, when on that very night, it was Raquel and his baby in harm's way. So in the early dawn of the day that Abby was to leave for the wedding, he delivered his letter to her front door. There was no way she would not discover it.

*Dear Abby,*

*I know we haven't talked of anything important for weeks, four tediously long weeks. But there are some things you ought to know. First and foremost, I am healing. When you return, when you have time, when you feel you are ready to let me in the front door of your world, I want to tell you why I have acted in the manner that I have. I need to tell you of the storage chest and the contents that I have ignored, foolishly and fearfully, for more than 30 years. I want you to know that being apart from you has made me miserable. You are the one woman who has made me feel lonely. I feel empty when I am not a part of your life. You may not know this, but you have given me the courage to finally face my bitterness and anger at life's tragedies. For that I am forever grateful.*

*I know that Tom and Nina's wedding will be very special and that your family will celebrate the love they have for each other. I know that you will think of Jack and how much you miss him. I would be a poor substitute for him.*

*I hope the damage I have done to your heart is not such that you can't forgive me, and I do promise that I will no longer keep my secrets from you.*

*I love you more than you know.*

*Greg*

---

The letter was folded on Abby's lap. Every time she read it, a lump formed in her throat such that she had difficulty swallowing. If only she hadn't read it so many times.

She glanced back out the plane's window on this January morning, two days before Tom and Nina's wedding. Now it was the Golden Gate Bridge that was out of view. She slipped Greg's letter into her purse and folded her reading glasses. He had given her something unexpected, and for the first time in a month, the skies above seemed blue despite all the fog into which they descended.

# Chapter 29

## *The Trigger —2002*

*How to break the ice? Just call him.*

"Greg, hi."

"Hello, Abby."

"We need to talk."

"Yes, we do."

"Please come over...soon." It was a Saturday. Abby had been home for a week since the wedding. She had to reorient herself to work, to being alone, to figuring out what to do about this man she was so drawn to.

The wedding had been wonderful. To have everyone in her life all gathered in one festive, joyous room, dancing, laughing, and promising to make the effort to remain closer—all of this brought solace to Abby's soul. Nevertheless, the one person missing was not Greg, but Jack.

Abby reflected on Greg's pronouncement that he was a mere understudy—that his attendance would be a distraction from the man who forged this family.

*Perhaps Greg was right. It may have been too soon. If we had been together for longer, then maybe it would have been different.*

Abby was unaware that she was not the only person who had gone to a family reunion.

---

When a plane leaves San Diego heading to Mexico, it also navigates west over the ocean and bends to the south so that the Coronado Bay Bridge is visible. Gregory Larson also glanced at the exact spot where his life crashed into Abby Adams' and his journey into sobriety began. This trip's purpose was not to celebrate the joining of two young lovers; rather it was to reunite two much older lovers for the first time in thirty years.

Greg had last made contact with the Mendez family seven years ago, when Raquel's father had passed away. He had only personally met them twice—once at their wedding and once at Raquel's funeral in Los Angeles. Occasionally, he sent Christmas cards, and sometimes Raquel's mother wrote back. She was always a buffer between her husband, who could never overcome the grief of losing his daughter, and her widowed son-in-law. There had always been tension between the two of them, even before Raquel's marriage. Her father had hoped that she would meet a fine Mexican-American man at UCLA. Raquel's father viewed Greg as a baseball pitcher who flunked out of university and then joined the Army. He didn't think military service was dishonorable, but under the circumstances, he felt that Greg allowed himself to fail. Besides, Vietnam seemed to Raquel's father like a mistake for America. After the accident, his animosity hardened. He could never accept the fact that Gregory Larson had been thousands of miles away from his daughter in a foreign land. "If he had been there, with our daughter," he told his wife, "this never would have happened to our Raquel...and the baby."

*He was right on every count.* Greg knew exactly how Raquel's father felt because he felt the same way.

After the funeral, Greg acquiesced to her parents' wishes to have Raquel buried in Mexico City. Her family had for decades been buried in the famous *Panteón Civil de Dolores*, the largest cemetery in Mexico. Greg knew that that cemetery contained the *Rotonda de las Personas Ilustres*, meaning the Rotunda of Illustrious Persons. It was a matter of honor for the Mendez family to have their daughter buried there. There could be no one more illustrious than Raquel, yet he had never once visited her grave.

When Greg called Raquel's mother before he left home, she was naturally taken aback that he would visit Raquel's grave after all these years. He told her that he had never remarried and that he still deeply loved Raquel. He told her that he had to see her grave and that he wished he had found the courage to come years ago. Raquel's mother felt the sorrow in his voice. She asked if he needed her to be there. Greg thanked her but explained that he needed to go alone.

----

The gravestone was simple. *Raquel Mendez Larson. Born April 7, 1947. Died with unborn child June 14, 1969.* Gregory Larson placed the red roses delicately next to the gravestone. He made the sign of the cross, not because he was a true believer, but because he knew that that is what Raquel would want of him. He knelt.

*Raquel, my love. I know I should never have left you alone then and now, but I was on a fool's errand. I come for forgiveness. I come to face my past, to tell you that I will always love you. You were the love of my life.*

Greg looked up to the cloudless sky. He had made his confession. Now he had to ask for permission to move on.

*Raquel, know that I have been alone and desolate. Know that I have inflicted much pain upon myself. But know that I come here to ask for your blessing. I must move forward. I think that is what you would have wanted me to do. That is why you called to me. You are part of my restoration.*

One last sigh. His eyes remained closed.

*Her name is Abby Adams. You would have been the same wonderful teacher that she is. I know it was your dream. Like you, she is my heroine. I love her.*

He stood.

*I will always love you. Goodbye, Raquel.*

He made the sign of the cross again. And he softly walked back through the gates of the *Panteón Civil de Dolores*.

Abby opened the door for him. He came without Molly. It was just the two of them.

"Hello, Greg."

"Hello, Abby."

There was an awkwardness that had not been there since the earliest days of their courtship. Abby motioned for Greg to follow her into the kitchen. She gestured toward the barstools and asked if he wanted anything to drink. She wanted wine, but they settled on iced tea.

He began, "So I assume the wedding was wonderful."

"Yes, it was."

"And Tom and Nina are on their honeymoon?"

"Yes. They decided to go to Cancun. They will be there another four days."

"Mexico, not Hawaii?"

"Less expensive…and Tom's company has some connections there. It's a new place for both of them." Abby noticed something different about Greg's manner. She knew that he tensed up when things got personal, although this wasn't particularly prickly.

"Mexico, huh?" Greg's body language seemed to recede into a softer, contemplative posture.

Abby took a sip of her iced tea. She wasn't thirsty, but her throat hurt. "I won't bore you with the details of the wedding…"

"Oh, no. Please do tell me…"

"No. No. Not now."

"Okay," Greg relented. He realized it was Abby who seemed nervous.

"So, what have you been up to?" Abby wanted to tell him that his intuition about being at the wedding was not entirely off base, but her walls were up. This was a time to reconnect, not to expose herself.

Greg had a completely different mindset. "Well, let's see. Let me work backwards. I came back from Mexico about the same time you came home."

Abby interrupted, "Mexico?"

"Actually, Mexico City. Before that, I went through my storage chest."

"Your storage chest." Abby cocked her head to the right, as if doing so would allow her to see the puzzle's missing pieces and place them in some sensible context.

"Yeah. I was looking for something important." Greg was perfectly satisfied with the fact that he was being coy. He wanted to lighten the mood since the overall tone of this conversation could become blue. "And I found it—right where I put it thirty-three years ago."

"Greg, what are you talking about?" Abby was confused, and whatever he was up to would not allow her to lower her guard.

"But really, it all started with 9.11 and some research I did." Greg sipped his iced tea and then said apologetically, "Abby, I know I am being evasive, but just hear me out because the last few weeks, the last six months—well, since the day I asked you where you saw us going—I have been trying to make amends. I have been trying to come to peace with my past so that I can begin living in the present." Greg smiled at her.

Abby hesitantly let the next word roll out of her mouth in the lengthiest manner possible, implying disbelief mixed with confusion, "O-kay…"

Greg stood. "Can we talk on the couch? It feels more comfortable." They quickly moved there; Abby sat with her legs tucked under her. A foot of space separated her from Greg. Greg sat with one leg up and one leg down, just like Molly's ears. He began:

"Abby, I know we both watched *MASH*, right? Yes, okay. Well, do you remember watching the final episode called 'Goodbye, Farewell, and Amen?' The one where Hawkeye Pierce has a nervous breakdown and is treated in a mental hospital?"

Abby had to think for a minute. "That episode was, like, the most watched TV show in history, right? Yes, of course I remember it, but faintly. Go on."

"Well, the key was that there was a trigger...a trigger that caused Hawkeye to crack—well, not really to crack, but to actually face his great fear...the event that he blocked out of his mind. If he hadn't have blocked it out, he would have never been able to operate and function. Do you remember what it was?"

"No."

"It was something he smelled. An odor that he hadn't come into contact with for the longest time. A smell that brought him back to the memory he had buried so far down that it was almost imperceptible. But the smell triggered it. Sometimes our senses pick up something— like an antenna that leads us to what we seek or to what we are afraid of facing. That's the trigger."

Abby was taking all this in. "Um, I am a little lost."

"So was I. Anyway, it happened to me. It happened on one of the nights when I was watching the news. I think I was here with you, and they were finally releasing the tapes of the 9.11 phone calls. It was the voices of people who were trying desperately to make sure that their husbands, wives, children—whomever—knew that they would forever love them. Some of them knew that they were going to die; others had only a small hope of survival. When I heard those messages, I knew. I knew. That was the trigger."

A beat.

Abby did not want to intrude on the moment.

"Abby, I know this is gonna sound like I'm nuts—and maybe I am—but I knew I had buried something important a long time ago. It was like a phone call that was ringing in my ears. I couldn't ignore it, and the longer I waited, the louder it got. And then I knew who it was. It was Raquel."

He leaned closer. She did not. "Abby, I never told you something about the day she died. I never said it out loud because I never made myself think of it. If I had, I think I would have gone crazy. So as a matter of survival, I put it out of my mind…that's why I drank."

"What happened when she died?"

"She was killed on the way to deliver a letter to me. She didn't have a stamp. She was writing to me. Calling to me."

"And…"

"And I got the letter from the police, but I never opened it. Never. I just couldn't face hearing her voice, seeing her last words to me. I put the letter at the bottom of my storage chest, and it stayed there until the night before you left to go to the wedding."

"You read the letter?"

"Yes, I did. I did. And that night, I came to your house and put a letter on your door telling you how much you mean to me. At that point, I hadn't figured it all out yet."

The light had faded, and twilight had settled on the neighborhood in Coronado. Abby hadn't noticed that she was finally leaning toward Greg, but he did.

He continued, "It wasn't just Raquel who was calling me; it was the fact that, for the first time in my life, I had a reason to want to answer the phone. You were the first woman who ever made me feel lonely. I wasn't just trying to figure out my past, but also my future. And that is what drove me to do a little research. See, I knew about PTSD, which lots of soldiers have when they return from war. After 9.11, the first responders experienced it big time. It made me wonder if the things that happened in Vietnam could still be inside me, messing me up, because the war was what pulled me away from Raquel. Abby, I realized that deep down, I blamed myself for her death. If I hadn't screwed up and dropped out of school, then I might not have been drafted; I might not have been gone; she might not have been at that corner, trying to mail me a letter. What the hell was I doing thousands of miles away from her? When I read her letter and saw the things that I saved of hers back then, it reminded me of everything I tried so hard to forget. I couldn't shake the look on her father's face at the funeral—the look that blamed me for his daughter's death...and the baby's."

Abby hands had involuntarily moved to her mouth. "You said something about research?"

"Yes. Yes. See, this PTSD thing—sometimes it is dormant, maybe for decades, and then, for some reason—a trigger—it manifests itself when people like me are older—maybe in their fifties or so. Okay, so then I knew what I had to do—what I hadn't done. I bought a ticket to Mexico City and..." He took a breath, and Abby filled the void.

"And you went to her grave. Oh, my God. Greg, you had never been to her grave, right?"

Greg let the darkness of the evening answer the question.

"You didn't realize it at the time, Abby, but you saved me from myself and much more."

Abby nodded. She reached for his hand and squeezed it. Never once in all that time that Greg spoke to her did he tremble. Abby realized the importance of that.

A beat.

"I have to confess something, too, Greg. You know, I am a little stubborn..."

"Really? I hadn't noticed."

"...yes, you know that. Anyway, when I was at the wedding, I missed Jack. I wished he was there, dancing with me. Oh, others tried to take his place: Nina's father, Tom, Jake, my dad—they all took turns dancing with me. But you were right. No one could replace Jack. I guess you would have felt awkward—how did you put it? 'A poor substitute.' And I realized that I probably pushed you too much, too fast."

He let her apology settle as she reached to turn on the lamp.

"Greg, I was lonely. I am lonely. So the question I have is this: where do we go from here?" Abby released his hand and leaned back. No walls. Just emotional exhaustion.

Greg was equally spent. "How about I take you to dinner…and then you can tell me all about the wedding?"

"Okay, but I'm not all that hungry," Abby replied.

"Well, I am, and I bet after hearing everything I told you, you could probably use a drink." Greg smiled knowingly.

---

As it turned out, the smell of pizza made Abby's appetite return. And Greg soaked in the story of Tom and Nina's wedding, complete with pictures that Abby had taken.

Abby, like all great teachers and mothers, could do numerous things simultaneously. In this case, while storytelling, she wondered about all that Greg had experienced and how he had come through it. As she nibbled on the last piece of crust, she asked him, "Greg, how did reading Raquel's letter make you feel? I mean, you're glad you read it, right?"

"Abby, honestly, I was mesmerized as I sorted through her things. I was also scared of what I would find. I hadn't looked at those things for so long. You must know exactly what I mean, looking at Jack's clothing and sorting through the things that meant so much to him."

A beat.

"Anyway, all the memories came back, and it was overwhelming. The letter was the final thing I looked at. I'm very glad I read it. She was so happy to be pregnant and so worried about me in 'Nam. It was all about us starting a new life the moment I came home."

Abby sighed, and sadness draped over her shoulders like the sweater she wore.

"In the end, I just sat there stunned. Thirty years, Abby. Another lifetime. Another me. It was like seeing a movie that you once loved and you still love—but all the actors are dead. So you hold onto the illusion that the movie creates. That she can come back. That lovers can never die. But I finally understood. I knew that I couldn't accept that the movie was over until…"

"Until you went to her grave?" Abby knew how the film ended.

"Yes."

"And what was that like? I'm sorry if I am asking too many questions. It's just that you went through all this alone and you've held it all in for so long, Greg." Abby realized once again that their faces were so close that their foreheads were practically touching. She wanted to caress his face, but she held back.

"No. No. I need to talk about it, Abby. That is part of the healing for me. I have shut all this out. And I want you to be the one I can talk to about it."

She smiled.

"So, anyway, Raquel's family has always been influential in Mexican politics and such. Her parents are not rich, but they are successful. And the cemetery she is buried in is the most famous one in Mexico. People can no longer be buried there; it closed in '77. Her grave was simple; it was peaceful. I brought her flowers. I said a prayer to her. I asked for her forgiveness for not being there."

A beat.

"Abby, do you believe that people can hear voices? I don't mean literally; I mean…"

Abby nodded. "I know what you are saying. Yes, I think so. I feel Jack's presence in my life. I felt him at the wedding."

"Yes. I just know that Raquel wanted me to find her. She wanted me to find myself. I think she would have wanted me to find you, too."

Abby could not help herself. She empathized with this man, who had the fortitude to go back in time and admit all his mistakes, even ones that were beyond his control. She wanted to shove all her walls down and embrace him, but something held her back.

"Greg, how do you feel now?" Abby asked softly.

"I feel like…like, like I've been—okay, this is going to sound really strange, so bear with me—but my dad, he had triple bypass surgery. I remember visiting him in the hospital numerous times. He held this red pillow in the shape of a heart close to his chest. And as the months went by, he slowly recovered. He got stronger. He had no idea, he told me later, how bad he had felt before the operation. It took the better part of a year, but when it was all said and done, he told me he felt like a new man."

Greg looked up at Abby. "I know now exactly how my dad felt."

# Chapter 30

## *The Crown Room —2002*

The walls of the Movie Palace were no longer bare. The stencil designs for the murals were complete, the curtains were ordered, the three screens would soon be in place, and seats would arrive next month if all went as planned. But most importantly, the sound system, which had been one of the many stumbling blocks, was now working as clear as a bell.

In some respects, old Joe hardly recognized the place. There were three smaller projection rooms attached by a corridor. He stood next to Greg and Abby and just marveled at what had been accomplished so far.

"Joe, we still have a big hurdle to get over. We will need the Coronado Community Development Agency to put up the grant money to really complete all this. They have been great, but the fundraising still needs one final push," Greg told him.

"Ah, yeah. So I heard from Norm. I suppose that's the reason for the big shindig down at the Hotel Del." Joe doffed his Navy hat and rubbed his white hair. "Well, I know you can do it—you two. But I gotta beg off the Del thing. Too pricey for my pension, kids."

Abby put her hand in the crook of Joe's arm and leaned into him. "You are an honorary guest, Joe. We wouldn't think of not having the original projectionist there. Besides, no one tells better stories of all the famous people who have come in these doors." Abby looked at Greg. She had been chronicling Joe's stories for the last year and was hoping to publish an article in some of the local magazines once the restoration became a reality.

"Not only that, Joe, but the CEO of the company that is going to run the theater is going to be there, and he wants to meet you. He runs five vintage theaters; he restored them all. One out in Hollywood and the others across some of the beach cities on the Pacific Coast Highway."

"No kidding? Really? Norm didn't tell me that. Hmm…" Joe's Navy hat returned to his head. His hand softly stroked his goatee.

Abby squeezed Joe's arm tightly against her. "So we are doing something for you today, and you are not going to say *no*, Joe," Abby insisted. "We are taking you out to rent a tuxedo…don't even think of arguing."

"Oh, guys. You gotta be kidding. Me in one of those monkey suits?"

Greg countered, "Lots of us will be just as uncomfortable, Joe. But it is for a good cause. Besides, the store cut us a deal, and yours was no charge."

Joe bowed to the unavoidable. "Well, okay. Now I can see that you two have ambushed me. Well, while I'm here, I may as well tell you about some of the murals you are planning. A few are just perfect, and a few are not exactly what they used to look like. Oh, and I like what you have done to the box office out front. The old gal looks sharp."

With that, Joe proceeded to expound on the beauty of the old Movie Palace, a place he knew better than any home in which he had ever dwelled.

---

Abby knew there were two forces pulling at her: her heart and her head. Why they sometimes didn't align properly was the crux of Karen's message to her as they slowly walked arm and arm down the sands of the Coronado beach.

"Abby, there are things that don't add up or make sense in this world. On the other hand, the lives you two have lived have intersected so many times that it would be a pity to ignore. He is a good man, Abby. That much I know. Now, whether he is *your soul mate*—no one other than you can answer that question."

Abby stopped and grabbed Karen's hand, pulling her to the sand. She let the wind blow her hair back and saw the crashing of waves as an invitation to discuss whether her life's tides were coming in or rushing away. "I know that, Karen. Look, that night he told me everything at my house—and at the pizza place—I wanted to keep my walls up. I did. I thought he had too much baggage for me. I mean, he is so complicated: Mexico, Raquel, bachelorhood." Abby waved her right hand to the breeze that blew in from the ocean, as if those issues were gusts of wind buffeting against her. "I mean, for God's sake, the man almost killed me—literally! But that night, he gave me something I hadn't expected. He let me into a place that he never believed he would revisit. And then he told me that I was the reason why. I mean, after that, how else could I feel? I wanted to kiss him so badly..."

Abby spread her fingers wide, placed them parallel to her temples, and then sunk them deeply into her hair, allowing her head to rest between these pillars. But at the same time, she felt the sensation that her mind would burst with a dangerous mixture of frustration and desire. "Karen, it took all my self-control to not throw myself into his arms when we got back to my house. But then I wondered: did I move too quickly before the holidays? Am I moving too slowly now? Do I even know what I want from him? Honestly, Karen, I don't know what to do."

Karen too wondered about the fates. She was lucky; she had her husband, Kevin. As much as she sympathized with the misfortune that had befallen Abby with Jack's passing, she simply could not wrap her mind around what it was like for Abby to be home alone, to start all over again with someone new, to trust him completely. It was incomprehensible to her. Karen knew that no one can avoid the eventual loss of their lover; that heartbreaking fear resides in each of us, veiled for a time. It is merely a question of when we come face to face with it.

There was no answer to Abby's dilemma. The tides just rushed in. They were either swept up in life's drama, or they ran from it.

Greg's anxiety grew with each passing week. He had laid out his cards—put them right before Abby Adams. Now he held his breath, wondering how she would react. He expected her to be cautious; that was her nature. However, he knew he had done the right thing. He felt that one huge weight had slid right off his shoulders, only to be replaced with a nagging, painful sting that pricked his muscles, forewarning him that maybe she could not or would not ever be his. Each time he felt the stinging—and it was real—he winced. And try as he might to rub it out, once his mind settled on her face—her lovely face, her eyes, her smile—the pain grew more intense. So it was best to pay attention to the business of the theater, the fundraiser, and the hardware store.

Sometimes he found himself talking to Molly, just as he had with Aussie. Strange as it seemed, the moment he spoke the word *Abby*, Molly would turn her head as if to say to him, "I miss her. Why did you scare her away?"

*Why, indeed?*

---

Helen knew that the phone call was a subterfuge. Ostensibly, Abby wanted to tell her about the gala that the Hotel Del Coronado was hosting in several weeks for the restoration of the Village Theater. Abby pretended to ask her mother's advice about what she should wear.

Helen wasn't fooled in the slightest.

It took an hour to get the entire story that Greg had told Abby out—about Raquel, about the storage chest, about the letter, about the trip to Mexico, about the grave, about the confession. Finally, Abby admitted to her mother that perhaps Greg had been right about not attending Tom and Nina's wedding.

During Abby's soliloquy, Helen listened intently. She had some misgivings about Greg, but she also knew that he was a person best described as high risk, high reward. She didn't question Greg's integrity; she questioned his resolve to face whatever demons had to be confronted. Helen knew Abby needed her advice, but what was on Helen's mind wasn't Greg's tenacity, but rather her daughter's.

Helen began slowly, "Abby, I've listened very patiently, and I hear your words, but I also feel your words. So I am going to tell you what I think and also tell you that no matter what I believe, you—and you alone—have to be at peace in your heart."

Abby did not utter a sound.

Then Helen began her homily: "The restoration of this theater, my dear, reminds me of a simple fact. We all age. We crumble and die. Nothing can change that. We lose those we love. I will lose your father soon. I know that. It will be hard. I will survive, and I will not give in to a widow's death. I live not waiting to die, but willing myself to expand my lungs and breathe life into a new day. And when I do, Abby, I restore myself. I open my life up to people, new and old, and to the sensation of being able to see that the sky is blue most days. Sometimes we all need to restore our faith in others and in ourselves. This man— Greg—he has done exactly that. And Abby, he did it because of you. You have motivated him to believe in himself. And look at all he did. I think he is waiting for you now. Whatever you do, Abby, don't give in to your fears. You have an obligation to live a full life—without Jack— and not feel sorry for yourself. Jack will always be there—in your soul. But this is a chance to find out just how much your soul can grow."

Abby had begun to cry right when Helen had mentioned that her father would die soon. By the time Helen finished tissues were balled up in front of her on her coffee table. She tried to hide that she was crying from her mother, but it was no use.

"Oh, Mom. Mom, I want to grow up and be like you."

"You already are, dear. I admire you and love you and pray for you all the time." Helen's eyes were moist.

A beat.

Abby blew her nose. Twice. Helen cleared her throat.

"So, what should I wear?"

"Go out and buy something new, sweetheart. Something new—in a color you've never worn before."

---

Greg asked Abby if she would be his date to the gala; he laughed as he said it to her over coffee the week before. "It's like going to the prom," he chuckled.

"Yes, but you're getting there really early to set up some of the fundraising, and I thought I would drive over with Karen and Kevin—if you don't mind."

"No, of course not. I'm really happy they are going—I know the event is expensive."

"Well, after all you've done, they said they wanted to contribute. To tell you the truth, Karen told Kevin that this is a pre-anniversary gift for them."

"Abby, that's great. I am sure Karen and you will look stunning."

"Well, I don't know about that, but we'll see what we can do." Abby smiled softly as she glanced at her watch. "Oh, shoot, I have to go now and do a few errands." She paused, realizing that she was, again, being far too abrupt. She also knew that she had not told Greg what she had intended to say when they had agreed to meet for coffee.

"Greg, I know we haven't talked much—I mean seriously—since the…well, since the big talk we had. But I want you to know that I have been thinking a lot about you, and I am really looking forward to Saturday night. Okay?" Abby's last word was said in a tone that implied that she had more to say, but now was neither the time nor the place.

Greg nodded. "Okay." Greg's last word was said in a tone that implied that he wished she would say more, but now was neither the time nor the place.

Abby kissed him quickly and smiled. She waved back to him as she pushed open the café's door.

Her dress was ready to be picked up.

---

The Crown Room, built in 1888, featured a spectacular, thirty-foot, sugar pine ceiling that bowed itself into an oval. Its name originated from the crown-shaped chandeliers designed by *The Wonderful Wizard of Oz* author L. Frank Baum. The room had been the Hotel Del Coronado's dining hall in the days when it had held state dinners, royal events, and even the celebration of Lindbergh's famous flight. Since then, the Del, as locals called it, had become the seaside resort visited by celebrities, dignitaries, and presidents of the United States.

On this evening, the Crown Room's enchanting Victorian setting was to host the final financial push for the restoration of the Art Deco-designed Village Theater. The attendees would have a range of interests: some would have deep pockets and a spirit of philanthropy, others an appreciation for the arts. Some would have strong community ties, and there would be a few local celebrities—not to mention one hardware store owner who looked around nervously as the final touches were being put into place.

Greg had insisted on music, and to his pleasant surprise, the high school's orchestra and its alumni musicians had volunteered to entertain the guests. The set list tonight would be comprised of songs that made movies magical. As the band set up, Greg couldn't help but smile at the blend of young musicians and older veterans, all of whom had the same deep appreciation for melody and movies. The school's choir director even recruited two professional singers, who were warming their voices to the song "Paper Moon."

Greg thought of Abby. *Was it a make-believe world he was living in? Did Abby really believe in him?*

Greg reminded himself that the mayor would handle the master of ceremonies duties and that the Community Development Agency was manning the donation table at the door. All he needed to do was make sure that all the final odds and ends were as planned. This, he quickly realized, required little of his attention since the attentive staff at the Hotel Del mirrored its legendary setting. So he found a seat, adjusted his black bow tie, which sharply contrasted with his white dinner jacket à la Humphrey Bogart's Rick Blaine in *Casablanca*, and anxiously awaited the guests.

---

The orchestra began the evening appropriately with the *Beauty and the Beast* anthem "Be Our Guest." The clumping of elegantly dressed couples all turned and smiled at the not-so-subtle motif of the evening: "Please give generously." Greg was surrounded by well-wishers, but he spent the majority of his time on his tip toes, craning his neck for his date. Just as the band played the final notes of the opening song, he thought he spotted her. Making excuses, he wedged himself between and around tables, waiters, and guests, keeping his gaze on the entrance to the Crown Room.

As the band began playing "Tonight" from *West Side Story*, Gregory Larson escaped the last entanglement of the evening's attendees and was within a few steps of Abby Adams, who just then pivoted to her left, away from Karen and Kevin, and saw Greg.

Karen nudged Kevin, as if her elbow could send a silent, unmistakable signal: "Don't move toward them; stay here—give them this moment." Kevin got the message.

Abby and Greg stood face to face.

Greg spoke first. "You look beautiful, Abby."

He took her hands and kissed her.

"Thank you. You look quite the dashing leading man yourself." Abby noted that Greg's silver goatee was neatly trimmed, his salt and pepper hair was shorter, just grazing the tops of his ears, and his smile was soft and reassuring. She knew that his gaze was fixed on her and her alone.

Abby's azure vintage cocktail dress featured a lace overlay with a sweetheart neckline underneath. She wore no jewelry other than pearl earrings. Her hair was up. She was understated and elegant.

"Everything looks fantastic, Greg. The table settings, the music, and the turnout are amazing."

"I know." He could not look away from her. "But you are the one person who makes the evening perfect."

Abby leaned in to kiss him delicately, aware of Karen's and Kevin's presence. Then she took Greg's arm and once again pivoted toward her friends.

"Guys, I cannot thank you enough for your support and friendship. Karen, you look lovely, and Kevin, you are a good sport to get into a tux tonight," Greg said as he hugged Karen and clasped Kevin's hand.

Small talk ensued. Dinner awaited. Tables were found. More hands were shaken. But the whispers between Abby and Greg trumped all distractions.

"Abby, I cannot stop staring at you."

"You're making me blush."

"Sorry about that."

"No, you're not."

She squeezed his hand.

"Moon River" from *Breakfast at Tiffany's* played. They looked at each other and smiled.

"Oh, I loved Audrey Hepburn in that movie," Abby told Greg.

"I loved the ending," Greg whispered.

The mayor opened the festivities as the salads appeared on the Crown Room tables. "Hello, everyone. What a night here at the Hotel

Del Coronado—the jewel of our town. As you have been hearing, this wonderful band has been regaling us with some of the finest songs from Hollywood's movies. Let's give them a round of applause."

The mayor waited out the applause. "They will be back with some favorites that we can all dance to after dinner. This event shows just how much we value the arts, this community, our history, and what we often call 'the island'…when we all know it is a peninsula." Chuckles rippled under the crown-shaped chandeliers. "Some of you may not know that the Village Theater opened in 1947 and was shuttered in 1998. Here we are, four years later, and the restoration is in full swing. Those old-timers like Joe Pappas over there at the table with Norman Barnett—stand up, Joe. Folks, Joe is the original projectionist from way back when. You too, Norm—stand up please. These guys have been around since the beginning. They're almost older than the Del…" A few more guffaws from the audience.

"Anyway, they have both helped us restore the Village Theater to its original Art Deco look. We have the basics done, but the glitter and gloss costs money, and that's where your generosity has been critical. So let me thank you for all you have—or will—contribute to the cause." A few more knowing laughs. "When will the theater be completed, you ask? We are hoping in two years—tops. It will once again be the 'Movie Palace,' as Joe calls it. It will be one of the many highlights of our Orange Avenue." More applause.

"I know Greg Larson is out there. Greg, take a bow. He has been the main driver of this project from the very beginning. Some of you only know Greg because you see him walking his dog, Molly, around town, but he does work for a living. He is the owner of Coronado Hardware, and he has worked quite a few deals to get everyone on board. He even convinced the Del to host this event. Let's give him a round of applause."

This time, the clapping was not obligatory, but hearty and heartfelt. Greg merely waved and was quick to disappear to chair level. Abby leaned into him and said, "You deserve it, Greg." He returned her compliment by touching her thigh under the table.

Thankfully, the mayor decided that he was too hungry to continue rambling on, so dinner was served. All were relieved that no more speeches were imminent.

---

The band returned with "Somewhere over the Rainbow" followed by "My Heart Will Go On" from *Titanic*. The audience appreciated their dinner serenade. A quick reminder about the existence of the donation table ensued; then the lead singer of the band invited the guests onto the dance floor as the band played the apropos "A Kiss to Build a Dream On."

Karen took the bait and grabbed Kevin. "Let's dance," she said. And off they went. Karen looked back at Abby, unsure of what Abby would do but certain that Abby wanted to be alone with Greg for at least a few minutes.

"We have never danced before, have we?" Greg asked.

"No, we haven't. I am waiting to, though." Abby told him.

"We need the right song."

"Hmm."

"I love your dress."

"Me too. Thought I would treat myself."

"Oh?"

"Yes. Took my mother's advice. Wearing something old, something new, and something blue."

"You know, I love your mom. Wise woman."

"Well, she says some very nice things about you." Abby took a sip of her wine.

"Really?"

"Yep."

"Like?" Greg smiled.

"Oh, I don't want to inflate your ego too much."

"No, you wouldn't want to do that."

"Let's just say that she thinks you are high risk, high reward."

"Ah, which is it?"

"I'm not sure yet."

A beat.

The band played the enduring *Casablanca* theme, "As Time Goes By."

"Abby, I do believe this is our song. Would you care to dance?" Greg offered his hand.

Abby took his hand. "I thought you'd never ask."

She tucked her head under his chin. He began by holding her several inches away—traditionally, with one arm released forward. She followed his movements gracefully, but then asserted herself, stepping closer to his body and pulling their outstretched hands into a tight embrace. Their palms were moist. They were locked together. Warm. Affectionate. Moving in a soft rhythm.

Greg whispered into her ear, "I love you. Do you know that?"

Abby did not look up at him, but merely said, "I do."

The song ended. Applause. They remained there, stepping apart only slightly.

Abby looked up and straightened his bow tie. "I want to keep dancing with you, but let's take a walk outside first," she whispered.

Greg nodded.

The time had come.

They walked through the lobby and into the famed rectangular courtyard, which provided a path to stroll down.

They held hands. Few words were said—except to comment on how the majestic hotel's white courtyard must be filled with memories. Then they sat on one of its wooden benches under a star jasmine canopy.

Abby knew it was her scene. She began, "I know it may be strange for me to talk to you now—of all times—about something Jack once asked me." She paused to see Greg's reaction. He did not blink. "But many, many years ago, we went to the movies and saw *Saving Private Ryan*. As a matter of fact, I think it was the night the Village Theater closed." She paused for a minute, putting a bookmark in her mental calendar.

Greg realized that he had been there on the same evening. He remembered old Joe coming out and telling everyone that it was closing night. He recalled walking home alone with Aussie.

Abby continued, "Jack and I talked about that movie. He never liked to talk much about movies—not like me, you know." Her right hand had been nestled in Greg's left hand all this time. "Anyway, at the end of the movie, I think Tom Hanks tells the young soldier they are saving—Private Ryan—that he needs to earn all that they have sacrificed for him."

Greg remembered the scene vividly but remained silent.

"So, Jack looks at me, and out of the blue, he says to me, 'Did I earn it?' And I was blown away. I looked at him and said something like, 'Of course you did.'" Abby took in a breath. Both were conscious of the sweet scent of the star jasmine as its white petals perfumed the air.

"I always knew he was a man of honor—of humility. But regardless, he still needed to know that he had done his best by me—by his kids."

Then Abby turned to Greg, let go of his hand, and put her soft hands on his cheeks. "Greg, that will be the last time I speak of Jack in the present tense. I loved him. But I am telling you right now that I love you. Because you earned it. We have faced tragedy. We both had lovers taken from us. We were both heartbroken. But we never, ever gave up."

In an instant, the space between them vanished, as did all the fears, doubts, and memories. They kissed each other with a passion that eclipsed all that they had ever felt between them.

She had saved him.

He had earned her.

---

Three years later, they stood in line for the Grand Opening of the Village Theater. They nestled shoulder to shoulder to see the debut of the newest version of *Pride and Prejudice*.

Abby had found her Mr. Darcy.

Greg had found his Elizabeth.

And Abby's fingers fell into the gaps between his.

And Greg's finger finally wore a wedding ring.

# Acknowledgements

I have always wanted to learn to play an instrument…and, of course, be in a band. Unfortunately, my musical talents never blossomed. However, I got my "Metaphor Café Band" back together for this novel. I added a few key players for this tour. I would be lost without them, and this book could never have been written without their wisdom and talents backing up my "lead vocals."

**Readers:** Linda Englund, Mark and Kathy McWilliams, Pam Pacilio

**Editor:** Christa Tiernan

**Artists:** Caitlyn Harvey (cover illustration) and Bob Bjorkquist (cover editor)

**Layout Design:** Tony Loton and his staff in London at LOTON*tech* (interior design)

**Web Designer:** Lovelle Cardoso

**The Chorus:** These folks gave me important information about the historical events that impact the lives of my characters and have stood behind my work over the years: Bob Bjorkquist, Laura Strachan, Bob Parkington, Faye Visconti, Ken Bettencourt, and Babette Davidson.

**The Behind-the-Scenes Story:** The story of the Village Theater on Coronado Island is essentially true. Lance Alspaugh, CEO of Vintage Cinemas, organized the 10-year courtship with property owners and the City of Coronado after its closing in 1998. His company manages the Village Theater and was a major financial contributor to the project. With generous support from Coronado's Community Development Agency and the encouragement of the entire community, the Village Theater reopened in 2008. The original Art Deco design and murals were the work of distinguished theater designer Joseph Musil. He died before seeing the project completed, but he was able to lay down a creative direction for his talented team to pursue. For those of us who love the movies on the silver screen and our buttered popcorn, we cannot thank these folks enough.

# About the Author

Bob Pacilio taught English and Debate for 30 years and was the 1998 San Diego County Teacher of the Year. He then penned the young adult novel *Meetings at the Metaphor Café* and its sequel *Midnight Comes to the Metaphor Café*, which have been adopted as part of the curriculum for several school districts. He regularly speaks at teachers' conventions and enjoys visiting schools, where he reads portions of his novels to students, answers their questions, and turns classrooms into the "Metaphor Café." He lives in San Diego with his wife, and they find themselves quite often driving across the Coronado Bay Bridge to enjoy the beauty of the island's beaches, its landmark Hotel Del Coronado, and the Village Theater, *The Restoration*'s centerpiece.

Photograph: Christa Tiernan

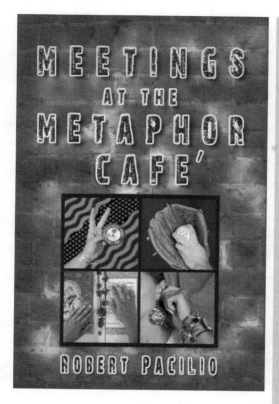

**ROBERT PACILIO**

**Also available as a Kindle from Amazon**

**Visit www.robertpacilio.net for ordering information**

Made in the USA
San Bernardino, CA
01 September 2015